Édition de Luxe

DRAMAS

IN FOUR VOLUMES

VOL. IV.

THE FOOL'S REVENGE — MARION DE LORME
LUCRETIA BORGIA

BY VICTOR HUGO

WITH ILLUSTRATIONS

WILDSIDE PRESS

ÉDITION DE LUXE.

Limited to One Thousand Copies.

No. **61**

*TYPOGRAPHY, ELECTROTYPING, AND
PRINTING BY JOHN WILSON AND SON,
UNIVERSITY PRESS, CAMBRIDGE, U.S.A.*

CONTENTS.

LIST OF ILLUSTRATIONS.

THE FOOL'S REVENGE.

(LE ROI S'AMUSE.)

AS ADAPTED BY TOM TAYLOR.

DRAMATIS PERSONÆ.

BERTUCCIO, *the Duke's jester.*
GALEOTTO MANFREDI, *Lord of Faenza.*
GUIDO MALATESTA, *an old Condottiere.*
SERAFINO DELL' AQUILA, *poet and improvisatore.*
BALDASSARE TORELLI, } *nobles.*
GIAN MARIA ORDELAFFI, }
BERNARDO ASCOLTI, *a Florentine envoy.*
ASCANIO, *a page.*
FRANCESCA BENTIVOGLIO, *wife of Manfredi.*
FIORDELISA, *daughter of Bertuccio.*
BRIGITTA, *Bertuccio's servant.*
GINEVRA, *wife of Malatesta.*

FAENZA, 1488.

THE FOOL'S REVENGE.

ACT I.

SCENE. — *The stage represents a loggia opening on the gardens of* MANFREDI'S *palace ; a low terrace at the back, and beyond a view of the city and country adjacent. Moonlight. The gardens and loggia illuminated for a festa.*

SCENE I.

Nobles and Ladies discovered R. *and* C., *and moving through the gardens and loggia. Music at a distance.* TORELLI *and* ORDELAFFI *discovered. Enter* ASCOLTI, L.

TORELLI.

Messer Bernardo, you shall judge between us:
Is Ordelaffi's here, a feasting face ?
I say, 't is fitter for a funeral.

ASCOLTI.

An Ordelaffi scarce can love the feast
That greets Octavian Riario,
Lord of Forli and Imola.

ORDELAFFI.

Because our line were masters there of old,
Till they were fools enough to get pulled down.
I was born to no lordship but my sword.
Thanks to my stout black bands, I look to win

New titles, and so grieve not over lost ones.
My glove upon 't!   I 'll prove a lighter dancer,
A lustier wooer, and a deeper drinker
Than e'er a landed lordling of you all.
Is it a wager?
[GINEVRA *passes with* MANFREDI *from* L. *to* R.   MALATESTA
 appears L., *watching them.*

TORELLI.

My hand to that!   There 's Malatesta's wife,
The fair Ginevra.   Let 's try lucks with her.

ASCOLTI.

Ware hawk!   Grey Guido 's an old-fashioned husband;
Look how he glares upon the Lord Manfredi.
Each of his soft words to the fair Ginevra 's
A dagger in the old fool's heart.

ORDELAFFI.

Sublime!   Ripe sixty wedded to sixteen,
And thinks to shut the foxes from his grapes!

TORELLI.

The Duke, too, for his rival!   Poor old man!

ASCOLTI.

Let the Duke look to it.   Ginevra's smiles
May breed him worse foes than Count Malatesta.
[*Whispering.*]   The Duchess!

TORELLI.

Faith!   't is ill rousing Bentivoglio blood.

ORDELAFFI.

And she 's as jealous as her own pet greyhound.

TORELLI.

And sharper in the teeth.   I wonder much
She leaves Faenza, knowing her Manfredi
So general a lover.

ASCOLTI.

She leaves Faenza

TORELLI.

So they say, — to-morrow
Rides to Bologna to her grim old father,
Giovanni Bentivoglio.

ASCOLTI.

To complain
Of her hot-blooded husband?

TORELLI.

Nay, I know not ;
Enough, she goes, and — fair dame as she is —
A murrain go with her, say I.   There never
Was good time in Faenza, since *she* came
To spoil sport with her jealousy.   Manfredi
Will be himself again when she is hence.

ASCOLTI.

Hush ! here she comes —

ORDELAFFI.

With that misshapen imp,
Bertuccio.   Gibing devil !   I shall thrust
My dagger down his throat, one of these days !

TORELLI.

Call him a jester ?   He laughs vitriol !

ASCOLTI.

Spares nothing ; cracks his random scurrile quips
Upon my master, great Lorenzo's self.

ORDELAFFI.

Do the knave justice; he's a king of tongue-fence.
Not a weak joint in all our armours round,
But he knows, and can hit. Confound the rogue!
I'm blistered still from a word-basting he
Gave me but yesterday. Would we were quits!

TORELLI.

Wait! I've a rod in pickle that shall flay
The tough hide off his hump. A rare revenge!

ASCOLTI.

They're here — avoid!
[ASCOLTI, ORDELAFFI, and TORELLI *retire up* C. *and min-
gle with the guests. Enter* FRANCESCA *and* BERTUCCIO,
R., *followed by her two women.*

FRANCESCA (*looking off, as if watching, and to herself*).
Still with her! changing hot plans and long looks!
Hers for the dance, hers at the feast, — all hers!
Nothing for me but shallow courtesies,
And hollow coin of compliment that leaves
The craving heart as empty as a beggar
Bemocked with counters!

BERTUCCIO (*counting on his fingers and looking at the moon*).
Moon — Manfredi — moon!

FRANCESCA.

Ha, knave!

BERTUCCIO.

By your leave, Monna Cecca, I am ciphering.

FRANCESCA.

Some fool's sum?

BERTUCCIO.

           Yes, running your husband's changes
Against the moon's. Manfredi has it hollow.
It comes out ten new loves 'gainst five new moons!

FRANCESCA.

Where do I stand?

BERTUCCIO.

First among the ten; your moon was a whole honey one.
Excluding that, it 's nine loves to four moons.

FRANCESCA.

You pity me, Bertuccio?

BERTUCCIO.

           Not a whit.
I pity sparrows, but not sparrow-hawks.

FRANCESCA.

I read your riddle. I am strong enough
To right my own wrongs! So I am, while here.

BERTUCCIO.

Then stay!

FRANCESCA.

           My father, at Bologna, looks for me.

BERTUCCIO.

Then go!

FRANCESCA.

           And leave him here — with her — both free,
And not a friend that I can trust to watch
And give me due report how things go 'twixt them?
Had I one friend —

BERTUCCIO.

You have Bertuccio.

FRANCESCA.

Men call you faithless, bitter, loving wrong
For wrong's sake, Duke Manfredi's worst counsellor,
Still prompting him to evil.

BERTUCCIO.

How folks flatter!

FRANCESCA.

How, then, am I to trust you?

BERTUCCIO.

Monna Cecca,
You know the wild beasts that your husband keeps
Down in the castle fosse? There's a she-leopard
I lie and gaze at by the hour together;
So sleek, so graceful, and so dangerous!
I long to see her let loose on a man.
Trust me to draw the bolt, and loose *my* leopard.

FRANCESCA.

I'll trust your love of mischief — not of me.

BERTUCCIO.

That's safest!

FRANCESCA.

I must know how fares this fancy
Of Duke Manfredi for yon pale Ginevra.
Mark him and her, — their meetings, communings;
I know you're private with my lord.

BERTUCCIO (*with a dry chuckle*).
He trusts me!

FRANCESCA.

Here! take my ring; your letters sealed with this,
My page Ascanio will bring me straight.
'T is but three hours' hard riding, and in six
I 'm here again.   Mark! write not on suspicion.
Let evil thought ripen to evil act,
That in the full flush of their guilty joys
I may strike sudden and strike home.
No Bentivoglio pardons.

BERTUCCIO.
                    Have a care!
Faenza is Manfredi's!   These court-flies,
                              [*Pointing to the guests.*
Who flutter in the sunshine of his favour,
Have stings; the pudding-headed citizens
Love his free ways, — he leaves *their* wives alone.
You play your own head, touching *his*.

FRANCESCA.

Give me my vengeance, — then come what come may.
Enough! I am resolved.   Now for the dance!
They shall not see a cloud upon my brow,
Though my heart ache and burn.   I can smile, too,
On him and her.   Bertuccio, remember!
            [*Exit* FRANCESCA, *followed by her women,* R.

BERTUCCIO (*looking at the ring*).
A blood-stone — apt reminder!
                        Does she think
That none but her have wrongs?   That none but her
Means to revenge them?   What! "No Bentivoglio
Pardons?"   There is a certain vile Bertuccio,

A twisted, withered, hunch-backed court buffoon, —
A thing to make mirth, and to be made mirth of;
A something betwixt ape and man, — that claims
To run in couples with your ladyship.
You hunt Manfredi; I hunt Malatesta.
Let's try which of the two has sharper fangs!
    [MANFREDI *and* GINEVRA *appear in the background,* R.
The Duke and Malatesta's wife!   [*He retires up stage.*
[MANFREDI *and* GINEVRA *come forward;* MALATESTA
    watching them, L.

MANFREDI.

Not yet, — but one more round! The feast is blank
For me when you are gone. The flowers lack perfume,
Missing your fragrant breath. The music sounds
Harsh and untunable when your sweet voice
Makes no more under melody. Oh, stay!

GINEVRA.

I am summoned, sir; my husband waits for me.

MANFREDI.

What spoil-sports are these husbands! [*Aside.*] And
    these wives
Per Bacco! I could wish Count Malatesta
Would lend my duchess escort to Bologna,
So we were both well rid. [MALATESTA *beckons to* GINEVRA.

GINEVRA.

             Your pardon, sir.
My husband beckons. It is I, not you,
Must bear his moods to-night; I dare not stay.

MANFREDI.

I would not bring a cloud to your fair brow
For all Faenza. Fare you well, sweet lady!
             [*He leads her to* MALATESTA.

I render up your jewel, Malatesta;
See that you guard it as befits its price.

MALATESTA.

Trust me for that, my lord.

MANFREDI (*to* GENEVRA).
Sweet dreams wait on you.

MALATESTA (*aside*).

This night sees *her* safe past Faenza's walls;
She 's too fair for this liquorish court of ours.
[*Exeunt* MALATESTA *and* GINEVRA, L.

MANFREDI.

A peerless lady!

BERTUCCIO (*coming forward*).
And a churlish spouse!

MANFREDI.

Bertuccio!

BERTUCCIO.
"At your elbow, sir!" quoth Satanus.

MANFREDI.

Come, fool, let 's rail at husbands.

BERTUCCIO.
Shall I call
Your wife to help us?

MANFREDI.
Out on thee, screech-owl!
Just when I felt my chains about to fall
Thou mind'st me of my jailer. Thank the saints,
I shall be free to-morrow, for a while

I 'm thirsty to employ my liberty.
Come, my familiar, help me to some mischief, —
Some pleasant deviltry, with just the spice
Of sin to make the enjoyment exquisite.

BERTUCCIO.

Let 's see ! Throat-cutting 's pleasant, but that 's stale;
Plotting has savour in it, but 't is too tedious;
Say, a campaign with Ordelaffi's band,
So you may feed all the seven sins at once ?

MANFREDI.

Out, barren hound ! thy wits are growing dull.

BERTUCCIO.

A man can't always be finding out new sins, —
Think they 're as hard to hit on as new pleasures.
My head on 't, Alexander had not run
So wide a round of pleasures as you of sins,
And yet he offered kingdoms for a new one.
You must invoke Asmodeus, not Beelzebub.

MANFREDI.

What 's he ?

BERTUCCIO.

The devil specially charged with love;
He has more work to do than all the infernal legion.
There 's Malatesta's wife; she 's young and fair,
And good, they say. Rare matter for *sin* there,
Though 't is the oldest of them all.

MANFREDI.

But show me
How to win *her !* She 's cold as she is fair;
I have spent enough sweet speech to have softened stone,
And all in vain.

BERTUCCIO.

The monks say Hannibal
Melted the rocks with vinegar, not sugar.

MANFREDI.

But she is adamant!

BERTUCCIO.

When all else fails,
You 've still force to fall back on.   Carry her off
From under Guido's grizzled beard.

MANFREDI.

By Bacchus,
There 's metal in thy counsel, knave !   I 'll think on 't.

BERTUCCIO.

It needs no brains neither, — only strong hands
And hard hearts.   Here come both.
      [*Enter* TORELLI, ASCOLTI, *and* ORDELAFFI, C.

MANFREDI.

What say you, gentlemen ; may I trust your arms ?

TORELLI.

They 're yours in any quarrel.

ASCOLTI.

So are mine !

ORDELAFFI.

And mine !

BERTUCCIO.

One at a time.   You said " *arms !* "   Of Torelli
You should ask *legs !*   His did such famous service
In carrying him out of danger at Sarzana,
I think they may be trusted. [*All laugh except* TORELLI.

TORELLI.

Scurrile knave!
But I 'll be even with thee!

BERTUCCIO.

That were pity.
A hump would be a sore disfigurement
Upon a back that you 're so fond of showing!

ASCOLTI.

This rogue needs gagging.

BERTUCCIO (*to* ASCOLTI).

What, for speaking truth?
I cry you mercy! I forgot how ugly
It must sound to a Florentine Ambassador —

MANFREDI.

Well thrust, Bertuccio!

ORDELAFFI (*angrily*).

My lord! my lord!
The slave is paid to find us *wit* —

BERTUCCIO (*interrupting*).

Hold there!
No man is bound to impossibilities, —
'T is a known maxim of the Roman law;
How then can I find wit for Ordelaffi?

[*All laugh but* ORDELAFFI.
But look! there 's Serafino, big with a sonnet:
I must help him to reason for his rhymes.

MANFREDI.

Stay!

BERTUCCIO.

Not I! You 're for finding out new sins :
With three such counsellors, I am superfluous.
[*Aside.*] The evil seed is sown ; 't will grow ! 't will
 grow !   [*Exit* BERTUCCIO.

TORELLI.

Toad !

ASCOLTI.

Foul-mouthed scoffer !

ORDELAFFI.

      Warped in wit and limb !

ASCOLTI.

My lord, you give your monkey too much rope.
He 'll soon forget all tricks in the scurvy one
Of making his grinders meet in our soft parts.

MANFREDI.

Nay, give the devil his due ; if he hits hard,
He hits impartially. I take my share
Of buffets with the rest. Best cure the smart
By laughing at your neighbour that smarts worse ;
But about this business, where *your* arms may help me.

ASCOLTI.

Is it an enemy to be silenced ?

ORDELAFFI.

        A castle
To be surprised ? A merchant to be squeezed ?

ASCOLTI.

Or aught in which ducats or brains of Florence
Can help ?

MANFREDI.

No.   Who was queen of the feast to-night,
In your skilled judgment, Messer Gian Maria ?

ORDELAFFI.

I ought to say your duchess, fair Francesca ;
But if another tongue had asked the question —-

MANFREDI.

Speak out thy honest judgment !

ORDELAFFI.

Not a lady
In all Faenza 's worthy to compare
With proud Ginevra Malatesta !

TORELLI.

I think I know a fairer — but no matter !

MANFREDI.

I hold with Ordelaffi.   I have mounted
Ginevra's colours in my cap and heart ;
But she 's too proud, or fearful of old Guido,
To smile upon my suit.   'T is the first time
I 've found so coy a dame.

ASCOLTI.

Trust one who knows them :
The coyest are not always chastest.

MANFREDI.

How say you, if I spared her shame of yielding
By a night escalade ?

ORDELAFFI (*shaking his head*).
Carry her off?
A Malatesta! Were it an enemy's town —

MANFREDI.

Hear him! How modestly he talks! Why, man,
Since when shrank'st thou from climbing balconies,
And forcing doors without an invitation?

ORDELAFFI.

Oh, citizens, I grant you; but a noble's!
One of ourselves!

ASCOLTI.

Remember, Malatesta
Is cousin to the old lord of Cesena.
The affair might breed a feud, and so let in
The sly Venetian.

TORELLI.

Be advised, my lord;
If you must breathe your new-fledged liberty,
Try safer game! Old Malatesta's horns
Might prove too sharp for pastime!

MANFREDI.

Out, you faint hearts!
Do you fall off? Then, by St. Francis' bones,
I and Bertuccio will adventure it.

TORELLI.

Bertuccio! My jewel to his hump,
T was he put this mad frolic in your head!

MANFREDI.

And if it were? At least he 'll stand by me.
Perchance his wits may be worth all your brawn.

ASCOLTI.

Here comes one who may claim to be consulted
Upon this business.   [*Enter* MALATESTA, L.

MANFREDI (*disconcerted*).

Guido Malatesta!
Why, how now, Count? You left our feast so soon,
I thought you warm i' the sheets this good half hour.

MALATESTA.

I had forgot my duty to your lordship,
So now repair my lack of courtesy.
To-morrow I purpose riding to Cesena,
And would not go without due leave-taking.

MANFREDI (*aside*).

This jumps well with my project.
[*Aloud.*] What, to-morrow!
You ride alone?

MALATESTA.

No, with my wife.

MANFREDI (*aside*).

The devil!
[*Aloud.*] Why, this is sudden. She spoke no word of this
To-night.

MALATESTA.

Tush! Women know not their own minds,
How should they know their husband's?

MANFREDI.

But your reason?

MALATESTA.

Your air here in Faenza is too warm,
And scarce so pure as fits my wife's complexion.

She 'll be better in my castle at Cesena;
The walls are five feet thick, and from the platform
There 's a rare view.   She 'll need no exercise.

MANFREDI (*aside*).

The jailer!   [*Aloud.*]   But what says the lady's will?

MALATESTA.

I never ask that, and so escape all risk
Of finding it run counter to my own.

MANFREDI.

Faenza will have great miss of you both.

MALATESTA.

Oh, fear not; I 'll return.   Your wine 's too good
To be left lightly.   I 'll be back to-morrow,
Before the gates are shut.   Meanwhile, accept
This leave-taking by proxy from my wife.

MANFREDI.

Not so; I must exchange farewell with her
To-morrow.

MALATESTA.

              We shall start an hour ere dawn;
You 'll scarce be stirring.

MANFREDI (*aside*).

              Plague upon the churl!
He meets me at all points.   [*Aloud.*]   At least, I hope
This absence of your wife will not be long;
My duchess cannot spare her.   [*Aside.*]   Saints forgive
    me!

MALATESTA.

When your fair lady wants her, she can send:
I 'll answer for her coming on *that* summons.
Good-night, sweet lords. [*Aside.*] How crestfallen he
    looks !
Mass ! 't is ill cozening an old condottiere !
Did he think I had forgot to guard my baggage ? [*Exit.*

MANFREDI.

A murrain go with him ! May the horse stumble
That carries him, and break his old bull-neck !
Oh, this is cruel ! with my hand stretched out,
To have to draw 't back empty. I could curse !

TORELLI.

What if I helped you to a substitute
For coy Ginevra, passing her in beauty ?
One, too, whose conquest puts no crown to risk,
And helps withal a notable requital
That we all owe Bertuccio, you included.

MANFREDI.

What mean you ?

TORELLI.

Guess what 's happened to Bertuccio.

ORDELAFFI.

He 's grown good-natured ?

ASCOLTI.

Or has dropped his hump ?

MANFREDI.

He has found a monkey uglier than himself ?

TORELLI.

No, something stranger than all these would be,
If they *had* happened, — he has found a mistress!
[*All burst out laughing.*

MANFREDI.

My lady's pet baboon? Bertuccio
Graced with a mistress? [*He laughs.*

ASCOLTI.

She is blind, of course?

ORDELAFFI.

And has a hump, I hope, to match his own?
What a rare breed 't will be, of two-humped babes,
Like Bactrian camels!

MANFREDI.

Bertuccio with a mistress! Why, the rogue
Ne'er yet made joke so monstrous or so pleasant!
[*They laugh again.*

TORELLI.

Laugh as you please, sirs; on my knightly faith,
He *has* a mistress, — and a rare one, too!
Nay, if you doubt my word — Here comes Dell' Aquila;
He knows, as well as I.

MANFREDI.

We 'll question him.
[*Enter* SERAFINO DELL' AQUILA, C.
Good-even to my poet. You walk late.

DELL' AQUILA (*pointing to the moon*).

I tend my mistress: poets and lunatics,
You know, are her liege subjects.

MANFREDI.

They are happy!

DELL' AQUILA.

Why?

MANFREDI.

They have a new mistress every month,
And each month's mistress no two nights alike.
But jesters can find mistresses, it seems,
As well as poets. There 's Torelli swears
Bertuccio has one, and that you know it.

DELL' AQUILA.

I know he has a rare maid close mewed up,
But whether wife or daughter —

MANFREDI.

Tell not me!
A mistress for a thousand! But what of her?
How did you find her out?

DELL' AQUILA.

'T was some weeks since,
Attending vespers in your house's chapel,
At San Costanza, I beheld a maiden
Kneeling before that picture of Our Lady
By Fra Filippo, — oh, so fair, so rapt
In her pure, passionate prayers! I tell you, sirs,
I was nigh going on my knees beside her,
And asking for an interest in her orisons:
Such eyes of softest blue, crowned with such wreaths
Of glossy chestnut hair; a cheek of snow
Plushed tenderly, as when the sunlight strikes
Upon an evening alp; and over all,
A grace of maiden modesty that lay

More still and snowy round her than the folds
Of her white veil.   And when she rose, I rose
And followed her, like one drawn by a charm,
To a mean house, where entering, she was lost.

MANFREDI.
She was alone?

DELL' AQUILA.
Only a shrewish servant
That saw her to the church, and saw her home.

MANFREDI.
A most weak wolf-dog for so choice a lamb !

DELL' AQUILA.
Methought, my lord, she needed no more guard
Than the innocence that sat, dove-like, in her eyes,
That shaped the folding of her delicate hands,
And timed the movement of her gentle feet.

MANFREDI.
You spoke to her?

DELL' AQUILA.
I dared not ; some strange shame
Put weight upon my tongue.   I only watched her,
And sometimes heard her sing.   That was enough.

MANFREDI.
Poets are easy satisfied.   Well, you watched?

DELL' AQUILA.
And then I found that I was not alone
Upon my nightly post : there were two more ;
One stayed outside, like me, and one went in.

TORELLI.

True to the letter!   I was the outsider ;
The third, and luckiest, was Bertuccio !

MANFREDI.

The hump-backed hypocrite !

ORDELAFFI.

                        The owl that screeched
The loudest against women !

ASCOLTI.

                        But is 't certain
That 't was Bertuccio ?

TORELLI.

                        I can swear to that !

DELL' AQUILA.

And I !

ASCOLTI.

How do you know him ?

TORELLI.

                        By his hump,
His gait — who could mistake that crab-like walk ?
I could have knocked my head against the wall
To think I had been fool enough to trust
A woman's looks for once.   Dell' Aquila,
I know, holds other faith about the sex.

DELL' AQUILA.

I would stake life upon her purity ;
Yet, 't is past doubt Bertuccio is the man,
The ugly jailer of this prisoned bird.

MANFREDI.

Why, that's enough to make it a mere duty
To break her prison-house, and shift her keeping
To fitter hands, — say, mine. I'm lord of the town;
None else has right of prison here, but me.

DELL' AQUILA.

What would you do?

MANFREDI.

First see if she bears out
Your picture, Serafino; if she do,
Be sure I will not wait outside to mark
Her shadow. Shadows may suit poets; I
Want substance.

TORELLI.

She's meat for Bertuccio's master,
Not for Bertuccio. When shall it be?

MANFREDI.

To-morrow
I'm a free man! Meet me at midnight, here.

DELL' AQUILA.

You would not harm her? Only see her face;
You will not have the heart to do her wrong.

MANFREDI.

What call you " wrong"? — to save so choice a creature
From such a guardian as Bertuccio?
He would have prompted me to play the robber
Of Malatesta's pearl. Let him guard his own!

ORDELAFFI.

If he resists, we'll knock him over the sconce;
Let me have *that* part of the business.

MANFREDI.

Nay, I'd not have the rascal harmed; he's bitter,
But shrewdly witty, and he makes me laugh.
No, spare me my buffoon; who does him harm,
Shall answer it to me.

TORELLI.

'T were a rare plot to make the knave believe
Our scheme still held against old Malatesta, —
That his Ginevra was the game we followed.

ORDELAFFI.

So give him a rendezvous a mile away;
And while he waits our coming, to break open
The mew where he keeps close his tassel-gentle.

ASCOLTI (*aside to* MANFREDI).

Ne'er trust a poet.   What if he betrayed us?

MANFREDI.

He's truth itself; and where he gives his faith,
'T is better than a bond of your Lorenzo's.

ASCOLTI.

Swear him to secrecy.

MANFREDI (*to* DELL' AQUILA).
                    Your hand upon it:
You 'll not spoil our sport by breaking to Bertuccio
What we intend?

DELL' AQUILA.
                    But think, oh, think, my lord,
What if this were no mistress — as — if looks
Have privilege to reveal the soul — she is none!

MANFREDI.

Mistress or maid, man, I will not be balked;
'T is for her good. I know the sex; she pines
In her captivity. I 'll find a cage
More fitting such a bird as you 've described.
Your hand on 't: not a whisper to Bertuccio!

DELL' AQUILA.

You force me! There 's my hand! I will not speak
A word to him!

MANFREDI (*taking his hand*).
                        That 's like a trusty liegeman
Of blind Lord Cupid!—Hark! a word with you.
                        [MANFREDI *and Lords talk apart*, C.

DELL' AQUILA.

I 'll save her from this wrong, or lose myself.
What tie there is betwixt these two, I know not, —
How one so fair and seeming gentle 's linked
With one so foul and bitter, a buffoon,
Who makes *his* vile office viler still
By prompting to the evil that he mocks.
But I will 'gage my life that she is pure,
And still shall be so, if my aid avail!
                        [MANFREDI *and Lords separate.*
Once more, my lord: you 'll not be stayed from this
That you propose?

MANFREDI.
                        Unconscionable bard!
What! when you 've set my mouth a-watering
You 'd have me put the dainty morsel from me?
Go, feed on signs and shadows! Such thin stuff
Is the best diet for you singing birds;
We eagles must have flesh!

DELL' AQUILA (*to all*).

     Good-night, my lords!
[*Aside.*] Keep to your carrion, kites! She 's not for *you*.
       [*Exit* DELL' AQUILA.

MANFREDI.

But how to get sight of Bertuccio's jewel!
I 'd see, before I 'd snatch.

TORELLI.

      Trust me for that.
I am no poet. When I found the damsel
Admitted such a gallant as Bertuccio,
I thought it time to press my suit, and so
Accosted her on her way from San Costanza —

MANFREDI.

She listened ?

TORELLI.

    Long enough — the little fool ! —
To learn my meaning, then she flushed and fled ;
I followed — when, as the foul fiend would have it,
Ginevra Malatesta coming by
From vespers, with her train, sheltered the pigeon,
And spoiled my chase.

MANFREDI.

    You did not give it up ?

TORELLI.

I changed my plan ; the mistress being coy,
I spread my net to catch the maid, — oh, lord !
The veriest Gorgon ! You might swear none e'er
Had given *her* chase before ; no coyness there.
A small expense of oaths and coin sufficed
To make her think herself a misprized Venus,

And me the most discriminating wooer
In all Faenza. 'T will not need much art
For me to win an entrance to the house ;
And when I 'm in it, it shall go hard, my lord,
But I find means to get you access too.

MANFREDI.

About it straight; at dusk to-morrow night
Be here, armed, masked, and cloaked.

ORDELAFFI.

      While poor Bertuccio
Awaits our coming near San Stefano, —
A stone's throw from the casa Malatesta.

ASCOLTI.

He 's here !   [*Enter* BERTUCCIO, L.

BERTUCCIO.

   Not yet a-bed !
Since when were the fiend's eggs so hard to hatch ?
I left a pleasant little germ of sin
Some half an hour since ; it should be full-grown
By this time. Is it ?

MANFREDI.

    Winged and hoofed and tailed.
If proud Ginevra Malatesta sleep
To-morrow night beneath old Guido's roof,
Then call me a snow-water-blooded shaveling.

BERTUCCIO.

Ha ! 'T is resolved then ?

TORELLI.

    We have pledged our faith
To carry off the fairest in Faenza —

ASCOLTI.

Before the stroke of midnight.

ORDELAFFI.

'T was my plan
To gather one by one to the place of action;
Lest, going in a troop, we might awake
Suspicion, and put Guido on his guard.

BERTUCCIO.

A wise precaution, although it *was* yours.
I wronged you, gentlemen; I thought you shrunk
Even from sin, when there was danger in 't.
It seems there *are* deeds black enough to make
Even Torelli brave, Ascolti prompt,
And Ordelaffi witty. But the place?

MANFREDI.

Beside San Stefano.

BERTUCCIO.

The hour of meeting?

MANFREDI.

Half an hour after vespers. There await us.
And now good rest, my lords; the night wanes fast:
My duchess will be weary.

ALL (*going*).

Sir, good-night!

BERTUCCIO.

Sleep well, Torelli. Dream of charging home
In the van of some fierce fight.

TORELLI.
My common dream.

BERTUCCIO.
'T is natural, — dreams go by contraries.
And you, Ascolti, dream of telling truth ;
And, Ordelaffi, that you 've grown wise.

TORELLI.
And you, that your back 's straight, your legs a match.

ASCOLTI.
And your tongue tipped with honey.

ORDELAFFI.
Come, my lords ;
Leave him to spit his venom at the moon,
As they say toads do !

BERTUCCIO.
Take my curse among you,
Fair, false, big, brainless, outside shows of men ;
For once your gibes and jeers fall pointless from me.
My great revenge is nigh, and drowns all sense,
I am straight and fair and well-shaped as yourselves ;
Vengeance swells out my veins, and lifts my head,
And makes me terrible !   Come, sweet to-morrow,
And put my enemy's heart into my hand
That I may gnaw it !

ACT II.

SCENE.—*A room in the house of* BERTUCCIO, *hung with tapestry; a coloured statue of the Madonna in a recess, with a small lamp burning before it; carved and coloured furniture; a carved cabinet and large carved coffers; in the centre a window opening on the street, with a balcony; behind the tapestry, a secret door communicating with the street,* L. 2 E.; *a door,* R. 2 E.; *a lamp lighted; a lute and flowers; a missal on a stand before the statue; a recess concealed by the tapestry,* L. 3 E.

SCENE I.

TORELLI *and* BRIGITTA *discovered,* C.

BRIGITTA.

Hark, there's the quarter. You must hence, fair
  signor.

TORELLI.

But a few moments more of your sweet presence!

BRIGITTA.

Saint Ursula, she knows, 't is not my will
That drives you hence; but if my master found
That I received a man into the house,
'T were pity of my place, if not my life.

TORELLI.

Your master is a churl, that would condemn
These maiden blooms to wither on the tree.

BRIGITTA.

Churl you may call him! Why, he'd have the house
A prison. If you heard the coil he keeps

Of bolts and bars and locks ! Lord knows the twitter
I 've been in all to-day about the key
I lost this morning ; it unlocks the door
Of the turnpike stair that leads down to the street.

TORELLI.

'T was lucky I came by just when you dropped it.

BRIGITTA.

Dropped ! — nay, signor, 't was whipped off by some cut-
purse
That thought to filch my coin.

TORELLI.

That 's a shrewd guess !
He must have flung it from him where I found it,
Not knowing [*bowing to her*] of what jewel it unlocked
the casket !

BRIGITTA.

How can I ever pay your pains that brought it back ?

TORELLI.

By ever and anon giving me leave
To come and sun myself in your chaste presence.

BRIGITTA *(coquettishly)*.
Alas, sweet signor !

TORELLI *(in the same tone)*.
Oh, divine Brigitta !

BRIGITTA.

But I must say farewell. Vespers are over ;
My mistress will be waiting ; she 's so fearful.

TORELLI.

As if her unripe beauties were in danger,
While your maturer loveliness can walk
The streets unguarded.

BRIGITTA.

Nay, I'm a poor, fond thing; Lord knows the risk
I run to let you in.

TORELLI.

I warrant now
You've some snug nook where, if your master came,
You could bestow me at a pinch.

BRIGITTA.

I know none,
Unless 't were here [*lifting arras* L. 3 E.] behind the arras,
      look!
Here's a hole, too, whence you could peep to see
When the coast's clear.

TORELLI (*aside*).

There's room enough for two.
[*Sternly.*]   Brigitta!

BRIGITTA.

Signor!

TORELLI (*with feigned suspicion*).

How if this had served
For hiding others before me?

BRIGITTA.

I swear
By the eleven thousand virgins —

TORELLI.

That's
Too many by ten thousand and ten hundred
And ninety-nine! Vouch but your virgin self,
And I am satisfied.

BRIGITTA (*whimpering*).

Alack-a-day!
To be suspected after all these years.

TORELLI.

Pardon a lover's jealousy; this kiss
Shall wipe away the memory of my wrong.
[*Aside.*] What will not loyalty drive a man to?
[*Kisses her.*
There!

BRIGITTA (*aside*).

He has the sweetest lips! And now begone,
Sweet signor, if you love me.

TORELLI.

If, Brigitta!
Banish me then to outer darkness straight!
Farewell, my full-blown rose — let others prize
The opening bud — the ripe, rich flower for me '

BRIGITTA.

Oh, the saints, how he talks! This way, sweet signor,
[*Taking a key from her girdle.*
The secret door; the key you found and brought me
Unlocks it. [*Unlocking secret door*, L. 2 E.

TORELLI (*taking another from his girdle, aside*).

Else, why did I filch it from you —
And have this, its twinb-rother, forged to-day!
VOL. XIV. — 3

BRIGITTA (getting the lamp).

I 'll light you out, and lock the door behind you,
" Safe bind, safe find."

TORELLI.

         Good-night, sweet piece of woman,
I leave my heart in pledge. [*Aside.*] Now for the Duke.
[BRIGITTA *holds open the door and lights him down, then
     locks it.*

BRIGITTA.

He 's gone, bless his sweet face ! To think what risks
Men will run that are lovers, and indeed
Weak women, too ! Lord ! if my master knew.
                [*Getting on her mantle.*
'T is lucky San Costanza is hard by,
I should be fearful else. Faenza 's full
Of gallants, and who knows what might befall
A poor young woman like myself, with naught
Except her innocence to be her safeguard ! [*Exit*, R. 2 E.
[*As soon as she has closed the door, the secret door*, C., *opens
     and* TORELLI *re-appears.*

TORELLI.

This way, my lord ; the dragon has departed.
        [*Enter* MANFREDI *from the secret door*, L. 2 E.

MANFREDI.

'T is time, I was weary of my watch.

TORELLI.

You were alone, at least. Think of *my* lot,
That had to make love to a tough old spinster.
I would we had changed parts. Why, good my lord,
I had to kiss her. Faugh ! When shall I get

The garlic from my beard?   But here 's the cage
That holds our bird.   We must ensconce ourselves,
For they 'll be here anon ; vespers were over
Before we entered.

MANFREDI.

Thanks to your device
Of the forged key.   Yet that was scarcely needed ;
I 've climbed more break-neck balconies than that
[Pointing to window.
Without a silken ladder! [Looking about.]   So — a lute —
A missal — flowers ! — more tokens of a maid
Than of a mistress !   Well, so much the better ;
I long to see the girl.   Is she as fair
As Serafino painted ?

TORELLI.

Faith, my lord,
She 's fair enough to justify more sonnets
Than e'er fat Petrarch pumped out for his Laura.
She is a paragon of blushing girlhood,
Full of temptation to the finger-tips.
I marvel at myself, that e'er I yielded
This amorous enterprise, even to you —
But that my loyalty outbears my love.

MANFREDI.

I will requite your loyalty ; fear not ;
But where shall we bestow ourselves ?

TORELLI (lifting the arras from the recess).

In here ;
The old crone showed it me but now there 's cover
And peeping-place sufficient.   Hark ! they come !
Stand close, my lord.
[They retire behind the arras. Enter FIORDELISA and
  BRIGITTA, R. 2 E.

BRIGITTA.

And he was there to-night?

FIORDELISA.

Oh, yes!   He offered me the holy water
As I passed in.   I trembled so, Brigitta,
When our hands met, I fear he must have marked it,
But that he seemed almost as trembling, too,
As I was.

BRIGITTA.

He! a brazen popinjay,
I 'll warrant me, for all his downcast looks!
I wonder how my master would endure
To hear of such audacious goings on!

FIORDELISA.

That makes me sad.   My father is so kind,
I cannot bear to have a secret from him.
Sometimes I feel as I would tell him all;
But then, I think, perhaps he would forbid me
From going out to church; and 't is so dull
To be shut up here all the long bright day:
From morn till dark, to mark the busy stir
Under the window, and the happy voices
Of holiday-makers, that go out and in
Just as they please.   Look at the birds, Brigitta!
Their wings are free, yet no harm comes to them;
I 'm sure *they 're* innocent!   And then to hear
Sometimes the trumpets, as the knights ride by,
And tramp of armed men; [*Lute sounds without.*] some-
    times a lute.
Hark! 't is his lute! I know the air, how sweet!
My good Brigitta, would there be much harm
If I touched mine, only a little touch,
To tell him I am listening?

BRIGITTA.

Holy saints,
Was e'er such boldness! I must have your lute
Locked up. These girls! these girls! Bar them from
    Court,
And they'll find matter in church; keep them from
    speech,
And they'll make cat-gut do the work of tongue.
Better be charged to keep a cat from cream,
Than a girl from gallants!

FIORDELISA.

Nay but, good Brigitta,
This gentleman is none.

BRIGITTA.

How do *you* know?

FIORDELISA.

He never speaks to me, scarce looks, or if
He do, it is but to withdraw his gaze
As hastily as I do mine. I've seen him
Blush when our eyes met; not like yon rude man
Who pressed upon me with such words and looks
As made me red and hot; you know the time
When that kind lady, Countess Malatesta,
Scarce saved me from his boldness.

BRIGITTA.

Tilly-vally.
There are more ways of bird-catching than one;
He's the best fowler who least scares his quarry.
But I must go and see the supper toward.
Your father will be here anon! [*Exit* BRIGITTA, R.

FIORDELISA.

Dear father!
Would he were here that I might rest my head
Upon his breast, and have his arms about me;
For then I feel there's something I may love
And not be chidden for it.   [*Lute sounds.*]   Hark! again.
If I durst answer!
How sad he must be out there in the dark,
Not knowing if I mark his music.

[*Takes her lute, then puts it away.*
No!
My father would be angry; sad enough,
To have one joy I may not share with him;
Yet there can be no harm in listening.
I thought to-night he would have spoken to me,
But then Brigitta came, and he fell back!
I'm glad he did not speak, and yet I'm sorry,
I should so like to hear his voice, just once.
He comes in my dreams, now, but he never speaks.
I'm sure 't is soft and sweet!   [*Listening.*]   His lute is
    hushed.
What if I touch mine, now that he is gone?
I must not look out of the casement!   Yes,
I'm sure he's gone?

[*Takes her lute and strikes a chord,* L.

MANFREDI (*aside, lifting the arras*).

She is worth ten Ginevras!

TORELLI (*holding him back*).

Not yet!

MANFREDI.

Unhand me, I *will* speak to her!
[BERTUCCIO *appears at the door,* R. 2 E.

TORELLI.

My lord! It is Bertuccio! In — quick!
[BERTUCCIO *stands for a moment fondly contemplating*
    FIORDELISA ; *his dress is sober and his manner com-*
    posed. He steps quietly forward.

BERTUCCIO.

My own!

FIORDELISA (*turning suddenly, and flinging herself into*
            his arms with a cry of joy).
        My father!

BERTUCCIO (*embracing her tenderly*).
                    Closer, closer yet!
Let me feel those soft arms about my neck,
This dear cheek on my heart! No, do not stir,
It does me so much good! I am so happy, —
These minutes are worth years!

FIORDELISA.

            My own dear father!

BERTUCCIO.

Let me look at thee, darling. Why, thou growest
More and more beautiful! Thou 'rt happy here?
Hast all that thou desirest, — thy lute, thy flowers?
She loves her poor old father? Blessings on thee,
I know thou dost, but tell me so.

FIORDELISA.
                    I love you —
I love you very much! I am so happy
When you are with me. Why do you come so late,
And go so soon? Why not stay always here?

BERTUCCIO.

Why not! Why not! Oh, if I could! To live
Where there's no mocking, and no being mocked;
No laughter but what's innocent; no mirth
That leaves an after bitterness like gall.

FIORDELISA.

Now, you are sad! There's that black ugly cloud
Upon your brow; you promised, the last time,
It never *should* come when we were together.
You know when *you're* sad *I'm* sad too

BERTUCCIO.

My bird!
I'm selfish even with thee; let dark thoughts come,
That thy sweet voice may chase them, as they say
The blessed church bells drive the demons off.

FIORDELISA.

If I but knew the reason of your sadness,
Then I might comfort you; but I know nothing,
Not even your name.

BERTUCCIO.

I'd have no name for thee
But "father."

FIORDELISA.

In the convent at Cesena,
Where I was reared, they used to call me orphan.
I thought I had no father, till you came,
And then they needed not to say I had one:
My own heart told me that.

BERTUCCIO.

I often think
I had done well to have left thee there, in the peace

Of that still cloister.   But it was too hard;
My empty heart so hungered for my child!
For those dear eyes that look no scorn for me,
That voice that speaks respect and tenderness,
Even for me!   My dove, my lily-flower,
My only stay in life.   Oh, God! I thank thee
Thou hast left me this at least!   [*He weeps.*

FIORDELISA.
                              Dear father!
You're crying now; you must not cry,— you must not.
I cannot bear to see you cry.

BERTUCCIO.
                              Let be!
'T were better than to see me laugh.

FIORDELISA.
                              But wherefore ?
You say you are so happy here, and yet
You never come but to weep bitter tears.
And I can but weep too, not knowing why.
Why are you sad ?   Oh, tell me, — tell me all!

BERTUCCIO.
I cannot.   In this house I am thy father;
Out of it, what I am boots not to say ;
Hated, perhaps, or envied ; feared, I hope,
By many ; scorned by more ; and loved by none.
In this one innocent corner of the world
I would but be to thee a father, — something
August and sacred !

FIORDELISA.
And you are so, father.

BERTUCCIO.

I love thee with a love strong as the hate
I bear for all but thee.   Come, sit beside me,
With thy pure hand in mine, and tell me still,
"I love you," and "I love you," — only that.
Smile on me — so! thy smile is passing sweet!
Thy mother used to smile so once ; oh, God!
I cannot bear it.   Do not smile ; it wakes
Memories that tear my heart-strings.   Do not look
So like thy mother, or I shall go mad!

FIORDELISA.

Oh, tell me of my mother!

BERTUCCIO (*shuddering*).
            No, no, no!

FIORDELISA.

She 's dead ?

BERTUCCIO.
      Yes.

FIORDELISA.
      You were with her when she died ?

BERTUCCIO.

No!   Leave the dead alone ; talk of thyself,
Thy life here.   Thou heed'st well my caution, girl, —
Not to go out by day, nor show thyself
There, at the casement.

FIORDELISA.

            Yes : some day, I hope,
You will take me with you, but to see the town ;
'T is so hard to be shut up here, alone.

BERTUCCIO.

Thou hast *not* stirred abroad ? [*Suspiciously and eagerly.*

FIORDELISA.

     Only to vespers ;
You said I might do that with good Brigitta
I never go forth or come in alone.

BERTUCCIO.

That's well. I grieve that thou should'st live so close,
But if thou knewest what poison 's in the air,
What evil walks the streets, how innocence
Is a temptation, beauty but a bait
For desperate desires — No man, I hope,
Has spoken to thee ?

     FIORDELISA.
    Only one.

BERTUCCIO (*fiercely*).

      Ha ! who?

FIORDELISA.

I know not. 'T was against my will.

BERTUCCIO (*eagerly*).

       You gave

No answer

     FIORDELISA.

 No, I fled.

BERTUCCIO (*in the same tone*).

    He followed you ?

FIORDELISA.

A gracious lady gave me kind protection,
And bade her train guard me safe home. Oh, father,

If you had seen how good she was, how gently
She soothed my fears, — for I was sore afraid, —
I 'm sure you 'd love her.

BERTUCCIO.

Did you learn her name ?

FIORDELISA.

I asked it, first, to set it in my prayers,
And then, that *you* might pray for her.

BERTUCCIO.

Her name ?   [*Aside.*]   I pray !   [*Contemptuously.*

FIORDELISA.

The Countess Malatesta.

BERTUCCIO (*aside*).

Count Malatesta's wife protect my child !
You have not seen her since ?

FIORDELISA.

No ; though she urged me
So hard to come to her ; and asked my name,
And who my parents were, and where I lived.

BERTUCCIO.

You did not tell her ?

FIORDELISA.

Who my parents were ?
How could I, when I must not know myself ?

BERTUCCIO.

Patience, my darling ; trust thy father's love,
That there is reason for this mystery !

Bertuccio.

Photogravure by Goupil et Cie — From Drawing
by A. Gués.

The time may come when we may live in peace,
And walk together free, under free heaven
But that cannot be here — nor now !

FIORDELISA.
                                    Oh, when —
When shall that time arrive ?

BERTUCCIO (*bitterly*).
                              When what I live for
Has been achieved !

FIORDELISA (*timidly*).
                    What *you* live for ?

BERTUCCIO (*with sudden ferocity*).
                                      Revenge !

FIORDELISA (*averting her eyes with horror*).
Oh, do not look so, father !

BERTUCCIO.
                        Listen, girl,
You asked me of your mother ; it is time
You should know why all questioning of her
Racks me to madness.   Look upon me, child ;
Misshapen as I am, there once was one,
Who, seeing me despised, mocked, lonely, poor,
Loved me, I think, most for my misery ;
Thy mother, like thee, just so pure, so sweet.
I was a public notary in Cesena ;
Our life was humble, but so happy ; thou
Wert in thy cradle then, and many a night
Thy mother and I sat hand-in-hand together,
Watching thine innocent smiles, and building up
Long plans of joy to come !
                        [*His voice falters ; he turns away.*

FIORDELISA.

Alas! she died.

BERTUCCIO.

Died! There are deaths 't is comfort to look back on;
Hers was not such a death. A devil came
Across our quiet life, and marked her beauty,
And lusted for her; and when she scorned his offers,
Because he was a noble, great and strong,
He bore her from my side, by force, and after
I never saw her more; they brought me news
That she was dead.

FIORDELISA.

Ah me!

BERTUCCIO.

And I was mad
For years and years, and when my wits came back —
If e'er they came — they brought one haunting purpose,
That since has shaped my life, — to have revenge!
Revenge upon her wronger and his order;
Revenge in kind; to quit him, — wife for wife!

FIORDELISA.

Father, 't is not for me to question with you;
But think! revenge belongeth not to man
It is God's attribute, usurp it not!

BERTUCCIO.

Preach abstinence to him that dies of hunger,
Tell the poor wretch who perishes of thirst,
There 's danger in the cup his fingers clutch;
But bid me not forswear revenge. No word!
Thou know'st now why I mew thee up so close;
Keep thee out of the streets; shut thee from eyes

And tongues of lawless men, — for in these days
All men are lawless, —'t is because I fear
To lose thee, as I lost thy mother.

FIORDELISA.

                Father,
I 'll pray for her.

BERTUCCIO.

       Do, and for me ; good-night !

FIORDELISA.

Oh, not so soon, with all these sad dark thoughts,
These bitter memories.   You need my love ;
I 'll touch my lute for you, and sing to it.
Music, you know, chases all evil angels.

BERTUCCIO.

I must go : 't is grave business calls me hence.
[*Aside.*]   'T is time that I was at my post.   My own,
Sleep in thine innocence.   Good ! good-night !

FIORDELISA.

But let me see you to the outer door.

BERTUCCIO.

Not a step further, then.   God guard this place,
That here my flower may grow, safe from the blight
Of look, or word impure, — a holy thing
Consecrate to my service, and my love !
[*Exit* BERTUCCIO *and* FIORDELISA, R.   *Enter from behind
   the arras,* MANFREDI *and* TORELLI.

MANFREDI.

His daughter !   That so fair a branch should spring
From such a gnarled and misshapen stock !

TORELLI.

But did you mark how he raved of revenge
Upon our order?

MANFREDI.

By the mass, I think
That Guido Malatesta is the man
That played him the shrewd trick he told the girl of.
'T was at Cesena, marked you — the time fits.
That's why he hounds me on after the Countess.
What! must I be the tool of his revenge?
I'll teach the scurrile slave to strike at nobles.

TORELLI.

Hark! what's that?   [*Listening.*

MANFREDI.   ˙

'T is outside the window.

TORELLI (*listening*).

                                             Yes,
By Bacchus, some one climbs the balcony.

MANFREDI.   ˙

A gallant?

TORELLI.

In, sir; see the play played out.

MANFREDI.

But I'll not be forestalled!

TORELLI.

                    We've time enough.
[*They retire to the recess.   Enter* DELL' AQUILA *from the
    balcony.*

DELL' AQUILA.

Pardon, sweet saint, if I profane thy shrine.
I watched Bertuccio forth ; he passed me close,
I feared he would have seen me. I have sworn
Not to betray their foul design to him.
And to warn her, this means alone is left me.
Hark ! 't is her gracious step, she comes this way.
[*Enter* FIORDELISA ; *she kneels before the statue of the
Madonna.*

FIORDELISA.

Comfort of the afflicted, comfort *him !*
Turn his revengeful purpose to submission,
And grant that I may grow to take the place
My mother has left empty in his heart !
He 's gone ! And I had not the heart to speak
Of the young gentleman who follows me.
He asked if any spoke to me ; I told
The truth, — he never spoke to me.
[*Turning round and seeing* DELL' AQUILA.
[*In great terror.*]   Who 's there ?
Brigitta ! help !

DELL' AQUILA.

Silence ! but have no fear.
I am not here to harm you, do not tremble.
I would die, lady, rather than offend you.

FIORDELISA.

Oh, sir, how came you here ?

DELL' AQUILA.

I knew no other way
But by the balcony.   Desperate occasions
Dispense with ceremony.   My respect
Is absolute.   Fear not : I am not here

To say, " I love you," nor to tell you how
For months your face has been my beacon star.
My passion never would have found a tongue;
It is too reverent; but your safety, lady,
I can be bold for that.

FIORDELISA.

My safety!

DELL' AQUILA.

Threatened

With desperate danger.   Think you one so fair
Could even pray in safety in Faenza?
You have been seen: your beauty hath been buzzed
In the Court's amorous ear.   There is a project   .
To scale your balcony to-night.

FIORDELISA.

Oh, father!

DELL' AQUILA.

He cannot save you.   What were his sole strength
Against the bravos that the duke commands,
For any deed of ill?   My arm and sword
Are stronger than your father's, and are yours
As absolutely.   And yet what were these?
I could die for you, but I could not save you.

FIORDELISA.

What shall I do?

DELL' AQUILA.

Have you no friends, protectors,

To whom you might betake yourself?

FIORDELISA.

Alas!

I am a stranger here.

DELL' AQUILA.
Think, have you none?

FIORDELISA.
Ha! if the Countess Malatesta —

DELL' AQUILA.
What?
You know her?

FIORDELISA.
She once rescued me from insult
Of a rude man, and promised help whene'er
I chose to seek it.

DELL' AQUILA.
She is good and pure
And powerful, moreover. That's the chief.
Go to her straight; you have no time to lose.
Midnight is fixed for their foul enterprise.

FIORDELISA.
But how to find the house? And then the streets
Are dark and dangerous. I've but our servant,
Brigitta —

DELL' AQUILA.
Not a word to her! She's false.
Can you trust me? I'll lead you to the Countess.

FIORDELISA (aside).
Were this a stratagem!

DELL' AQUILA.
I see you doubt me;
I know you have good cause to doubt all men.
Oh, could I bare my heart, and show you there

Your image set amongst its holiest thoughts,
Beside my mother's well-remembered face.
Could truth speak with the tongue, look from the eyes,
You would not doubt me! What can oaths avail?
He who could cheat you, would not fear to cheat
God and his saints! Lady, it is the truth
That I have spoken! May Heaven give you faith
To trust me; but if not, I will stay,
And die in your defence.

FIORDELISA.

Sir, I will trust you!
And Heaven so deal with you as you with me!
Go with me to the Countess Malatesta.
I 'll seek the shelter of her roof to-night,
To-morrow must bring counsel for the future.

DELL' AQUILA.

Oh! bless you for this trust! Come, quick, but softly.
Put on your veil, fear not, I am your guard,
Your slave, your sentinel. I crave no guerdon,
Not even a look! Enough for me to save you.
                    [*Exit* FIORDELISA *and* DELL' AQUILA.

MANFREDI (*breaking from behind the arras;* TORELLI
            following him).
Why did you hold me back? Our project 's marred.
This moonstruck poet bears away the prize,
And I am fooled.

TORELLI.

            Nay, trust my cooler brain.
I 'll follow him to Malatesta's. Sure,
He 'll give her shelter?

MANFREDI.

In his lady's absence?

TORELLI.

Even so.   The old ruffian can be courteous
When there 's a pretty face in question!

MANFREDI.

Let him!

I 'll break his house, or any man that dares
Set his locks in the way of my good pleasure!

TORELLI.

Why not?   'T will give a double pungency
To our revenge upon Bertuccio.
We only looked to keep the foul-mouthed knave
Out of the way while we bore off his pearl;
But now we 'll use him for the robbery.
He shall see *us* scale Malatesta's windows;
But she whom we bear thence, muffled and gagged,
Shall be the hunch-backed scoffer's pretty daughter!

MANFREDI.

A rare revenge! and so this brain-sick poet
And my curst jester may console each other.
Watch them to Malatesta's!   I 'll to our friends,
And find Bertuccio by San Stefano!

[*Exit by secret door*, L. 2 E.

SCENE II.

*A street near the Church of San Stefano ; stage dark.
Enter* BERTUCCIO, L., *cloaked and masked.*

BERTUCCIO.

The hour has struck, — they will be here anon, —
Trust them to keep tryst for a villainous deed.
I had need to whet the memory of my wrong,
Or my girl's angel face and innocent tongue
Had shaken even *my* steadfastness of purpose !
And Malatesta's wife has done her kindness, —
I would that she had not ! But what's such slight service
To my huge wrong ? Let me but think of that !
I grow too human near my child. I lack
The sharp sting of court scorn to spur the sides
Of my intent ! With her I 'm free to weep ;
With them, I still must laugh, — still be their ape,
To mop and mow and wake their shallow mirth.
True, I can sometimes bite, as monkeys do.
They 'll make mirth of that, too ! O courtly sirs !
Sweet-spoken, stalwart gallants ! if you knew
The hate that rankles underneath my motley,
The scorn that barbs my wit, the bitterness
That grins behind my laughter, you would start
And shudder o'er your cups, and cross yourselves
As if the devil were in your company !
Once my revenge achieved, I 'll spurn my chain,
Fool it no more, but give what 's left of life
To thought of her I 've lost, and love of her
That yet is left me.
[*Enter* MANFREDI, ASCOLTI, *and* ORDELAFFI, *masked and
cloaked.*

MANFREDI.

Hist, Bertuccio!

BERTUCCIO.

Here, gossip Galeotto, — you are punctual;
Ascolti too; grave Signor Florentine,
We 'll show you how the gallants of Faenza
Treat greybeards who aspire to handsome wives.
Remember your beard 's grizzled — and beware —

ASCOLTI.

I will stand warned. You have the ladders here?

BERTUCCIO.

The lackeys wait in charge of them hard by.
But where 's Torelli? we shall want his help.

ORDELAFFI.

Pshaw! our three swords are plenty.

BERTUCCIO.

Cry you mercy!

'T is not Torelli's sword we want.

ORDELAFFI.

What then?

BERTUCCIO.

His marvellous quick scent of danger, man.
Stick to *his* skirts, I 'll answer for 't you 're safe.
Perhaps he smelt some risk of buffets here,
And so has ta'en him home to bed.

MANFREDI.

Away
Towards Malatesta's house! 't was there he promised

To meet us. Sirrah fool, be it thy post
To hold the ladder while we mount; and see
Thou play'st us no jade's trick, or 'ware the whip!

BERTUCCIO.

Fear not, magnanimous gossip! do your work
With as good will as I do mine. The Countess
Sleeps in the chamber of the balcony
Which rounds the angle of the southern front;
I came but now by the palace, — all was quiet.

MANFREDI.

Set on, then, cautiously, — use not your swords,
Unless on strong compulsion; blood tells tales,
And I want no more feuds upon my hands. [*Exeunt,* R.

SCENE III.

Exterior of the palace of MALATESTA, *with street. The
flat exhibits the corner of two streets. The palace of
MALATESTA is on a set piece,* L. U. E. *A window on the
first floor, with a balcony, practicable.* — *Night. Enter
FIORDELISA and DELL' AQUILA, followed by TORELLI
at a distance. Through the scene between FIORDELISA,
DELL' AQUILA, and MALATESTA, TORELLI watches and
listens behind a projecting piece of masonry.*

DELL' AQUILA.

Be of good cheer, — this is the house; I'll knock,
And summon forth the Count.   [*Knocks.*

FIORDELISA.

                              Oh, sir! what thanks
Can e'er repay this kindness?

DELL' AQUILA.
But remember
Who 't was that did it, I am thanked enough.

FIORDELISA.
I 'll pray for you after my father — hark !

DELL' AQUILA.
They come !   [*Enter a Servant from house.*
Two strangers who crave instant speech
Of the Count Malatesta.   [*Exit Servant.*

DELL' AQUILA.
And I should see your father ?

FIORDELISA.
Then you know him ?

DELL' AQUILA.
Yes.

FIORDELISA.
And his business — occupations ?   [*He bows.*
[*Sadly.*]   'T is more than I do, sir, that am his child.
I do not even know his name.

DELL' AQUILA.
What he
Keeps secret from you 't is not mine to tell ;
'T were well you should not question him too closely ;
He shall learn you are safe.

FIORDELISA.
And tell him, too,
That 't was *you* saved me, sir.   Promise me that !
[*Enter* MALATESTA, L.

MALATESTA.

Who is it would have speech of Malatesta ?

DELL' AQUILA.

You know me, Count ?

MALATESTA.

Dell' Aquila, well met!
But your companion ?   [*Aside.*]   Ha ! a petticoat!
So ho, my poet !

DELL' AQUILA.

Pardon, if I pray
This lady's name may rest a secret, Count ;
She is in grievous danger, — one from which
Your house can shelter her.   She owes already
Your countess much, for good help given at need,
So craves to increase the debt.

MALATESTA.

My house is hers,
But she should know my countess is not here.

FIORDELISA.

Not here !

MALATESTA.

But if she dare trust my grey hairs
She shall have shelter.

DELL' AQUILA.

Nay, she cannot choose.

MALATESTA.

I 'll give her my wife's chamber, if she will ;
Her woman to attend her.

DELL' AQUILA.

All she needs
Is your roof's shelter for the night; to-morrow
Must see her otherwise bestowed.

MALATESTA.

Go in,
Fair lady; my poor house, with all that 's in it,
Is at your service.   Had my wife been here,
You had had gentler 'tendance; as it is,
I 'll lead you to her chamber and there leave you.

TORELLI (*aside*).

Now to the hunters; I 've marked down the deer.
[*Exit* TORELLI, L. U. E.

MALATESTA (*to* AQUILA).

You will not stay and crush a cup with me?

DELL' AQUILA.

No, not to-night.
[*To* FIORDELISA.]   Did you not well to trust me?
Farewell; think of me in your prayers!

FIORDELISA.

I cannot
Choose but do that, sir.   [*Aside.*]   Oh, the thought of
him
Will come, henceforth, betwixt my prayers and Heaven!
[*Exit* MALATESTA, L., *leading in* FIORDELISA.

DELL' AQUILA.

His child!   Since when did grapes grow upon thistles?
And yet I 'm glad to know the tie that binds
The two together such a holy one!
Sweet angel, — sister angels guard thy sleep!

Now to seek out Bertuccio, and tell him
The danger she has 'scaped, and thank the saints
That made *me* her preserver.
[*Exit* DELL' AQUILA, R.   *Enter cautiously,* L. U. E., BER-
    TUCCIO, MANFREDI, ASCOLTI, ORDELAFFI, *and* TORELLI,
    with Servants carrying ladders.

MANFREDI.

Softly, you knaves! with velvet tread, like tigers —

BERTUCCIO.

Say rather, " cats."
                          [*A light appears at the window,* L. 2 E.

TORELLI.

Which is the balcony?

BERTUCCIO (*pointing*).

That!   I have noted in this summer weather
The window's left unbarred.

ASCOLTI.

                          Ha! there's a light!
If she were stirring!

BERTUCCIO.

                          What an' if she were?
A sudden spring, — a cloak flung o'er her head;
If she have time to scream, you are but bunglers.

MANFREDI.

My cloak will serve.   [*Takes it off.*

ASCOLTI.

                          If she alarm the house
It might go hard with us.

BERTUCCIO.

O cats that long
For fish, yet fear to wet your feet! I'll shame you.
Let me mount first; give me your cloak, Galeotto!

MANFREDI.

By your leave, fool, I'll net my own bird. Back!
Hold thou the ladder; that is lackeys' work,
And fits thee best. Ascolti and Torelli,
Guard the approaches! I and Ordelaffi
Will be enough to mount, and snare the game.
[*The light is extinguished; the Servants set a ladder to
the balcony.*
BERTUCCIO (*holds it*).
All's dark now, — up!
MANFREDI.
Why, rogue, how thy hand shakes!
Is 't fear?
BERTUCCIO.
'T is inward laughter, Galeotto.
To think how blank Guido will look to-morrow
To find the nest cold, and his mate borne off.
[MANFREDI *mounts the ladder, followed by* ORDELAFFI.
They enter the balcony.

BERTUCCIO (*eagerly listening*).
Ha! they are in by this time!
Cautious fools!
I had done 't myself in half the space! So, Guido,
You love your young wife well, they say; that's brave.

[MANFREDI *and* ORDELAFFI *appear on the balcony, bearing*
FIORDELISA *in their arms, muffled in* MANFREDI'S
cloak. She struggles, but cannot scream. ORDELAFFI
descends first, MANFREDI *hands* FIORDELISA *to him.*
They come down the ladder.

BERTUCCIO.

'T is done!

MANFREDI.

Away all, — to my garden house,
There to bestow our prize!
[*Exeunt* MANFREDI *and* ORDELAFFI, L. U. E. — *The Servants carry off the ladder.*

BERTUCCIO.

Now, Malatesta,
[*Shaking his fist at the house.*
Learn what it is to wake and find her gone
That was the pride and joy of your dim eyes, —
The comfort of your age!   I welcome you
To the blank hearth, — the hunger of the soul, —
The long dark days and miserable nights!
These you gave me; I give them back to you!
I, the despised, deformed, dishonoured jester,
Have reached up to your crown and pulled it down,
And flung it in the mire, as you flung mine!
Now, murdered innocent, *thou* art avenged!
But I have private wrongs, too, to repay;
This proud Manfredi, — he you spat upon,
He you spurned such a day, set in the stocks,
Whipped, — *he* is even with your mightiness!
Here is Francesca's ring; and here the letter,
To tell her that *her* vengeance, too, is ripe.
The blow shall come from her; but mine 's the hand
That guides the dagger's point straight to *his* heart!
I cannot sleep!   I 'll walk the night away;
It is no night for me, — my day has come!   [*Exit*, R.

ACT III.

SCENE. — *A room in the garden-house of* GALEOTTO MANFREDI,
*decorated with arabesques in the style of the earlier renaissance, —
folding-doors at the back, communicating with an inner chamber;
side entrances,* R. *and* L., *covered by curtains; a table, and chairs
of the curule form.*

SCENE I.

Enter FIORDELISA, *from* R.

FIORDELISA (*pressing her hands to her temples*).
Where am I?   What has happened? let me think!
Those men! — that blinding veil, — the fresh night air
That struck upon my face!   Then a wild struggle,
In strong and mastering arms!   Then a long blank!
I must have fainted; when I woke I lay
On a rich couch in that room.   Has he brought me
Into the very danger that he said
He came to take me from?   Oh, cruel!   No;
Falsehood could ne'er have found such words, such looks.
Father! — oh, when he comes and finds me gone!
I must go hence!
　　[*Looking round.*]   That door! —
　　　　[*She runs to side entrance,* L.]   'T is locked!
　　　　　　　　　　[*Shaking door.*]   Help! help!
How dare they draw their bolts on me!   My father
Shall punish them for this!   I will go forth!
　　　　[*Shakes door again; the door opens from without.*
At last! — Whoe'er you are, sir, help me hence!
　　　　　　　　　　　　[*Enter* MANFREDI, L.

Take me back to my father! He will bless you!
Reward you —

MANFREDI.

Nay, your own lips must do that.

FIORDELISA.

Oh, they shall bless you too, sir —

MANFREDI.

To be blessed
With that sweet mouth were well, yet scarce enough.

FIORDELISA.

Oh, sir, we waste time! Set what price you will
On the great service, I am sure my father
Will pay you.   [MANFREDI *re-locks the door.*

MANFREDI.

If we're to discuss your ransom
'T were fairest we should do it with closed doors;
The terms can scarce be settled till you know
Your prison, jailer, in what risk you stand.
First, for your prison, — Know you where you are?

FIORDELISA.

No.

MANFREDI.

In the Duke Manfredi's palace. Next,
Know you your jailer?

FIORDELISA.

Who?

MANFREDI.

Manfredi's self.

FIORDELISA (*wringing her hands*).

Woe 's me !

MANFREDI.

What ?   Is the news so terrible ?

FIORDELISA.

I 've heard Brigitta, and my father, too,
Speak of the Duke Manfredi.

MANFREDI (*aside*).

Here 's a chance
To hear a genuine judgment of myself !
[*To her.*]   They said —

FIORDELISA.

That he was cruel, bold, unsated
In thirst for evil pleasures, — it was odds
Whether more feared or hated in Faenza.

MANFREDI (*aside*).

Trust the crowd's garlic cheers and greasy caps !
The knaves shall know me worse ere they have done.
I thank you, pretty one, — I am the Duke !

FIORDELISA.

Then Heaven have mercy on me !

MANFREDI.

If report
Speak truth, your prayer were idle ! — but report
Is a sad liar.   Do I look the ogre
They painted to you ?   Nay, my fluttered dove,
Smooth but those ruffled feathers ; look about you !
Is this so grim a dungeon ?   Was your couch

Last night so hard, — your 'tendance so ungentle?
I am *your* prisoner, fairest, — not you mine.

FIORDELISA.

Then let me go!

MANFREDI.

               Not till you know at least
What you will lose by going.   All Faenza
Is mine, and she I favour may command
Whate'er Faenza holds of wealth or pleasure.
I 'll pour them at her feet, and after fling
Myself there too, to woo a gracious word!
What 's life, ungraced by love? — a dismal sky
Without sun, moon, or starlight!   'T is a cup
Drained of the wine that reddened in its gold!
A lute shorn of its strings, — a table stripped
Of all its festal meats, — mere life in death
A jewel like thy beauty is not meet
To be shut in a chest; it should be set
To shine in princely robes, — to grace a crown.
I would set thee in mine.　　　　　*[Approaching her.*

FIORDELISA.

             Stand back, my lord!

MANFREDI.

Why, little fool, I would not harm a hair
On thy fair head.   Think what thy life has been!
How dull and dark and dreary!   It shall be
As bright and glad and sunny as the prime
Of summer flowers.   Only repel not joy
Because it comes borne in the hand of Love!

FIORDELISA.

Oh, you profane that name!   Is Love the friend
Of night and violence and robbery?

Let me go hence, I say! I have a father
Who 'll make you terribly aby this wrong,
Lord as you are!

MANFREDI.

Your father! By the Mass!
She makes me laugh! Your father, girl! Bertuccio!

FIORDELISA.

That I should learn my father's name from him!
Yes, Duke, my father!

MANFREDI.

Why, he is my slave, —
A thing that crouches to me like my hound,
To beg for food, or deprecate the lash, —
My butt, — my whipping-block, — my fool in motley!

FIORDELISA.

It is *not* true! This is a lie, like all
That you have said. Let me go forth, I say!

MANFREDI.

You 're in my palace. Here are none but those
To whom my will is law; your calls for help
Will only bring more force, — if I could stoop
To use force with a lady —

FIORDELISA.

Then you *have*
Some manhood in you. Look, sir, at us two.
You are a duke, you say, — your power but bounded
By your own will. I am a poor weak girl,
E'en weaker than I knew, if what you say
Touching my father be the truth. What honour
Is to be won on me? Yet, won it may be,

By yielding to my prayers to be set free, —
To be sent home. Oh, let me but go hence
As I came hither; I will speak to none
Of this night's outrage, — even to my father.

MANFREDI.

Ask anything but this.

FIORDELISA.

      Nothing but this!
You have a wife, my lord; what if she knew?

MANFREDI.

The more need to take care that you tell her not!
Come, little one, give up these swelling looks,
Though they become you mightily.
         [Approaching her.
FIORDELISA.

        Stand off!
        [He pursues her; she flies.
Help! Help!   *[Running to the* C. *door.*
    A door! ha!
  [She forces it open, rushes in, and closes it violently.

MANFREDI (locking it outside).

       Deeper in the toils!
[Laughs.] The lamb seeks shelter in the wolf's own den.

TORELLI (at L. door outside).

My lord!

MANFREDI (unlocks the door).

  Torelli's voice! How now, Torelli?
         [Enter TORELLI, L.
TORELLI.

My lord, the Duchess is returned.

MANFREDI.
Why, man,

Thy news is stale; the Duchess has been here
These five hours; she arrived, post-haste, ere sunrise.
She must have ridden in the dark. 'T was that
Prevented me from making earlier matins
Before my little saint here.

TORELLI.
Do you know

What brought the Duchess back so suddenly?

MANFREDI.

Some jealous fancy pricked her, as I judge
From her accost when we encountered first;
And, as I gathered, she suspects contrivance
Betwixt me and the Countess Malatesta.
'T was a relief, for once, that I could twit her
With groundless fears. I told her Malatesta
Rode yesterday with his lady to Cesena,
And, for more proof, repeated what he said,
That on my wife's least summons, she 'd return;
So she *has* summoned her, in hopes, no doubt,
To catch me in a lie. Her messenger
Rode to Cesena just at daybreak. Soon
We may look for him back, bringing, I hope,
Ginevra Malatesta.

TORELLI.
This is rare.

So falls she off the scent, and leaves you here
To follow up your game with Fiordelisa.

MANFREDI.

Even so; I excused me from her presence
By work of State, for which to this pavilion

I had summoned you and the envoy of Florence, —
Staid work of State, being no less a one
Than to lend me your presences at the banquet
I mean to offer our fair prisoner.
Bid Ordelaffi and Ascolti hither,
And send my men with fruits and wines and sweetmeats,—
All that is likeliest to tempt the sense
Of this scared bird.

TORELLI.

How did you find her, sir ?

MANFREDI.

Beating her pretty wings against the bars ;
Still calling for her father.   Shrewdly minded
To peck, instead of kissing, silly fledgeling !
But I will tame her yet, till she shall come
To perch upon my finger.

TORELLI.

Where is she ?

MANFREDI.

In the inner room, whither she fled but now.
Fear not, — I turned the key on her ; she 's safe.

TORELLI.

I 'll send what you command, and warn the rest
That you attend them.   Good speed to your wooing !
[Exit TORELLI, by entrance, L.

MANFREDI.

Now for my prisoner ! by gentle means
To gain her ear.   Asmodeus, tip my tongue
With love's persuasion.

[*Exit into inner room*, C. *Enter* THE DUCHESS FRANCESCA,
masked, and BERTUCCIO, *who has resumed his fool's
dress*, R.

FRANCESCA (*unmasking*).

Was 't not Torelli went hence, even now ?

BERTUCCIO.

By the great walk ?   I think it was.   Be sure
He saw us not in the pleached laurel alley.

FRANCESCA.

Then you still bear me out, my husband lies ?
That Malatesta's wife has *not* gone hence ?

BERTUCCIO.

Trust a fool's eyes before a husband's tongue.
I say again, I was at hand last night
When your lord bore from Malatesta's house
Said Malatesta's wife.   I saw the deed.
I heard the order given to bring her hither.

FRANCESCA.

Then 't was by force, not by the lady's will,
She came ?

BERTUCCIO.

Force ?   Quotha, — force ?   How many ladies
Have had to bless the " force " that saved their tongue
An awkward " yes ! "   See you not what an answer
" Force " finds for all ?   It stops a husband's mouth ;
Crams its fist down the town's throat ; nay, at a pinch,
Perks its sufficient self in a wife's face.
Commend me still to " force."   It saves more credits
Than e'er it ruined virtues.   After folly,
I hold force the best mask that wit has found
To mock the world with !

FRANCESCA.

There 's weight in that.
This violence would stand her in good stead,
Were she e'er called in question! Then what matter,
[BERTUCCIO, *who has been moving round the room, stops
opposite centre door.*
So I be wronged, if 't is by force or will!
Would I had certain proof!

BERTUCCIO.

Ha! you want proof?
Come here!   [THE DUCHESS *approaches him.*
Stand where I stand. Now listen, — close.

FRANCESCA (*listening at door*).
My husband's voice in passionate entreaty!

BERTUCCIO.
Only *his* voice?
FRANCESCA (*starting*).
An answering voice! a woman's!
These are your State affairs, my gracious duke!

BERTUCCIO.

If you would have more proof, I 'll bring you where
You shall hear his humble tools in last night's business
Discuss the deed, — all noble gentlemen,
Who 'd pluck my hood about my ears if I
Durst hint a doubt of their veracity.

FRANCESCA.

Do so; and if they bear thy story out,
I know my part.
BERTUCCIO.
What! tears?

FRANCESCA.

> Tears ?   Death to both !

BERTUCCIO.

Take care ! His guards are faithful.   Can you trust
A hand to do the deed ?

FRANCESCA.

> I trust my own.

BERTUCCIO.

Women turn pale at blood.   Your heart may fail you
When the time comes to strike.

FRANCESCA.

> Daggers for men !

I know a surer weapon.

BERTUCCIO (*creeping up to her and whispering*).

> Poison ?

FRANCESCA (*putting her finger on her lip*).

> Hush !

The Borgia's physician gave it me !
It may be trusted !

BERTUCCIO (*withdrawing, aside*).

> My she leopard 's loosed !
> [*Exit* BERTUCCIO, L.

FRANCESCA (*still at the door,* C., *listening*).

Past doubt, a woman's tongue ! And now my husband's !
How well I know the soft, smooth, pleading voice, —
The voice that drew my young heart to my lips
When, at my father's court, I plighted troth

To him, and he to me! Oh, bitterness!
Now spurned for each new leman of the hour!
Oh, he shall learn how terrible is hate
That grows of love abused!
[*Taking a phial from her bosom.*
Come, bosom friend,
That hast lain cold, of late, against my heart,
As if to whisper to it, "Be thou stone,
When the time calls for *me*." [*Looking at the phial.*
Each drop's a death!
What matter who she be? Enough for me
That she usurps the place that should be mine
In Galeotto's love! Hark! some one comes.
[*She conceals the phial, and resumes her mask. Enter two
Chamberlains with white wands,* L., *followed by
Attendants bearing a banquet, and pass into the
inner room; after them a* PAGE, *with wine in a
golden flagon; goblets, fruit, etc., on a salver. She
stops him as he is going through the folding-doors.*
Hold, sir; set down your charge.

PAGE.

By your leave, madame:
'T is for my lord.
FRANCESCA.
Since when was that an answer
To give thy lady? [*Removes her mask.*
PAGE (*aside*).
'T is the Duchess! [*Respectfully.*] Pardon,
I knew you not.
FRANCESCA.
Enough, sir, set it down,
And wait without till I bid thee bear in.
[*Exit* PAGE, L., *after placing the salver on the table.*
What need of further proof? Is 't heaven or hell

That sends this apt occasion? Galeotto,
I warned thee in the springtime of our loves,
This hand could kill as easy as caress;
You laughed, and took it in your ampler palm,
And said that death were pleasant from such white
And taper fingers. Try it now!
[*She pours some of the contents of the phial into the flagons
of wine.*

                            'T is done!
[*Re-enter* BERTUCCIO, L., *hastily.*

BERTUCCIO.

Hide, here, Madonna: here their lordships come!
I met them on the way, so brave and merry!
My gossip Galeotto bids them here,
To feast with him and *her!*
[*Exit* BERTUCCIO L. FRANCESCA *starts as if stung, then
goes to the door and beckons. Re-enter,* PAGE, L.
She signs to him : he bears in the wine.

FRANCESCA (*aside*).

                      Their doom is sealed!
[*She retires behind curtained entrance,* R. *Re-enter* BER-
TUCCIO, *with* ASCOLTI *and* ORDELAFFI, L.

BERTUCCIO.

It is your due; you that go out bat-fowling
Lack wine o' mornings to keep up your hearts.

ORDELAFFI.

Why, thou wert there, knave; yet try thou to enter
Into the presence, and they 'll whip thee back;
His Highness wants no fool to-day!

BERTUCCIO.
                              That's true, —
With you two for his company.   But tell me,
How will the lady relish, o'er her wine,
The cut-throat faces that she saw last night?
Methinks 't will mar her appetite.

ASCOLTI.
                                   Be sure
She will not look so scared at *us*
As *thou* would'st at the sight of *her.*

BERTUCCIO.
                              Who — I?
Nay, I but held the ladder; we poor knaves
Must take the leavings of your rogueries,
As of your feasts; but prithee, Ordelaffi,
How looked she in her night-rail?

ORDELAFFI.
                              Would'st believe it?
Methought she had a something of thy favour,
As — if so crook'd a thing could have a daughter —
Thy daughter might have had.
                    [*All laugh.*   BERTUCCIO *starts.*

ASCOLTI.
                    How now?   He winces!
There cannot, sure, be issue of thy loins!
Nature's too merciful; she broke the mould
When she turned *thee* out!

BERTUCCIO.
                              Nature, sir, proportions
Her witty fools to her dull ones; while she makes
Ascoltis, she must needs produce Bertuccios

To sting their hard hides now and then.   But tell me,
Think you Ginevra needed all that force ?

ORDELAFFI.

She struggled stoutly ; but a lady's struggles,
I take it, are much like her " no," — which often
Must be read " yes."

ASCOLTI.
Let 's in, at once, my lords.

BERTUCCIO.

I 'll marshal you.   Who said that cap and bells
Should be shut out ?
ASCOLTI.
Stand back, Sir Fool ; 't were best.
You may repent your pressing on too far.

BERTUCCIO.

I fain would see the lady ; 't is not often
That one can carry a beauty off at night,
And make her laugh i' the morning.

ORDELAFFI.
Neither she
Nor you, I think, are likely to breed much mirth
Out of each other.
BERTUCCIO.
Say you so ?   Here goes !
[*He runs up to the door ; a* PAGE *opens it and motions
him back, two Chamberlains appearing at the open
door.*
Why, how now, sirrah ?   I 'm the fool ! ·

PAGE.
Stand back !

BERTUCCIO.

I ! — why I 'm free o' the palace ; every place
Except the council chamber, and in that
I sit by proxy !

PAGE.

'T is the Duke's strict order
You enter not this room.

[BERTUCCIO *is pressing forward.*

Back ! or the grooms
Shall score thy hunch to motley.   [*He closes the door.*

ASCOLTI.

How now, sirrah !
Call you this marshalling ?

BERTUCCIO.

I am right served !
I forgot that fools in silks should take precedence
Of fools in motley !   Lead the way, my lords !

ORDELAFFI.

Look ! here comes Malatesta.

BERTUCCIO.

Ha ! — but stay,
To hear me gird at him !   You call me bitter ;
Now you shall see how merciful I 've been.

ASCOLTI.

Waste not your ears on him ; the Duke awaits us
Beside his beauty, — metal more attractive
Than this cursed word-catcher.

ORDELAFFI.

Ay, ay ! let 's in.
[*Exeunt* ORDELAFFI *and* ASCOLTI.   BERTUCCIO *goes hastily
to* R. *entrance.   Enter* FRANCESCA.

BERTUCCIO.

Now, now, Madonna, have you proof enough ?

FRANCESCA.

Mountains of proof on proof, if proof were needed ;
But had disproof come with them, and not proof,
'T is all too late.

BERTUCCIO.

How ?

FRANCESCA.

I have drugged their wine
They will sleep sound to-night.   [*She retires up stage.*

BERTUCCIO (*aside*).

Choose woman's hands,
You that would have grim work nimbly dispatched !
Here 's Malatesta, — looking black as night !
So, Lord, I hope you liked your waking news ?
Now — now — to gloat over his agony !
                    [*Enter* MALATESTA, L.

MALATESTA (*not seeing* THE DUCHESS).

Ha, knave, I 'd see the Duchess.

BERTUCCIO (*looking at him curiously*).

Marvellous !

MALATESTA.

How now ?

BERTUCCIO.

To think that they can make such caps
To hide all trace of them !

MALATESTA.

Of what knave ?

BERTUCCIO.

                                  Horns.

MALATESTA.

Rascal!

BERTUCCIO.

    I hope your lordship had good rest,
And that my lady, too, slept undisturbed?

MALATESTA.

What mean you, sirrah?

BERTUCCIO.

                Nay, strain not so hard
To keep it down; you are among friends here.
A grievous loss, no doubt; but at your age
You could scarce look to keep her to yourself.
Others have lost wives, too, — poor knaves who thought
To stick in their thrum-caps jewels that caught
The eyes of nobles; needs were they must yield
Daughters or wives —

MALATESTA.

              Art mad, or drunk, or both?
My errand's to thy mistress, not to thee.
Where is she?

FRANCESCA (*coming down stage*).
       Here, my lord!   [*They talk apart.*

BERTUCCIO.
              He bears it bravely,
But wounds will bleed under an iron corselet:
And how his must be bleeding! For he loved her —
The whole Court vouches it — as old men love,
Husbanding their spent fires into a heat,
The fiercer that it has short time to burn.
      [FRANCESCA *and* MALATESTA *come forward.*

FRANCESCA.

You say your lady slept not here, last night,
But at Cesena ?

MALATESTA.

Or the devil 's in 't.
I saw her safe bestowed there ; I can trust
My own eyes, — or still better, my own bolts.

BERTUCCIO (*amazed and aside*).

Is this old man, too, of Manfredi's council,
To cheat his wife ?

MALATESTA.

I little thought to bring her back so soon,
But on your summons, I have straight recalled her.

BERTUCCIO (*breaking in eagerly*).

And she is here ; hold him to that, Madonna!

MALATESTA.

Malapert dog !

FRANCESCA.

Pardon his licensed tongue.
I fain would see the lady.

MALATESTA (*bowing*).

You shall see her ;
I have not far to fetch her.   [*Exit* L.

BERTUCCIO (*furiously*).

'T is a lie, —
A cursed lie, to hide his own foul shame !
Believe him not !

FRANCESCA.

But if he bring the lady ?

BERTUCCIO (*laughing*).
Ay, if he bring the lady, then believe him !
[*Aside.*]   He robs me of my right, — taking his wrong
With outward show of calm : *mine* turned my brain.
I looked to see him mad, or drive him so !

MANFREDI (*within*).
More wine, knave !
        [*Enter a* PAGE *from* C. *door, passes out* L.

FRANCESCA.
Ginevra, or another, — what of that ?
The wrong 's the same ; why not the same revenge ?

BERTUCCIO.
The same to you, but not the same to me !
I tell you, Malatesta's wife sits yonder, —
Sits at your husband's side ; I saw her — I —
Borne off last night !   I *saw !*   There is no faith
In eyes or ears or truth, if 't were not she !
[*Re-enter* MALATESTA, L., *with* GINEVRA.   BERTUCCIO'S
    back is towards the door.

MALATESTA.
Madame, my wife !

BERTUCCIO (*turning in amaze*).
            Ginevra here ! Then who
Was that they carried from her bed last night ?
Who is 't sits yonder ?

FRANCESCA.
            Tell me, gracious lady,
Where did you sleep last night ?

GENEVRA.

Where I scarce thought
To leave so soon, your Highness; in Cesena,
Within my husband's castle.

FRANCESCA.

Pardon, madame,
That I have set you on a hurried journey,
Still more that *I* have wronged you in my thoughts!
[*Passing her hand over her brow. Laughter heard within.*
[*Aside.*] They laugh! Laugh on, my lord, while it is
   time.

GINEVRA.

Will 't please you, grant me audience; you shall hear
To the minute how my hours went yesterday,
Down to this moment.

FRANCESCA.

Come out in the air;
I stifle within hearing of their mirth.
[*To* BERTUCCIO.] Stay here; see that the other 'scape
   me not.   [*Exit* FRANCESCA *and* GINEVRA, L.

BERTUCCIO.

The other! Not Ginevra?
   [*To* MALATESTA.] Good, my lord,
Your wife slept at Cesena, yet her chamber
Was not untenanted last night, I 'll swear!

MALATESTA.

And so thou might'st, yet break no oath.

BERTUCCIO.

Who slept in 't?

MALATESTA.

I know not. Ask Dell' Aquila; 't was he
Brought me the lady, craving shelter for her
From some great danger.

BERTUCCIO.
But you saw her face ?

MALATESTA.

And if I did, think'st thou I 'd trust her name
To *thy* ass-ears ? [*Exit* MALATESTA, L.
BERTUCCIO.
Fooled — mocked of my revenge !
The sweetest morsel on 't whipped from my teeth !
Oh, I could brain myself with my own bawble !
[*Enter* DELL' AQUILA, L.
[*Aside.*] Dell' Aquila. *He* knows.

DELL' AQUILA.
Well met, Bertuccio ;
I 've sought thee since this morning, — nay, since mid-
night.
BERTUCCIO.
Ha !
DELL' AQUILA.
For a matter much concerns thy peace.
Thou hast a daughter. [BERTUCCIO *starts.*] How I know
thou hast
Matters not to my story.

BERTUCCIO (*hastily*).
Hush ! hush ! hush !
If you know this, as you 're a Christian man,
And poet, — poets should have softer hearts
Than courts and camps breed now-a-days, — oh, keep
The knowledge to yourself !

DELL' AQUILA.

It is too late.
Torelli knew it; had set wolfish eyes
On her —

BERTUCCIO.

Well? well?

DELL' AQUILA.

Had rung her beauty's praise
Here in the Court.   Thou hast no friends here.

BERTUCCIO (*eagerly*).

Well?

DELL' AQUILA.

They plotted how to lure thee from the house,
And in thy absence to surprise her window,
And bear her off!   They bound me by an oath
To keep it secret from *thee* — not from *her*.
I swore to save her or to lose myself,
So found a desperate means of speech with her,
And warned her of her danger.

BERTUCCIO.

Thanks! thanks! thanks!
But only warned her!

DELL' AQUILA.

Placed her, too, in safety.

BERTUCCIO.

Oh, heaven! where?

DELL' AQUILA.

In the house of Malatesta.

BERTUCCIO (*hoarsely*).

My child in Malatesta's house last night?

DELL' AQUILA.

Secure; — even in the Countess's own chamber!

BERTUCCIO (*with a wild cry*).

My child! my child! wronged! murdered!

DELL' AQUILA.

Ha! by whom?

BERTUCCIO (*wildly*).

By me! by me! Her father — her own father!
That would have grasped Heaven's vengeance, and have drawn
The bolt on my own head, and hers — and hers!

DELL' AQUILA.

What do you mean?

BERTUCCIO.

I counselled the undoing
Of Malatesta's wife. I stood and watched,
And laughed for joy, and held the ladder for them;
And all the while 't was my own innocent child!
Look not so scared —'t is true; I am not mad!
She 's here — now — in their clutches! [*Laughter within.*
Hark! they laugh.
'T is the hyænas o'er their prey — my child! —
And I stand here and cannot lift a hand!

DELL' AQUILA.

Here 's mine, and my sword, too!

BERTUCCIO.

Oh, what were that
Against their felon blades?

DELL' AQUILA.

                       True, true! what aid?
Ha, there 's the Duchess!

BERTUCCIO (*shrieks*).

                      I had forgotten her!
[*Drawing* DELL' AQUILA *to him and whispering hoarsely.*
Man, she has drugged their wine; the bony Death
Plays cupbearer to them: if she drinks, she dies!
                    [*Enter a* PAGE *with wine*, L.
Look! look! Perchance that is the very wine!
[*He runs between the* PAGE *and the door, and assumes the*
    FOOL'S *manner.*
Halt there! for the fool's toll. No wine goes in
But pays the fool's toll.

                PAGE.

                Out knave! Stand aside!
[BERTUCCIO *snatches the flagons from the salver.*

                BERTUCCIO.

'T is forfeit by the law!
[*The* PAGE *tries to recover the wine; in the struggle* BER-
    TUCCIO *pretends to upset the flagons by accident, and*
    the wine is poured out on the stage.

                PAGE.

                Thy back shall bleed
To make it up. Now must I go fetch more, —
And brook the cellarer's chiding for thy folly.
                        [*Enter* TORELLI, L.

               BERTUCCIO (*to* DELL' AQUILA).
If he goes in — could we but enter with him!
A word of mine might save her from the poison.
                  [BERTUCCIO *gets between him and the door..*

TORELLI.

Good-day, Sir Poet ; stand aside, Sir Fool.

BERTUCCIO.

You are going in ?

TORELLI.

Ay !

BERTUCCIO.

There 's a shrewd hiatus
Needs filling at the table.   You have War
And Love, but, lacking Poetry and Folly,
War is but butchery, and Love goes lame.
Tuck us beneath your wings, sweet Baldassare,
And you 'll be trebly welcome.
[*Seizing him by one arm, and motioning* DELL' AQUILA
to take the other.

TORELLI.

The Duke for once has shut his doors against
Both Poetry and Folly.   He is cloistered
For grave affairs.

BERTUCCIO.

Tush ! tell me not, sweet gossip.
Why, man, *I* know that there 's a petticoat —
And more, I know the wearer.

TORELLI.

Thou !

BERTUCCIO.

You 've lost
The rarest sport.   Ascolti and Ordelaffi
Have had their will of me.   For once I 'll own
You 've turned the tables fairly on the fool !
That our Ginevra should be Fiordelisa,

And poor Bertuccio not know! Ha, ha!
Oh, excellent! It was a sleight of hand
I shall remember to my dying day.

TORELLI.

Nay, an' thou tak'st it so —

BERTUCCIO.

How should I take it?
Besides the pleasantness of it, there's the honour.
Think! my poor daughter in the Duke's high favour!
Why, there are counts by scores had pawned their 'scutcheons
To come into such grace. I warrant now,
You thought I'd swear, and storm, and rend you all,
So shut me out. But, lo you! I am merry;
And so shall *she* be, if you'll let me in.
But let me in — I'll school the silly wench —
Teach her what honour she has come to; thank
The gracious duke, and play the merriest antics.
You'll swear you never saw me in such fooling —
But take me in.

TORELLI.

Why, now! the fool's grown wise!
I'll tell the Duke; perchance he'll let thee in.
[*Exit* TORELLI, C. BERTUCCIO, *exhausted by his emotions,
falls into a chair and writhes convulsively.*

DELL' AQUILA.

Lives hang on minutes here. Said you the Duchess
Had mixed the poison, or but meant to mix it?

BERTUCCIO.

There it is, man, — I know not which. E'en now
Death may be busy at her lips. Once in,

In my mad antics I might spurn the board,
And spill the flagons as I did e'en now;
But here I'm helpless.   Oh, Beelzebub!
Inspire them with desire to see a father
Make laughter of the undoing of his child!
Ha, some one comes!   They'll let me in!

[c. *door opens.*

TORELLI (*at the door*).

The Duke
Will none of thy ape's tricks.
[*He retires, closing the door.*   BERTUCCIO *wrings his hands
and screams.*

DELL' AQUILA (*rushing forward*).

What ho!   Torelli!
And you within, you, my lord duke, 'fore all!
I do proclaim you cowards, ruffians, beasts.
Come out, if you be men, and drive my challenge
Back in my throat, if you 've one heart among you!

BERTUCCIO.
You speak to men; they 're fiends.

DELL' AQUILA.

No hope! no hope!
Yes! here 's the Duchess; she 's a woman still —
[*Enter* FRANCESCA *and* GINEVRA, L.

BERTUCCIO.
Madame, and you, too [*To* GINEVRA.], plotting your un-
doing,
I 've compassed the destruction of my child, —
The daughter that I loved more than my life.
'T was she they seized last night, and she 's in there.
[*Pointing to* c. *door.*

FRANCESCA.

Your child ?

BERTUCCIO.

From death, if not wrong worse than death,
You still may save her. Have the doors burst open.
You can command here — next the Duke ; if not,
At least [*aside to her*] forbear the poison !

FRANCESCA (*aside to him*).

'T is too late.
The wine was here !

BERTUCCIO.

Then this alone remains.
[*He rushes up to the door and shouts.*
Come forth, my lords ! The Duke's life — all your lives
Hang by a thread ! Come forth — all ! For your lives !
[TORELLI, ASCOLTI, *and* ORDELAFFI *appear at the door.*
Your wine is poisoned !

TORELLI.

Ha ! Who did the deed ?

BERTUCCIO.

I ! Drink not — for your lives !
[*They are rushing upon him, drawing their swords.*

FRANCESCA.

He lies ! 'T was I !
[*A shriek is heard within.*

BERTUCCIO.

My child ! my child !

TORELLI (*who has turned back at the sound, flinging the
door wide open*).

Look to the Duke, my lords !

[*As the doors are flung open, the interior of the inner room
   is seen with* THE DUKE *senseless on his seat, and*
   FIORDELISA *lying at his feet.* TORELLI, ASCOLTI, *and*
   ORDELAFFI *support* THE DUKE. BERTUCCIO *and* DELL'
   AQUILA *rush up to* FIORDELISA.

BERTUCCIO.

Too late! too late!

TORELLI.

He 's dead!

FRANCESCA.

                              Before all men,
I 'll answer this!

BERTUCCIO.

          Before Heaven's judgment seat,
How shall I answer *this?*   [*Pointing to* FIORDELISA.
[DELL' AQUILA *has brought* FIORDELISA *forward.* BER-
   TUCCIO *takes her in his arms.*

                              Dead — dead — my bird!
My lily flower! Gone to thy last account,
All sinless as thou wert. My fool's revenge
Ends but in this! Cold! cold!
[*Putting his hand on her heart.*]   Ha! Yes! a beat!
                    [*Putting his lips to her mouth.*
A breath! A full deep breath!
                              She lives! she lives!
Say, some of you, *she* drank not, and I 'll bless
The man that says so, — yea, so pray for him
As saints ne'er prayed! She breathes still! Hark!
     hark!

FIORDELISA (*faintly*).

Father!

TORELLI.

She never drank! Thou hast her pure as when
She kissed thy lips last night!

BERTUCCIO.

Oh, bless you, bless you!
She lives — lives — lives! Leave us to pray together.

TORELLI (*to* FRANCESCA).

Madame, you are our prisoner: the Duke
Lies foully murdered.

FRANCESCA.

Ha! what call you "foully"?
Who but myself can estimate my wrongs?
For those who stand, like him, past reach of justice,
Vengeance takes Justice's sharp sword.

BERTUCCIO.

No, no!
Vengeance is hellish! Justice is from heaven!
Look, Guido Malatesta, I am he
Whose wife, long years ago, *you* stole from him:
I am Antonio Bordiga!

MALATESTA.

You?

BERTUCCIO.

I thirsted for revenge; for that I wrought
Upon the Duke to carry off *your* wife, —
Your innocent Ginevra. Seeking that,
See to what verge of terrible disaster
I've brought my own dear daughter! — seeking that,
I've compassed the Duke's death, whose blood must lie
Still on my head!

FRANCESCA (*proudly*).
                    I take it upon mine!
My father, Giovanni Bentivoglio,
Stands at your gates, in arms!   Let who will, question
Francesca Bentivoglio of this deed.

FIORDELISA.
Father, let's pray for her!

BERTUCCIO.
                    For her — for me!
We need it both!   Ah, thou said'st well, my child!
Vengeance is not man's attribute, but Heaven's!
I have usurped it.   [*Hiding his face in her bosom.*
          Pray — oh, pray for me!

THE END.

MARION DE LORME.

DRAMATIS PERSONÆ.

MARION DE LORME.
DIDIER.
LOUIS XIII.
MARQUIS DE SAVERNY.
MARQUIS DE NANGIS.
L' ANGELY.
M. DE LAFFEMAS.
DUKE DE BELLEGARDE.
MARQUIS DE BRICHANTEAU,
COUNT DE GASSÉ,
VISCOUNT DE BOUCHAVANNES, } *Officers of the Regiment of Anjou.*
CHEVALIER DE ROCHEBARON,
COUNT DE VILLAC,
CHEVALIER DE MONTPESAT,
DUKE DE BEAUPRÉAU.
VISCOUNT DE ROHAN.
ABBÉ DE GONDI.
COUNT DE CHARNACÉ.
SCARAMOUCHE,
GRACIEUX, } *Provincial comedians.*
TAILLEBRAS,
COUNCILLOR OF THE GREAT CHAMBER.
TOWN CRIER.
CAPTAIN.
A JAILER.
A REGISTRAR.
THE EXECUTIONER.
FIRST WORKMAN.
SECOND WORKMAN.
THIRD WORKMAN.
A LACKEY.
DAME ROSE.

Provincial Comedians, Guards, Populace, Nobles, Pages.

1638.

MARION DE LORME.

ACT I.

THE MEETING.

SCENE. — *Blois. A bed-chamber. A window opening on a balcony at the back. To the right, a table with a lamp, and an arm-chair. To the left a door, covered by a portière of tapestry. In the background a bed.*

SCENE I.

MARION DE LORME, *in a very elegant wrapper, sitting beside the table, embroidering.* MARQUIS DE SAVERNY, *very young man, blond, without moustache, dressed in the latest fashion of* 1638.

SAVERNY (*approaching* MARION *and trying to embrace her*).
Let us be reconciled, my sweet Marie!

        MARION (*pushing him away*).
Not such close reconciliation, please!

        SAVERNY (*insisting*).
Just one kiss!
        MARION (*angrily*).
   Marquis!

        SAVERNY.
           What a rage! Your mouth
Had sweeter manners, not so long ago!

MARION.

Ah, you forget!

SAVERNY.

No, I remember, dear.

MARION (*aside*).

The bore! the tiresome creature!

SAVERNY.

Speak, fair one!
What does this swift, unkind departure mean?
While all are seeking you at Place Royale,
Why do you hide yourself at Blois?   Traitress,
What have you done here all these two long months?

MARION.

I do what pleases me, and what I wish
Is right.   I'm free, my lord!

SAVERNY.

Free!   Yes.   But those
Whose hearts you've stolen, are they also free?
I?   Gondi, who omitted half his Mass
The other day, because he had a duel
Upon his hands for you?   Nesmond, D'Arquien,
The two Caussades, Pressigny, whom your flight
Has left so wretched, so morose, even
Their wives wish you were back in Paris, that
They might have gayer husbands!

MARION (*smiling*).

Beauvillain?

SAVERNY.

Is still in love.

MARION.

Céreste?

SAVERNY.

Adores you yet.

MARION.

And Pons?

SAVERNY.

Oh, as for him, he hates you!

MARION.

Proof
He is the only one who loves me! Well,
The President?
    [*Laughing.*] The old man! What's his name?
                  [*Laughing more heartily.*
Leloup!

SAVERNY.

He's waiting for you, and meanwhile
He keeps your portrait and sings odes to it.

MARION.

He's loved me two years now, in effigy.

SAVERNY.

He'd much prefer to burn you. Tell me how
You keep away from such dear friends.

MARION (*serious, and lowering her eyes*).

That's just
The reason, Marquis; to be frank with you,
Those brilliant follies which seduced my youth
Have given me much more misery than joy.
In a retreat, a convent cell, perhaps,
I want to try to expiate my life.

SAVERNY.

I 'll wager there 's a love-tale behind that.

MARION.

You dare to think —

SAVERNY.

That never a nun's veil
Surmounted eyes so full of earthly fire.
It could not be.   You love some poor provincial!
For shame!   To end a fine romance with such
A page!

MARION.

It is n't true!

SAVERNY.

Let 's make a wager!

MARION.

Dame Rose, what time is it?

DAME ROSE (*outside*).

Almost midnight!

MARION (*aside*).

Midnight!

SAVERNY.

That is a most ingenious way
Of saying, " Time to go."

MARION.

I live retired,
Receiving no one, and unknown to all.
Besides, 't is dangerous to be out late:
The street is lonely, full of robbers.

SAVERNY.
Well,
They can rob me.

MARION.
And oftentimes they kill!

SAVERNY.
Good! they can kill me.

MARION.
But —

SAVERNY.
You are divine!
But I 'll not stir one foot before I know
Who this gay shepherd is, who 's routed us!

MARION.
There 's no one!

SAVERNY.
I will be discreet.   We courtiers,
Whom people think so mad, so curious
And spiteful, are maligned.   We gossip, but
We never talk!   You 're silent?
            [*Sits down.*]   Then I 'll stay!

MARION.
What does it matter?   Well, it 's true!   I love!
I 'm waiting for him!

SAVERNY.
That 's the way to talk!
That 's right!   Where is it you expect him?

MARION.
Here!

SAVERNY.
When?

MARION.

Now !   [*She goes to the balcony and listens.*
Hark ! that is he perhaps.
                    [*Coming back.*]   'T is not.
Now are you satisfied ?

SAVERNY.

Not quite !

MARION.

                                   Please go !
SAVERNY.

I want to know his name, this proud gallant,
For whose reception I am thus dismissed.

MARION.

Didier is all the name I know for him.
Marie is all the name he knows for me.

SAVERNY (*laughing*).

Is 't true ?

MARION.

             Yes, true !

SAVERNY.

               This is a pastoral,
And no mistake.   'T is Racan, pure !   To enter,
I have no doubt he scales the wall.

MARION.

                         Perhaps.
Please go !   [*Aside.*]   He wearies me to death !

SAVERNY (*becoming serious*).

                                   Of course
He 's noble.

MARION.

I don't know.

SAVERNY.

What?
[*To* MARION, *who is gently pushing him towards the door.*
I am going!
[*Coming back.*
Just one word more! I had forgotten. Look!
[*He draws a book out of his pocket and gives it to* MARION.
An author who is not a fool, did this.
It's making a great stir.

MARION (*reading the title*).
"Love's Garland"—ah!
"To Marion de Lorme."

SAVERNY.
They talk of nothing
But this in Paris. That book and "The Cid"
Are the successful efforts of the day.

MARION (*taking the book*).
It's very civil of you; now, good-night!

SAVERNY.
What is the use of fame? Alack-a-day!
To come to Blois and love a rustic! Bah!

MARION (*calling to* DAME ROSE).
Take care of the Marquis, and show him out!

SAVERNY (*saluting her*).
Ah, Marion, you've degenerated! [*He goes out.*

SCENE II.

MARION, *afterwards* DIDIER.

MARION (*alone, shuts the door by which* SAVERNY *went out*).

                                        Go —
Go quickly! Oh, I feared lest Didier —

[*Midnight strikes.*
                                        Hark!
It's striking midnight! Didier should be here!

[*She goes to the balcony and looks into the street.*
No one!

[*She comes back and sits down impatiently.*
            Late! To be late — so soon!
[*A young man appears behind the balustrade of the balcony, jumps over it lightly, enters, places his cloak and sword on the arm-chair. Costume of the day: all black: boots. He takes one step forward, pauses and contemplates* MARION, *sitting with her eyes cast down.*
                                        At last!

[*Reproachfully.*
To let me count the hour alone!

            DIDIER (*seriously*).
                        I feared
To enter!

            MARION (*hurt*).
    Ah!

            DIDIER (*without noticing it*).
            Down there, outside the wall,
I was o'ercome with pity. Pity? yes,
For you! I, poor, accursed, unfortunate,

The Rendezvous.

Etched by H. Toussaint — From Drawing by
François Flameng.

Stood there a long time thinking, ere I came!
" Up there an angel waits," I thought, " in virgin grace,
Untouched by sin, — a being chaste and fair,
To whose sweet face shining on life's pathway
Each passer-by should bend his knees and pray.
I, who am but a vagrant 'mongst the crowd,
Why should I seek to stir that placid stream ?
Why should I pluck that lily ? With the breath
Of human passion, why should I consent
To cloud the azure of that radiant soul ?
Since in her loyalty she trusts to me,
Since virtue shields her with its sanctity,
Have I a right to take her gift of love,
To bring my storms into her perfect day ?

MARION (*aside*).

This is theology, it seems to me!
I wonder if he is a Huguenot ?

DIDIER.

But when your tender voice fell on my ear,
I wrestled with my doubts no more, — I came.

MARION.

Oh, then you heard me speaking, — that is strange !

DIDIER.

Yes ; with another person.

MARION (*quickly*).
                    With Dame Rose !
She talks just like a man, don't you think so ?
Such a strong voice ! Ah, well, since you are here
I am no longer angry ! Come, sit down.
                    [*Indicating a place at her side.*
Sit here !

DIDIER.

No! at your feet.

[He sits on a stool at MARION'S *feet and looks at her for*
some moments in complete silence.

                                  Hear me, Marie!
I have no name but Didier, — never knew
My father nor my mother. I was left,
A baby, on the threshold of a church.
A woman, old, belonging to the people,
Preserved me, was my mother and my nurse.
She brought me up a Christian, then she died
And left me all she had, — nine hundred francs
A year, on which I live. To be alone
At twenty is a sad and bitter thing!
I travelled — saw mankind: I learned to hate
A few and to despise the rest. For on
This tarnished mirror we call human life,
I saw nothing but pride and misery
And pain; so that, although I'm young, I'm old,
And am as weary of the world as are
The men who leave it. Never touched a thing
That did not tear and lacerate my soul!
Although the world was bad, I found men worse.
Thus I have lived; alone and poor and sad,
Until you came, and you have set things right.
I hardly know you. At the corner of
A Paris street you first appeared to me.
Then afterwards I met you, and I thought
Your eyes were sweet, your speech was beautiful!
I was afraid of loving you, and fled!
But destiny is strange: I found you here,
I find you everywhere, as if you were
My guardian angel. So at last, my love
Grew powerful resistless, and I felt
I must talk with you. You were willing. Now

They 're at your service, both my heart and life.
I will do anything that you wish done.
If there is any man or anything
That troubles you, or you have any whim
And somebody must die to satisfy it, —
Must die, and make no sign, — and feel 't was worth
Death any time to see you smile ; if you
Need such a man, speak, lady : I am here !

MARION (*smiling*).

You 've a strange nature, but I love you so !

DIDIER.

You love me ! Ah, take care ! One dare not say
Such words in any careless way ! Love me ?
Oh, do you know what loving means ? What 't is
To feel love take possession of our blood,
Become our daily breath ? To feel this thing
Which long has smouldered burst to flame, and rise
A great, majestic, purifying fire ?
To feel it burn up clean within our hearts
The refuse other passions have left there ?
This love, hopeless indeed, but limitless,
Which outlives all things, even happiness, —
Is this the kind of love you mean ?

MARION (*touched*).
                                    Indeed !

DIDIER.

You do not know it, but I love you so !
From that first time I saw you, my dark life
Was shot with sunlight streaming from your eyes ;
Since then all 's different. To me you seem
Some wonderful creation, not of earth.
My life, in whose dark gloom I groaned so long,

Grows almost beautiful when you are by.
For 'til you came, I 'd wandered, suffered, wept ;
I 'd struggled, fallen, — but I had not loved.

MARION.

Poor Didier !

DIDIER.

Speak, Marie !

MARION.

Well, then, I do.
I love with just this love, — love you as much
And maybe more than you love me !   It was
Not destiny that brought me here.   'T was I
Who came, who followed you, and I am yours !

DIDIER (*falling on his knees*).

Oh, do not cheat me !   Give me truth, Marie !
If to my ardent love your love responds,
The world holds no possession rich as mine !
My whole life, kneeling at your feet, will be
One sigh of speechless, blinding ecstasy.
But do not cheat me !

MARION.

Do you want a proof
Of love, my Didier ?

DIDIER.

Yes !

MARION.

Then speak !

DIDIER.

You are —
Quite free ?

MARION (*embarrassed*).

Free ?   Yes !

DIDIER.

Then take me for a brother,
For a protector — be my wife ?

MARION (*aside*).

His wife !
Ah, why am I not worthy ?

DIDIER.

You consent ?

MARION.

I — can —

DIDIER.

Don't say it, please — I understand !
An orphan, without fortune !   What a fool !
Give back my pain, my gloom, my solitude !
Farewell !   [*He starts to go ;* MARION *holds him back.*

MARION.

Didier, what are you saying ?
                    [*She bursts into tears.*

DIDIER.

True !
But why this hesitation ?   [*Going back to her.*
                    Can't you feel
The ecstasy of being, each to each, a world,
A country, heaven ; in some deserted spot
To hide a happiness kings could not buy

MARION.

It would be heaven !

DIDIER.

Will you have it ?   Come !

MARION.

[*Aside.*]   Accursed woman !   [*Aloud.*]   No, it cannot be.
[*She tears herself from out his arms, and falls on the
      arm-chair.*

DIDIER (*freezingly*).

The offer was not generous, I know.
You 've answered me.   I 'll speak of it no more !
Good-bye !

MARION (*aside*).

Alack, the day I pleased him !   [*Aloud.*]   Stay !
I 'll tell you.   You have hurt me to the soul.
I will explain —

DIDIER (*coldly*).

What were you reading, madame,
When I came ?   [*Takes the book from the table and reads.*
      " To Marion de Lorme.
Love's Garland !"   Yes, the beauty of the day !
      [*Throwing the book violently to the floor.*
Vile creature ! a dishonour to her sex !

MARION (*trembling*).

But — she —

DIDIER.

What are you doing with such books ?
How came they here ?

MARION (*inaudibly, and looking down*).
They came by chance.

DIDIER.

Do you, —
You who have eyes so pure, a brow so chaste, —

Do you know what she is — this woman ?   Well,
She 's beautiful in body, and deformed
In soul !   A Phryne, selling everywhere,
To every man, her love, which is an insult,
An infamy !

MARION (*her head in her hands*).
My God!
[*A noise of footsteps, a clashing of swords outside, and cries.*

VOICE IN THE STREET.
Help!   Murder!   Help!

DIDIER (*surprised*).
What noise is that out there upon the square ?
[*Cries continue.*
VOICE IN THE STREET.
Help!   Murder!   Help!

DIDIER (*looking from the balcony*).
They 're killing some one!   Ha!
[*He takes his sword and steps over the balustrade.
MARION rises, runs to him and tries to hold him
back by his cloak.*

MARION.
Don't Didier, if you love me!   They 'll kill you!
Don't go!

DIDIER (*jumping down into the street*).
He is the one they 're going to kill!
Poor man!   [*Outside, to combatants.*
Stand off!   Hold firmly, sir, and push!
[*Clashing of swords.*
There, wretch !   [*Noise of swords, voices, and footsteps.*

MARION (*on the balcony, terrified*).
        Just Heaven!   They are six 'gainst two!

VOICE IN THE STREET.
This man — he is the devil!
[*The clashing of swords subsides little by little, then entirely
    ceases.   The sounds of footsteps become indistinct.
    DIDIER re-appears scaling the balcony.*

DIDIER (*outside of the balcony and turned towards the street*).
                    You are safe;
Now go your way!

SAVERNY (*from outside*).
            Not 'til I 've grasped your hand, —
Not 'til I 've thanked you, if you please!

DIDIER.
                    Pass on!
I will consider myself thanked.

SAVERNY.
                Not so!
I mean to thank you.   [*Scaling balcony.*
            DIDIER.
            Can't you speak from there
And say " I thank you " without coming up?

———

SCENE III.

MARION, DIDIER, SAVERNY.

SAVERNY (*jumping into the room, sword in hand*).
Upon my soul!   'T is a strange chivalry
To save my life and push me from the door!

The door, — that is to say, the window! No,
They shall not say one of my family
Was bravely rescued by a nobleman
And did not in return say " Marquis — " Pray,
What is your name ?

DIDIER.

Didier.

SAVERNY.

Didier — of what?

DIDIER.

Didier, of nothing! People kill you, and
I help you, — that is all! Now go!

SAVERNY.

Indeed!

That 's your way, is it ? Why not have let
Those traitors kill me ? 'T would have pleased me more.
For without you I 'd be a dead man now.
Six thieves against me! Dead! Of course! What else?
Six daggers against one thin sword —

[*Perceiving* MARION, *who has been trying to avoid him.*

Oh, ho!

You 're not alone! At last I understand!
I 'm robbing you of pleasure. Pardon me!
[*Aside.*] I 'd like to see the lady!
[*Approaches* MARION, *who is trembling : he recognizes her.*

It is you!

[*Indicating* DIDIER.

Then he 's the one!

MARION (*low*).

Hush! You will ruin all!

SAVERNY (*bowing*).

Madame !

MARION (*low*).

I love for the first time !

DIDIER (*aside*).

'Sdeath !

That man is looking at her with bold eyes.

[*He overturns the lamp with a blow.*

SAVERNY.

You put the lamp out, sir ?

DIDIER.

It would be wise

For us to leave together, and at once.

SAVERNY.

So be it, then !   I follow you !

[*To* MARION, *whom he salutes profoundly.*

Madame,

Farewell !

DIDIER (*aside*).

What a rare coxcomb !

[*Aloud to* SAVERNY.]   Come, sir, come !

SAVERNY.

You 're brusque, but I 'm in debt to you for life.

If ever you should need fraternal friendship,

Count upon me, Marquis de Saverny,

Paris, Hôtel de Nesle.

DIDIER.

Enough ; sir ! Come !

[*Aside.*]   To see her thus examined by a fool !

[*They go out by the balcony.   The voice of* DIDIER *is heard outside.*

Your road lies that way.   Mine lies here !

Marion de Lorme.

SCENE IV.

MARION, DAME ROSE.

MARION (*remains absorbed a moment, then calls*).

Dame Rose!

[DAME ROSE *appears.* MARION *points to the window.*
Go shut it!

[DAME ROSE *having shut the window, turns and sees* MARION
wiping away a tear.

DAME ROSE (*aside*).

She is weeping!

[*Aloud.*] It is time
To sleep, madame!

MARION.

Yes, time for you, — you people.

[*Undoing her hair.*
Come, help me to undress!

DAME ROSE (*helping her to undress*).

The gentleman
To-night was pleasant. Is he rich?

MARION.

Not rich.

DAME ROSE.

But gallant.

MARION.

No, nor gallant.

[*Turning to* DAME ROSE.
He did not
So much as kiss my hand!

DAME ROSE.

What use is he?

MARION (*pensive*).

I love him!

ACT II.

THE ENCOUNTER.

SCENE. — *Blois. The door of a public-house. A square. In the background the city of Blois is visible in the form of an amphitheatre, also the towers of St. Nicholas upon the hill, which is covered with houses.*

SCENE I.

COUNT DE GASSÉ, MARQUIS DE BRICHANTEAU, VISCOUNT DE BOUCHAVANNES, CHEVALIER DE ROCHEBARON. *They are seated at tables in front of the door: some are smoking, the others are throwing dice and drinking. Afterwards* CHEVALIER DE MONTPESAT, COUNT DE VILLAC; *afterwards* L'ANGELY; *afterwards* THE TOWN-CRIER *and The Populace.*

BRICHANTEAU (*rising, to* GASSÉ, *who enters*).
    Gassé!   [*They shake hands.*
               You are come to join
The regiment at Blois: our compliments
Upon your burial.   [*Examining his clothes.*
      Ah!

GASSÉ.
         . It is the style, —
This orange with blue ribbons.
       [*Folding his arms and curling his moustache.*
                You must know
That Blois is forty miles from Paris!

BRICHANTEAU.
Yes,
It 's China!

GASSÉ.
That makes womankind rebel:
To follow us they must exile themselves.

BOUCHAVANNES (*turning from the game*).
You come from Paris ?

ROCHEBARON (*taking out his pipe*).
Is there any news ?

GASSÉ (*bowing*).
No, nothing.   Corneille still upsets all heads.
Guiche has obtained the order ; Ast is duke.
Of trifles, plenty, — thirty Huguenots
Were hung ; a quantity of duels.   On
The third, D'Angennes fought Arquien on account
Of wearing point of Genoa ; the tenth,
Lavardie had a rendezvous with Pons,
Because he 'd taken Sourdis' wife from him.
Sourdis and D'Ailly met about a creature
In the theatre Mondori.   On the ninth,
Lachâtre fought with Nogent because he wrote
Three rhymes of Colletet's badly ; Margaillan
With Gorde, about the time of day ; D'Humière
With Gondi on the way to walk in church ;
And all the Brissacs 'gainst all the Soubises
For some bet on a horse against a dog.
Then Caussade and Latournelle fought for nothing, —
Merely for fun : Caussade killed Latournelle.

BRICHANTEAU.
Gay Paris !   Duels have begun again.

GASSÉ.

It is the fashion!

BRICHANTEAU.

Feasts and love and fighting!
There is the only place to live!
[*Yawning.*]   All one
Can do here is to die of weariness.
[*To* GASSÉ.]   You say Caussade killed Latournelle?

GASSÉ.

He did,
With a good gash!   [*Examining* ROCHEBARON'S *sleeves.*
What's that you wear, my friend?
Those trimmings are not fashionable now.
What! cords and buttons?   Nothing could be worse.
You must have bows and ribbons.

BRICHANTEAU.

Pray repeat
The list of duels.   How about the King?
What does he say?

GASSÉ.

The Cardinal's enraged
And means to stop it.

BOUCHAVANNES.

Any news from camp?

GASSÉ.

I think we captured Figuère by surprise —
Or else we lost it.
[*Reflecting.*]   Yes, that's it.   'T is lost!
They took it from us.

ROCHEBARON.

Ah!   What said the King?

GASSÉ.

The Cardinal is most dissatisfied.

BRICHANTEAU.

How is the Court?   I hope the King is well.

GASSÉ.

Alas! the Cardinal has fever and
The gout, and goes out only in a litter.

BRICHANTEAU.

Queer!   We talk King, you answer Cardinal!

GASSÉ.

It is the fashion!

BOUCHAVANNES.

So there's nothing new!

GASSÉ.

Did I say so?   There's been a miracle,
A prodigy, which has amazed all Paris
For two months past; the flight, the disappearance —

BRICHANTEAU.

Go on!   Of whom?

GASSÉ.

Of Marion de Lorme,
The fairest of the fair!

BRICHANTEAU (*with an air of mystery*).
Here's news for you.

She's here!

GASSÉ.

At Blois?

BRICHANTEAU.

Incognito!

GASSÉ.

What! she?
In this place? Oh, you must be jesting, sir!
Fair Marion, who sets the fashions! Bah!
This Blois is the antipodes of Paris.
Observe! How ugly, old, ungainly 't is!
Even those towers —

[Indicating the towers of St. Nicholas.
Uncouth and countrified!

ROCHEBARON.

That's true.

BRICHANTEAU.

Won't you believe Saverny when
He says he saw her, hidden somewhere with
A lover, and this lover saved his life
When thieves attacked him in the street at night? —
Good thieves, who took his purse for charity,
And just desired his watch to know the time.

GASSÉ.

You tell me wonders!

ROCHEBARON (*to* BRICHANTEAU).

Are you sure of it?

BRICHANTEAU.

As sure as that I have six silver bezants
Upon a field of azure. Saverny
Has no desire, at present, but to find
This man.

BOUCHAVANNES.

He ought to find him at her house.

BRICHANTEAU.

She 's changed her name and lodging, and all trace
Of her is lost.
[MARION *and* DIDIER *cross the back of the stage slowly*
    without being noticed by the talkers ; they enter a small
    door in one of the houses on the side.

GASSÉ.

To have to come to Blois
To find our Marion, a provincial !
[*Enter* COUNT DE VILLAC *and* CHEVALIER DE MONTPE-
    SAT, *disputing loudly.*

VILLAC.
                            No !

I tell you no !

MONTPESAT.

And I — I tell you, yes !

VILLAC.

Corneille is bad !

MONTPESAT.

                    To treat Corneille like that, —
The author of " The Cid " and of " Melite."

VILLAC.

" Melite ? "   Well, I will grant you that is good ;
But he degenerated after that,
As they all do.   I 'll do the best I can
To satisfy you : talk about " Melite,"
" The Gallery of the Palace," but " The Cid ! "
What is it, pray ?

GASSÉ (*to* MONTPESAT).
You are conservative.

MONTPESAT.
" The Cid " is good !

VILLAC.
I tell you it is bad !
Your " Cid," — why Scudéry can crush it with
A touch ! Look at the style ! It deals with things
Extraordinary ; has a vulgar tone ;
Describes things plainly by their common names
Besides, it is obscene, against the law !
" The Cid " has not the right to wed Chimène !
Now have you read Pyramus, Bradamante ?
When Corneille writes such tragedies, I 'll read !

ROCHEBARON (*to* MONTPESAT).
" The Great and Last Soliman " of Mairet,
You must read that : that is fine tragedy !
But for your " Cid."

VILLAC.
What self-conceit he has !
Does he not think he equals Boisrobert,
Mairet, Gombault, Serisay, Chapelain,
Bautru, Desmarets, Malleville, Faret,
Cherisy, Gomberville, Colletet, Giry.
Duryer, — indeed, all the Academy ?

BRICHANTEAU (*laughing compassionately and shrugging
his shoulders*).
Good !

VILLAC.
Then the gentleman deigns to create !
Create ! Faith ! after Garnier, Theophile,
And Hardy ! Oh, the coxcomb ! To create !

An easy thing!   As if the famous minds
Had left behind them any unused thing.
On that point Chapelain rebukes him well!

ROCHEBARON.

Corneille's a peasant!

BOUCHAVANNES.

                    Yet Monsieur Godeau,
Bishop of Grassé, says he's a man of wit.

MONTPESAT.

Much wit!

VILLAC.

                If he would write some other way, —
Would follow Aristotle and good style.

GASSÉ.

Come, gentlemen, make peace.   One thing is sure,
Corneille is now the fashion: takes the place
Of Garnier, just as in our day felt hats
Have replaced velvet *mortiers*.

MONTPESAT.

                    For Corneille
I am, and for felt hats!

GASSÉ (*to* MONTPESAT).

                You are too rash!
[*To* VILLAC.]   Garnier is very fine.   I'm neutral; but
Corneille has also his good points.

VILLAC.

                        Agreed!

ROCHEBARON.

Agreed! He is a witty fellow and
I like him!

BRICHANTEAU.

He has no nobility!

ROCHEBARON.

A name so commonplace offends the ear.

BOUCHAVANNES.

A family of petty lawyers, who
Have gnawed at ducats 'til they obtained sous.
[L'ANGELY *enters, seats himself at a table alone, and in
silence. He is dressed in black velvet with gold trim-
ming.*

VILLAC.

Well, if the public like his rhapsodies
The day of tragic-comedy is past.
I swear to you the theatre is doomed.
It is because this Richelieu —-

GASSÉ (*looking across at* L'ANGELY).
Say, *lordship,*
Or else speak lower.

BRICHANTEAU.
Hell take this eminence!
Is 't not enough to manage everything?
To rule our soldiers, finances, and us,
Without controlling our poor language too?

BOUCHAVANNES.

Down with this Richelieu, who flatters, kills :
Man of the red hand and the scarlet robe !

ROCHEBARON.

Of what use is the King ?

BRICHANTEAU.

In darkness, we —
That is, the people — march : eyes on a torch.
He is the torch : the King's the lantern which
In its bright glass protects the flame from wind.

BOUCHAVANNES.

Oh, could our swords blow such a wind some day
As to extinguish this devouring fire !

ROCHEBARON.

If every one had the same mind as I !

BRICHANTEAU.

We would unite —
[*To* BOUCHAVANNES.]   What do you think, Viscount ?

BOUCHAVANNES.

We 'd give him one perfidious, useful blow !

L'ANGELY (*rising, with gloomy tone*).

Conspiring !   Young men !   Think of Marillac !
[*All shudder : turn away, and are silent with terror ; all
fix their eyes on* L'ANGELY, *who silently resumes his
seat.*

VILLAC (*taking* MONTPESAT *aside*).

My lord, when we were talking of Corneille,
You spoke in tones that irritated me.
In my turn I would like to say two words
To you —

MONTPESAT.

With sword —

VILLAC.

Yes.

MONTPESAT.

Or with pistol?

VILLAC.

Both!

MONTPESAT (*taking his arm*).

Let's go and find some corner in the town.

L'ANGELY (*rising*).

A duel, sirs?   Remember Boutteville.

[*New consternation among the young men.* VILLAC *and*
   MONTPESAT *separate, keeping their eyes fixed on*
   L'ANGELY.

ROCHEBARON.

Who is this man in black who frightens us?

L'ANGELY.

I'm L'Angely.   I'm jester to the King.

BRICHANTEAU (*laughing*).

Then it's no wonder that the King is sad.

BOUCHAVANNES (*laughing*).

Great fun he makes, this rabid cardinalist!

L'ANGELY (*standing*).

Be careful, gentlemen!   This minister
Is mighty.   A great mower, he!   He makes
Great seas of blood, and then he covers them
With his red cloak and nothing more is said.   [*Silence.*

GASSÉ.

Good faith!

ROCHEBARON.
I 'm blessed if I shall stir !

BRICHANTEAU.
Beside

This jester Pluto was a funny man !
[*A crowd of people enter from the streets and houses, and
spread over the Square. In the centre appears* THE
TOWN-CRIER *on horseback, with four Town-servants in
livery, one of whom blows the trumpet, while the other
beats the drum.*

GASSÉ.
What are these people doing ?   Ah, the crier !
Well, pater-nosters are in order now !

BRICHANTEAU (*to a juggler with a monkey on his back,
who has joined the crowd*).
Which one of you shows off the other, friend ?

MONTPESAT (*to* ROCHEBARON).
I hope our packs of cards are still complete.
[*Indicating the four Servants in livery.*
It looks as though these knaves were stolen thence.

TOWN-CRIER (*in a nasal tone of voice*).
Peace, citizens !

BRICHANTEAU (*low to* GASSÉ).
He has a wicked look.
His voice wears out his nose more than his mouth !

TOWN-CRIER.
"Ordinance : Louis, by the Grace of God — "

BOUCHAVANNES (*low to* BRICHANTEAU).
Cloak *fleur-de-lis* concealing Richelieu !

L'ANGELY.

Attention !

TOWN-CRIER (*continuing*).
" King of France and of Navarre — "

BRICHANTEAU (*low to* BOUCHAVANNES).
A fine name, which no minister e'er hoards.

TOWN-CRIER (*continuing*).
" Know all men by these presents, we greet you !
> [*He salutes assembly.*

Having considered that all kings desired
And have tried to abolish duelling,
But yet, in spite of edicts signed by them,
The evil has increased in great degree,
We ordain and decree that from this time
All duellists who rob us of our subjects,
Whether but one of them or both survive,
Be brought for punishment unto our court,
And commoner or noble shall be hung.
In order to give force to this edict
We here renounce our right of pardon for
This crime. It is our gracious pleasure." — Signed,
LOUIS ; and lower, — RICHELIEU.
> [*Indignation among the nobles.*

BRICHANTEAU.
> What 's this ?

We are to hang up like Barabbas !

BOUCHAVANNES.
> We ?

Tell me the name of any place which holds
A rope by which to hang a nobleman !

TOWN-CRIER (*continuing*).

" We, provost, that all men may know these facts,
Command this edict to be hung up on
The Square."
[*The two Servants attach a great placard to an iron
    gallows protruding from the wall on the right.*

GASSÉ.

'T is the edict they ought to hang!
Well done!

BOUCHAVANNES (*shaking his head*).

Yes, Count; while waiting for the head
Which shall defy it.
[THE TOWN-CRIER *exits; the crowd retires.* SAVERNY
    enters. It begins to grow dark.

SCENE II.

The same. MARQUIS DE SAVERNY.

BRICHANTEAU (*going to* SAVERNY).

Cousin Saverny,
I hope you 've found the man who rescued you.

SAVERNY.

No; I have searched the city through in vain.
The robbers, the young man, and Marion, —
They have all faded from me like a dream.

BRICHANTEAU.

You must have seen him when he brought you back,
Like a good Christian, from those infidels.

SAVERNY.

The first thing that he did was to throw down
The lamp.

GASSÉ.

That's strange!

BRICHANTEAU.

You'd recognize him if
You met him?

SAVERNY.

No; I did n't see his face.

BRICHANTEAU.

What is his name?

SAVERNY.

Didier.

ROCHEBARON.

That's no man's name!
That is a bourgeois name.

SAVERNY.

It does n't matter.
Didier is this man's name.   There are great men
Who have been conquerors and bear grand names,
But they 've no greater hearts than this man had.
I had six robbers!   He had Marion!
He left her, and saved me.   My debt's immense!
This debt I mean to pay.   I tell you all:
I 'll pay it with the last drop of my blood!

VILLAC.

Since when do you pay debts?

SAVERNY (*proudly*).
                                        I 've always paid
Those debts which can be paid with blood.
Blood is the only change I carry, sir !
[*It is quite dark ; the windows in the city are lighted one
    by one ; a lamp-lighter enters and lights a street-lamp
    above the edict and goes out.   The little door through
    which* MARION *and* DIDIER *disappeared is re-opened.*
    DIDIER *comes forth dreamily, walking slowly, his arms
    folded.*

SCENE III.

The same.   DIDIER.

DIDIER (*coming slowly from the back ; no one sees or hears
                            him*).
Marquis de Saverny !   I would like much
To see that fool who looked at her so hard.
I have him on my mind.

BOUCHAVANNES (*to* SAVERNY, *who is talking with* BRI-
                        CHANTEAU).
                    Saverny !

DIDIER (*aside*).
                                        Ah,
That is my man !
[*He advances slowly, his eyes fixed on the noblemen, and
    sits down at a table placed under the street-lamp,
    which lights up the edict.*   L'ANGELY, *motionless and
    silent is a few steps distant.*

BOUCHAVANNES (*to* SAVERNY, *who turns around*).
                You know about the edict ?

SAVERNY.

Which one?

BOUCHAVANNES.

Commanding us to give up duels.

SAVERNY.

It is most wise.

BRICHANTEAU.

Hanging's the penalty.

SAVERNY.

You must be jesting.   Commoners are hung,
Not nobles.

BRICHANTEAU (*showing the placard*).

Read it for yourself.   It's there,
Upon the wall.

SAVERNY (*perceiving* DIDIER).

That sallow face can read
For me.   [*To* DIDIER, *elevating his voice.*
Ho! man there with the cloak!   My friend!
Good fellow!
[*To* BRICHANTEAU.]   Brichanteau, he must be deaf.

DIDIER (*slowly lifting his head, without taking his eyes
from him*).

You spoke to me?

SAVERNY.

I did!   In fair return,
Read that placard which hangs above your head.

DIDIER.

I?

SAVERNY.

You, — if you can spell the alphabet.

DIDIER (*rising*).

It is the edict threatening duellists
With gallows, be they nobles or plebeians.

SAVERNY.

No, you mistake, my friend.   You ought to know
A nobleman was never born to hang,
And in this world, where we claim all our rights,
Plebeians are the gallows' only prey.   [*To the noblemen.*
These commoners are rude.
    [*To* DIDIER, *with malice.*]   You don't read well;
Perhaps you are near-sighted.   Lift your hat,
'T will give you more light.   Take it off.

DIDIER (*overthrowing the table which is in front of him*).
                                        Beware !
You have insulted me !   I 've read for you;
I claim my recompense !   I 'll have it, too !
I want your blood, I want your head, Marquis !

SAVERNY (*smiling*).
We must be fitted to our station, sir.
I judge him commoner, he scents marquis
In me.

DIDIER.
        Marquis and commoner can fight.
What do you say to mixing up our blood ?

SAVERNY.

You go too fast, and fighting is not all.
I am Gaspard, Marquis de Saverny.

DIDIER.

What does that matter ?

SAVERNY.

Here my seconds are l'
The Count de Gassé, noble family,
And Count de Villac, family La Teuillade,
From which house comes the Marquis d'Aubusson.
Are you of noble blood ?

DIDIER.

What matters that ?
I am a foundling left at a church door.
I have no name ; but in its place, I 've blood,
To give you in exchange for yours !

SAVERNY.

That, sir,
Is not enough ; but as a foundling, you
May claim the right, because you might be noble.
It is a better thing to lift a vassal
Than to degrade a peer. You may command me !
Choose your hour, sir.

DIDIER.

Immediately !

SAVERNY.

Agreed !
You 're no usurper, that is clear.

DIDIER.

A sword !

SAVERNY.

You have no sword ? The devil ! that is bad.
You might be thought a man of low descent.

Will you have mine ?   [*Offers his sword to* DIDIER.
                    Well tempered and obedient !
[L'ANGELY *rises, draws his sword and presents it to* DIDIER.

                    L'ANGELY.

No ; for a foolish deed, you 'd better take
A fool's sword !   You are brave !   You 'll honour it !
[*Maliciously.*]   And in return, to bring me luck, pray let
Me cut a piece from off the hanging-rope !

            DIDIER (*bitterly, taking sword*).
I will.   [*To* THE MARQUIS.
        Now God have mercy on the good !

        BRICHANTEAU (*jumping with delight*).
A duel — excellent !

            SAVERNY (*to* DIDIER).
            Where shall we fight ?

                    DIDIER.
Beneath the street-lamp.

                    GASSÉ.
            Gentlemen, you 're mad !
You cannot see.   You 'll put your eyes out.

                    DIDIER.
                            Humph !
There 's light enough to cut each other's throat.

                    SAVERNY.
Well said !

                    VILLAC.
        You can see nothing.

DIDIER.
                    That's enough !
Each sword is lightning flashing in the dark.
Come, Marquis !
[*Both throw off their cloaks, take off their hats with which
    they salute each other, throwing them afterwards on
    the ground.   Then they draw their swords.*]

SAVERNY.
At your service, sir.

DIDIER.
                    Now !   *Garde !*
[*They cross swords and fence, silently and furiously.
    Suddenly the small door opens,* MARION *in a white
    dress appears.*]

———

SCENE IV.

The same.   MARION.

MARION.
What is this noise ?   [*Perceiving* DIDIER *under the lamp.*
                    Didier !
        [*To the combatants.*]   Stop !
            [*They continue.*]   Ho !   The guard !

SAVERNY.
Who is this woman ?

DIDIER (*turning*).
        Heaven !

BOUCHAVANNES (*running, to* SAVERNY).
All is lost!
That woman's cry went through the town.
I saw the archers' rapiers flash.
[*The Archers with torches enter.*

BRICHANTEAU (*to* SAVERNY).
Seem dead,
Or you will be so!

SAVERNY (*falling down*).
Ah!
[*Low to* BRICHANTEAU, *who bends over him.*
Oh, damn these stones.
[DIDIER, *who thinks he has killed him, pauses.*

CAPTAIN OF THE DISTRICT.
Hold!   In the King's name!

BRICHANTEAU (*to the noblemen*).
We must save the Marquis.
He 's a dead man if he is caught.
[*The noblemen surround* SAVERNY.

CAPTAIN OF THE DISTRICT.
Zounds, sirs!
To fight a duel 'neath the very light
Of the edict is bold indeed!
[*To* DIDIER.]   Give up
Your sword.
[*The Archers seize* DIDIER, *who stands apart, and disarm
him.* THE CAPTAIN *indicates* SAVERNY *stretched upon
the ground and surrounded by the noblemen.*
That other man with dull eyes, who
Is he?   What is his name?

BRICHANTEAU.

His name 's Gaspard,
Marquis de Saverny, and he is dead.

CAPTAIN OF THE DISTRICT.

Dead, is he ?   Then his trouble 's over.   Good !
This dead man 's worth more than the other.

MARION (*frightened*).

What !

CAPTAIN OF THE DISTRICT (*to* DIDIER).

The whole affair rests now with you, sir.   Come !
[*The Archers lead* DIDIER *off on one side, the noblemen
   carry* SAVERNY *off on the other.*

DIDIER (*to* MARION, *who is motionless from horror*).

Forget me, Marion.   Good-bye !   [*They exit.*

SCENE V.

MARION, L'ANGELY.

MARION (*rushing to detain him*).

Didier !

What do you mean ?   Good-bye ?   Why this good-bye ?
Wherefore forget you ?
[*The Soldiers push her off; she approaches* L'ANGELY
   with anguish.

Is he lost for this ?
What did he do ?   What will they do to him ?

L'ANGELY (*takes her hand and leads her in silence before
                   the edict*).

Read this !

MARION (*reads, and starts back with horror*).

My God! Just God! Condemned to death!
They 've taken him away. To kill him! Oh,
I brought this ruin on him with my cries!
I called for help, but my unhappy voice
Found death in the dark streets and brought her here.
Impossible! A duel is no crime! [*To* L'ANGELY.
They 'll not kill him for that?

L'ANGELY.

I think they will.

MARION.

He can escape!

L'ANGELY.

The prison walls are high!

MARION.

I 've brought this crime upon him with my sins.
God strikes him for my sake! My Didier! love!
[*To* L'ANGELY.] Nothing on earth seemed good enough
    for him!
A prison cell — my God! Death! Torture too!

L'ANGELY.

Perhaps! It all depends —

MARION.

I 'll find the King!
He has a royal heart; he pardons.

L'ANGELY.

Yes,
The King does, not the Cardinal.

MARION.

Then, what —
What can I do ?

L'ANGELY.

A capital offence,
Nothing can save him from the fatal rope.

MARION.

Oh, grief !
[*To* L'ANGELY.]   You freeze my blood, sir.   Who are you ?

L'ANGELY.

I 'm the King's jester !

MARION.

Oh, my Didier, love,
I 'm lost, unworthy ; but what God can do
With a weak woman's hands, I 'll show to you.
Go on, my love ; I follow !
            [*She goes out on the side from which* DIDIER *left.*

L'ANGELY (*alone*).

God knows where !
[*Picking up the sword which* DIDIER *left on the ground.*
Among all these, who 'd think I was the fool ?
            [*He goes out.*

ACT III.

THE COMEDY.

SCENE. — *The Castle of Nangis. A park in the style of Henry IV. In the background on an elevation, the Castle of Nangis, part new, part old, is visible. The old, a castle-keep with arches and turrets: the new, a large brick house with corners of wrought stone, and pointed roof. The large door of the castle-keep is hung with black: from afar one distinguishes a coat-of-arms, — that of the families of Nangis and of Saverny.*

SCENE I.

M. DE LAFFEMAS, *undress costume of a magistrate of the period.* MARQUIS DE SAVERNY, *disguised as an officer of the Regiment of Anjou; with black moustache and imperial, and a plaster on the eye.*

LAFFEMAS.

Then you were present, sir, at the attack?

SAVERNY (*pulling his moustache*).

I was his comrade: had that honour, sir!
But he is dead!

LAFFEMAS.

The Marquis de Saverny?

SAVERNY.

Yes, from a thrust in tierce, which burst the doublet,
Then carved its cruel way between the ribs
Through to the chest and to the liver, which,
As you well know, makes blood. The wound was fearful.
'T was horrible to see!

LAFFEMAS.

He died at once?

SAVERNY.

Almost. His agony was short. I watched
The spasm follow frenzy ; tetanos
Then came, and after opisthotonos
There followed improstathonos.

LAFFEMAS.
The deuce !

SAVERNY.

So that I calculate 't is false to say
The blood passes the jugular. Pequet
And learned men should be condemned when they
Dissect live dogs to study 'bout the lungs.

LAFFEMAS.

The poor marquis is dead.

SAVERNY.
A thrust is fatal.

LAFFEMAS.

You are a doctor, sir, of medicine ?

SAVERNY.

No.

LAFFEMAS.
You have studied it ?

SAVERNY.
Somewhat.

In Aristotle.

LAFFEMAS.
You can talk it well !

SAVERNY.

Faith! I've a most malicious sort of heart.
I like destruction; find delight in evil;
I love to kill! So that I thought I'd be
A soldier or a doctor, sir, at twenty.
But I hesitated long, and finally
I chose the sword. It's not so sure, but twice
As quick. There was a time, I will confess,
I longed to be a poet or an actor,
Or an exhibitor of bears, — but then,
I like dinner and supper every day.
A plague upon the poetry and bears!

LAFFEMAS.

With this hope in your mind you studied verse?

SAVERNY.

A little bit, in Aristotle. Yes —

LAFFEMAS.

The Marquis knew you?

SAVERNY.

                        He knew me as well
As a lieutenant knows an upstart soldier.
I belonged to Monsieur de Caussade first,
Who gave me to the Marquis' colonel. Poor
The present, but we do the best we can!
They made me officer, — I'm worth as much
As any, and I wear a black moustache.
That is my history.

LAFFEMAS.

                    They sent you here
To notify the uncle?

SAVERNY.

Yes; I came
With Brichanteau, the cousin, and the corpse.
He will be buried here — where, if he 'd lived
He would have had his wedding!

LAFFEMAS.

Tell me how
The old Marquis de Nangis bore the news.

SAVERNY.

With calmness, without tears.

LAFFEMAS.

He loved him though?

SAVERNY.

As much as we love life.   Having no children
Of his own he had but this one passion, —
His nephew, whom he dearly loved, although
They had not seen each other for five years.
[*In the background, the old* MARQUIS DE NANGIS *passes;
    white hair, pale countenance, arms folded across his
    breast, dress of the day of Henry IV.: deep mourning;
    the star and the ribbon of the order of the Holy Ghost.
    He walks slowly; nine guards in three rows follow;
    they are dressed in mourning, their halberds on their
    right shoulder, their muskets on their left; they keep
    within a short distance, stopping when he stops, and
    continuing when he continues.*

LAFFEMAS (*watching him pass*).
Poor man!
[*He goes to the back and follows* THE MARQUIS *with his eyes.*

SAVERNY (*aside*).
My good old uncle!
    [BRICHANTEAU *enters and goes to* SAVERNY.

SCENE II.

The same. BRICHANTEAU.

BRICHANTEAU.

Ah ! two words !
[*Laughing.*]   He 's looking pretty well for a dead man !

SAVERNY (*low, indicating* THE MARQUIS, *who passes*).
Why do you make me grieve him, Brichanteau ?
I think we might explain it to him now.
Oh let me try.

BRICHANTEAU.

No ; God forbid, my friend !
His grief must be sincere ; he must weep much.
His woe is one good half of your disguise.

SAVERNY.

Poor uncle !

BRICHANTEAU.

He will find it out ere long.

SAVERNY.

If sorrow has not killed him, then joy will.
These shocks are dangerous to such old men.

BRICHANTEAU.

It must be done !

SAVERNY.

I cannot bear to hear
Him laugh so bitterly, then weep ; then keep
So still !   I hate to see him kiss that coffin.

BRICHANTEAU.

Yes — a fine coffin with no corpse in it !

SAVERNY.

But I am dead and bleeding in his heart.
The corpse lies there.

LAFFEMAS (*coming back*).
                    Alas, the poor old man !
His eyes show plainly how he 's suffering !

BRICHANTEAU (*low to* SAVERNY).

Who is that surly looking man in black ?

SAVERNY (*with gesture of ignorance*).

Some friend who 's living at the castle ?

BRICHANTEAU (*low*).
                                        Crows
Are also black and love the smell of death.
Keep silence more than ever.   'T is a face
That 's treacherous and evil; it would make
A madman prudent.
[THE MARQUIS DE NANGIS *re-enters; he is still absorbed
    in a deep reverie.   He walks slowly, does not appear to
    notice any one, and seats himself upon a bank of turf.*

SCENE III.

The same. MARQUIS DE NANGIS.

LAFFEMAS (*approaching* THE MARQUIS).
                    Marquis, we 've lost much.
He was a rare man; would have comforted

Your old age. I mingle my tears with yours.
Young, handsome, good, naught more could be desired;
Obeying God, respecting women, strong;
Just in his actions, sensible in speech,
A perfect nobleman, whom all revere!
To die so young! Most cruel fate! Alas!
                [THE MARQUIS *lets his head fall on his hands.*

SAVERNY (*low to* BRICHANTEAU).
The devil take this funeral discourse!
These praises but augment the old man's grief.
Console him, you! Show him the other side.

BRICHANTEAU (*to* LAFFEMAS).
You are mistaken, sir. I was in the
Same grade. A bad comrade, this Saverny, —
A shiftless fellow, growing worse each day.
Courageous! Every man is brave at twenty;
His death is nothing much to boast about.

LAFFEMAS.
A duel! Surely, that is no great crime.
        [*Banteringly to* BRICHANTEAU, *pointing to his sword.*
You are an officer?

BRICHANTEAU (*in the same tone, pointing to* LAFFEMAS'S
wig).
                A magistrate?

SAVERNY (*low*).
Go on!
                BRICHANTEAU.
        He was capricious, thankless, and
A liar: not worth any real regret.

He went to church, but just to ogle girls.
He was a gallant, a mere libertine,
A fool!

SAVERNY (*low*).

Good! good!

BRICHANTEAU.

Intractable and stubborn;
Rude to his officers.   As to good looks,
He had lost his; he limped, had a large wen
Upon his eye; from blond had turned to red,
And from round-shouldered had become hump-backed.

SAVERNY (*low*).

Enough!

BRICHANTEAU

He gambled, — every one knows that.
He would have staked his soul on dice.   I'll wager
That cards had eaten up his property.
His fortune galloped faster every night.

SAVERNY (*low, pulling his sleeve*).

Enough!   Good God!   Your consolation is
Too strong.

LAFFEMAS.

To speak so ill of a dead friend!
Unpardonable!

BRICHANTEAU (*indicating* SAVERNY).

Ask this gentleman!

SAVERNY.

Oh, no; I beg to be excused!

LAFFEMAS (*affectionately, to the old* MARQUIS).

My lord,
We 'll comfort you.   We have his murderer,
And we will hang him.   We have kept him safe.
His end is sure.   [*To* BRICHANTEAU *and* SAVERNY.
But can one understand
The Marquis?   There are duels, we all know,
That cannot be avoided, but to fight
With any one named Didier —

SAVERNY (*aside*).

What?   Didier?
[*The old* MARQUIS, *who has remained silent and motionless during all this scene, rises and goes out slowly on
the side opposite where he came in.   His guards follow
him.*

LAFFEMAS (*wiping away a tear and following him with
his eyes*).
In truth, his sorrow deeply touches me.

LACKEY (*running*).

My lord!

BRICHANTEAU.

Why can't you leave your master quiet?

LACKEY.

It is the burial of the young marquis!
What is the hour?

BRICHANTEAU.

You 'll know it by-and-by.

LACKEY.

A few comedians have arrived here from
The city; they beg shelter for the night.

BRICHANTEAU.

The time's ill chosen for comedians, but
The law of hospitality holds good.
Give them this barn.   [*Indicating a barn on the left.*

LACKEY (*holding a letter*).
                    A letter! 'T is important!
[*Reading.*]   For a Monsieur de Laffemas.

LAFFEMAS.
                                    'T is I!
Give it to me!

BRICHANTEAU (*low to* SAVERNY, *who has remained
            thoughtful in a corner*).
            Saverny, let us go!
Come and arrange things for your funeral!
                        [*Pulling him by the sleeve.*
What is it?   Are you dreaming?

SAVERNY (*aside*).
                    Oh, Didier!
                        [*They go out.*

————

SCENE IV.

LAFFEMAS (*alone*).
The seal of State!   The great seal of red wax!
Come! this is business.   Let me know at once!
[*Reading.*]   "Sir Criminal Lieutenant: We make known
To you that Didier, the assassin of
The late Marquis Gaspard, has fled."   My God!
That is unfortunate!   "A woman is
With him, called Marion de Lorme.   We beg

You to return as soon as possible."
Quick ! Get me horses ! I, who felt so sure !
Another matter spoiled for want of sense.
Outrageous ! Of the two, not one ! One, dead !
Escaped, the other ! I will catch him, though !
[*He exits. Enter a troupe of strolling actors, men, women
and children in character costumes. Among them are*
MARION *and* DIDIER, *dressed as Spaniards.* DIDIER
wears a great felt hat and is covered with a cloak.

———

SCENE V.

The Comedians, MARION, DIDIER.

A LACKEY (*conducting the Comedians to the barn*).
This is your lodging.   You 're on the estate
Of the Marquis de Nangis.   Behave well
Try to be quiet, for some one is dead.
The burial is to-morrow.   Above all,
Don't mix your songs with the funereal chants
Which will be sung for him throughout the night.

GRACIEUX (*small and hump-backed*).
We 'll make less noise than do your hunting-dogs
Who bark around the legs of all who pass !

LACKEY.
Dogs are not actors, my good friend.

TAILLEBRAS (*to* GRACIEUX).
Be still !
You 'll cause us to sleep in the open air !   [LACKEY *exits.*

SCARAMOUCHE (*to* MARION *and* DIDIER, *who until now
have remained quietly apart*).

Come ! let us talk.   Now you belong to us.
Why Monsieur fled with Madame on behind,
If you are man and wife or lovers only,
Escaping justice, or black sorcerers
Who held Madame a prisoner, perhaps, —
Is not my business.   What I want to know
Is what you 'll act.   Chimènes are best for you,
Black eyes   [MARION *makes a courtesy.*

DIDIER (*aside, indignant*).
To hear that mountebank speak thus !

SCARAMOUCHE (*to* DIDIER).

For you : if you should want a splendid part,
We need a bully, — a long-legg̀ed man,
Tremendous strides, a thundering voice ; and when
Orgon is robbed of wife or niece, you kill
The Moor and terminate the piece.   Great part !
High tragedy !   'T will suit you splendidly.

DIDIER.
Just as you please !

SCARAMOUCHE.
                    Good !   Don't say " you " to me !
I like " thou " !   [*With a profound obeisance.*
Blusterer, hail !

DIDIER (*aside*).
                    What fools !

SCARAMOUCHE (*to the other actors*).
                                   Now eat ;
Then we 'll rehearse our parts.
            [*All enter the barn except* MARION *and* DIDIER.

SCENE VI.

MARION, DIDIER; *afterwards* GRACIEUX, SAVERNY, *afterwards* LAFFEMAS.

DIDIER (*with bitter laugh, after a long silence*).
                              Is 't bad enough ?
My Marion, have I dragged you low enough ?
You wished to follow me ?   My destiny
Precipitates itself and crushes you,
Bound to its wheel !   What are we come to now ?
I told you so !

MARION (*trembling and clasping her hands*).
        Do you reproach me, love ?

DIDIER.
Oh, may I be accursed !   Cursed first by Heaven
Then cursed 'mongst men : cursed throughout all my life ;
Cursed more than we are now, if a reproach
Shall ever leave my lips for you !   What matter
Though all the earth abandon me, you 're mine !
You are my saviour, refuge, all my hope !
Who duped the jailer, filed my chains for me ?
Who came from heaven to follow me to hell ?
Who was a captive with the prisoner,
An exile with the fugitive ?   Ah, who,
Who else had heart so full of love and wit,
Heart to sustain, console, deliver me ?
Great, feeble woman, have you not saved me
From destiny, alas ! and my own soul ?
Had you not pity on my nature, crushed ?
Have you not loved one whom all others hate ?

MARION (*weeping*).

It is my joy to love you — be your slave.

DIDIER.

Leave me your eyes, dear; they enrapture me!
God willed, when placing soul within my flesh,
A demon and an angel should guide me.
Yet he was merciful; his love concealed
The demon, but the angel he revealed.

MARION.

You are my Didier, master, lord of me!

DIDIER.

Your husband, am I not?

MARION (*aside*).
Alas!

DIDIER.
What joy,
When we have left this country far behind,
To have you, call you wife as well as love!
You will be willing? — answer.

MARION.
I will be
Your sister, and my brother you shall be!

DIDIER.

Oh, no! Refuse me not that ecstasy
Of knowing, in God's sight, you 're mine alone!
You 're safe to trust my love in everything.
The lover keeps you for the husband, pure!

MARION (*aside*).

Alas!

DIDIER.

If you knew how things torture me!
To hear that actor talk, affront you thus!
It is not least among our wretched woes
To see you mixed with jugglers such as these,
A chaste, exquisite flower 'mid this filth, —
You, 'mongst these women steeped in infamy!

MARION.

Be prudent, Didier!

DIDIER.

God! I struggled hard
Against my anger! He said "thou" to you,
When I, your love, your husband, hardly dare
For fear of tarnishing that virgin brow —

MARION.

Be pleasant with them; it means life to you,
And me as well.

DIDIER.

She's right. She's always right.
Although each hour brings us increasing woe,
You lavish on me love and joy and youth!
How happens it these blessings come to me,
When royal kingdoms were small pay for them, —
To me, who give but anguish in return?
Heaven gave you, — yes; but hell binds you to me.
For us to merit this unequal fate,
What good can I have done? What evil you?

MARION.

My only blessings come from you, my love!

DIDIER.

If you say that you think it, but it 's wrong!
Oh, yes, my star of destiny is bad.
I know not whence I come, nor where I go.
My whole horizon 's dark.   Love, hark to me!
There 's time yet; you can leave me and go back.
Let me pursue the gloomy route alone.
When all is ended and I 'm tired out,
The couch that 's waiting will be cold, — ice-cold,
And narrow; there 's not room enough for two.
Go back!

MARION.

That couch, dark, and mysterious,
I 'll share it with you; that at least is mine.

DIDIER.

Will you not listen?   Can't you understand?
You 're tempting Providence to cling to me!
The years of anguish, love, may be so long
Your sweet eyes may grow sightless, just from tears.
[MARION *lets her head fall on her hands.*

DIDIER.

I swear I draw the picture none too strong.
Your future frightens me.   I pity you!
Go back!

MARION (*bursting into tears*).

It were more kind to kill me, Didier,
Than to talk thus!   [*Weeping.*]   O God!

DIDIER (*taking her in his arms*).

My darling, hush!
So many tears!   I 'd shed my blood for one.
Do what you will!   Come, be my destiny,

My glory, life, my virtue, and my love!
Answer me now.   I speak!   Sweet, do you hear?
                        [*He seats her on a bank of turf.*

MARION (*withdrawing herself from his arms*).
You've hurt me!

DIDIER (*kneeling to her*).
                I, who'd gladly die for her!

MARION (*smiling through her tears*).
You made me cry, you cruel man!

DIDIER.
                        My beauty!
                [*Sits on the bank beside her.*
Just one sweet kiss upon your forehead, pure
As is our love!
[*He kisses her forehead.   They look at each other with
    ecstasy.*
                Yes, look at me!   Look thus,
Look harder; look until we die of looking!

GRACIEUX (*entering*).
Dona Chimène is wanted in the barn.
[MARION *rises hastily from* DIDIER'S *side.   At the same
    time that* GRACIEUX *enters,* SAVERNY *comes in; he
    stands in the background and looks attentively at*
    MARION *without seeing* DIDIER, *who remains sitting on
    the bank and is hidden by a bush.*

SAVERNY (*back, without being seen, aside*).
Faith, it is Marion!   What brings her here?
[*Laughing.*] Chimène!

GRACIEUX (*to* DIDIER, *who is about to follow* MARION).
                    Oh, no! stay there, my jealous friend,
I want to tease you!

DIDIER.
                    Devil take you!

MARION (*low to* DIDIER).
                                        Hush!
Restrain yourself.
                    [DIDIER *re-seats himself; she enters the barn.*

SAVERNY (*still back, aside*).
What makes her roam the country in this fashion?
Can he be the gallant who succoured me?
Who saved my life?   Didier!   It is indeed!

LAFFEMAS (*enters in travelling costume, and salutes*
                    SAVERNY.)
I take my leave, sir!

SAVERNY (*bowing*).
                    You are going away?
                                        [*He laughs.*

LAFFEMAS.
What makes you laugh?

SAVERNY.
                    A very silly thing.
I'll tell you.   Guess whom I have recognized
Among those jugglers who have just arrived.

LAFFEMAS.
Among those jugglers?

SAVERNY (*laughing still more*).
                    Yes.   Marion de Lorme!

LAFFEMAS (*with a start*).
Marion de Lorme!

DIDIER (*who has been looking at them fixedly all the time*).
　　　　　　Hein? [*He half rises from the bank.*

SAVERNY (*still laughing*).
　　　　　　　　I would like to send
That news to Paris.   Are you going there?

LAFFEMAS.
I am, and I will spread the news, trust me!
But are you sure you recognized her?

SAVERNY.
　　　　　　　　　Sure?
Hurrah for France!   We know our Marion.
　　　　　　　　[*Feeling in his pocket.*
I think I have her portrait, — tender pledge
Of love!   She had it done by the King's painter.
　　　　　　[*Giving* LAFFEMAS *a locket.*
Look and compare them.   [*Indicating the barn door.*
　　　　　　See her, through that door,
In Spanish costume, with green petticoat.

LAFFEMAS (*looking from the locket to the barn*).
'T is she — Marion de Lorme!
　　　　　　[*Aside.*]   I have him now!
[*To* SAVERNY.]   She must have a companion 'mongst
　these men.

SAVERNY.
It's likely.   Such fair ladies are not prudes,
And seldom travel round the world alone.

LAFFEMAS (*aside*).

I 'll guard this door.   It will go hard, indeed,
If I can't capture that false actor here.
He 's taken now — no doubt of that!   [*Goes out.*

SAVERNY (*watches the exit of* LAFFEMAS : *aside*).
                                    I think
I 've done a foolish thing.
[*Taking* GRACIEUX *aside, who all this time has stood in
    a corner gesticulating and running over his lines : in a
    whisper.*
                        Who is that lady
Sitting within the shadow there ?
                    [*Indicating the door of the barn.*

GRACIEUX.
                        Chimène ?
[*Solemnly.*]   My lord, I do not know her name.   Ask him,
This lord, her noble friend.
                    [*Exits on the side of the park.*

SCENE VII.

DIDIER, SAVERNY.

SAVERNY (*turning towards* DIDIER).
                    This gentleman ?
Tell me —   'T is strange how hard he looks at me !
Upon my soul, 't is he !   My man !
                [*Loud to* DIDIER.]   If you
Were not in prison, I should say that you
Resemble a —

DIDIER.

And if you were not dead, I 'd say
That you had the exact appearance of —
His blood be on his head ! — a man whom two
Short words of mine put in a tomb.

SAVERNY.

Hush ! You

Are Didier !

DIDIER.

Marquis Gaspard, you !

SAVERNY.

'T was you
Who were somewhere, a certain night !   'T is you
To whom I owe my life !

[He opens his arms.   DIDIER *draws back.*

DIDIER.

Excuse surprise !
I felt so sure I took it back.

SAVERNY.

Not so !
You saved me — did not kill me !   Let me know
What I can do for you.   Do you desire
A second — brother — a lieutenant ?   Speak !
What will you have, — my blood, my wealth, my soul ?

DIDIER.

Not any of those things.   That portrait there !
[SAVERNY *gives him the portrait ; he looks at it, speaking*
with bitterness.
Yes, there 's her brow, her black eyes, her white neck ;
Above all, there 's her candid glance !   How like !

SAVERNY.

You think so?

DIDIER.

This was made for you, you say?

SAVERNY (*bowing, and making an affirmative sign*).
It was! But now 't is you whom she prefers,
You whom she loves and chooses 'mongst us all.
You are a happy man.

DIDIER (*with loud and mocking laugh*).
Yes! Am I not?

SAVERNY.

Accept my compliments; she 's a good girl,
And loves no one but men of family.
Of such a mistress one can well be proud!
It 's honourable, and it gives one style.
'T is in good taste.   If men ask who you are
They say, " Beloved of Marion de Lorme."
        [DIDIER *gives him back the portrait; he refuses it.*
No, keep the portrait; since the lady 's yours,
It should belong to you.   Keep it, I pray.

DIDIER.

I thank you!   [*Puts it in his breast.*

SAVERNY.

She is charming in that dress.
So you are my successor!   One might say,
As King Louis succeeded Pharamond.
The Brissacs, both of them, supplanted me.
[*Laughing.*]   Then, yes, the Cardinal himself came next,
Then little D'Effiat, then the three Sainte-Mesmes,
The four Argenteans!   In her heart you 'll find
The best society. [*Laughing.*]   A little numerous.

DIDIER (*aside*).

My God!

SAVERNY.

      Tell me about it sometime.   Now,
To be quite frank with you, I pass for dead,
And in the morning shall be buried.   You
Must have escaped police and seneschals.
Your Marion can manage everything!
You joined a strolling company by chance;
What a delightful history!

DIDIER.

                  Yes, true
It is a history!

SAVERNY.

            To get you out
She probably made love to all the jailers.

DIDIER (*in a voice of thunder*).
Do you think that?

SAVERNY.

            You are not jealous — what?
Oh, joke incredible! — of Marion!
A man jealous of Marion!   The poor child!
Don't go and scold her!

DIDIER.

            Have no fear.
                  [*Aside.*]   The angel —
It was a demon!   Oh, my God!
[*Enter* LAFFEMAS *and* GRACIEUX.   DIDIER *goes out ;* SA-
      VERNY *follows him.*

SCENE VIII.

LAFFEMAS, GRACIEUX.

GRACIEUX (*to* LAFFEMAS).

My lord,

I do not understand you!

[*Aside.*] Humph! A costume
Of Alcaid and a figure of police ;
Small eyes, adorned with big eyebrows!   I think
He plays the part of Alguazil in this
Locality.

LAFFEMAS (*pulling out his purse*).

My friend !

GRACIEUX (*drawing near, low to* LAFFEMAS).

My lord — I see !

Chimène has interested you.   You wish
To know —

LAFFEMAS (*low, smiling*).

Who is her Roderick ?

GRACIEUX.

You mean

Her lover ?

LAFFEMAS.

Yes !

GRACIEUX.

Who groans beneath her spell ?

LAFFEMAS (*impatiently*).

There's one ?

GRACIEUX.

Of course !

LAFFEMAS (*approaching him eagerly*).
                    Then show him to me, quick !

GRACIEUX (*with profound obeisance*).
It 's I, my lord.   I 'm mad about her !

LAFFEMAS.
                              You !
[LAFFEMAS, *disappointed, turns away with annoyance ;
    then he comes back and shakes his purse in* GRACIEUX'S
    eyes and ears.
Know you the sound of ducats ?

GRACIEUX.
                    Heavenly tones !

LAFFEMAS (*aside*).
I 've got my Didier !
    [*To* GRACIEUX.]   Do you see this purse ?

GRACIEUX.
How much !

LAFFEMAS.
        Gold ducats — twenty !

GRACIEUX.
                              Humph !

LAFFEMAS (*jingling the gold in his face*).
                              Will you ?

GRACIEUX (*grabbing the purse from him*).
Most certainly !
[*With theatrical tone to* LAFFEMAS, *who listens anxiously.*
        My lord, if your back bore

Just in the centre a great hump, as big
As is your belly, and if those two bags
Were filled with louis, sequins, and doubloons,
In that case —

LAFFEMAS (*eagerly*).
Well, what would you do?

GRACIEUX (*putting the purse into his pocket*).
I 'd take
The whole of it, and I would say —
[*With profound obeisance.*
I thank you;
You are a gentleman!

LAFFEMAS (*aside, furious*).
Plague on the monkey!

GRACIEUX (*aside, laughing*).
The devil take the cat!

LAFFEMAS (*aside*).
They have agreed
On what to do, if any one suspects.
'T is a conspiracy.   They 'll all be dumb;
Accursed gipsy devils!
[*To* GRACIEUX *who is going away.*
Give me back
My purse!

GRACIEUX (*turning around, with tragic tone*).
What do you take me for, my lord?
What will the world think of us, pray, if you
Propose and I agree to anything
So infamous as sell for gold a life,
My soul?   [*Turns to go.*

LAFFEMAS.

That's as you please ; but give me back
My money !

GRACIEUX.

No, I keep my honour, sir,
And we have no accounts to settle.

[*He salutes him and re-enters barn.*

———

SCENE IX.

LAFFEMAS (*alone*).
Humph !
The wretched juggler !   Pride in such base souls !
If you some day should fall into my hands
Unoccupied with better sort of game —
But this will not find Didier !   Now, I can't
Take all this crowd and put them to the torture.
This is worse work than hunting needles in
A hay-stack.   Faith ! a chemist's crucible
Bewitched I ought to have, which, eating up
The lead and copper, would reveal at last
The golden ingot hid by much alloy.
Go to the Cardinal without my prize ?

[*Striking his brow.*

That's it !   The clever thought !   Oh, joy !   He's mine !

[*Calling through the barn door.*

Ho, gentlemen, comedians ! one word, please.

[*The actors crowd out of the barn.*

SCENE X.

The Same.　Comedians, among them MARION *and* DIDIER ; *afterwards* SAVERNY, *afterwards* MARQUIS DE NANGIS.

SCARAMOUCHE (*to* LAFFEMAS).
What do you want with us ?

LAFFEMAS.
　　　　　　　　　Without preamble :
My lord the Cardinal commissioned me
To find good actors, if there may be such
Within the provinces, to act the plays
Which he constructs in hours of leisure when
Allowed by State affairs.　In spite of care
And earnest thought, his theatre declines,
And is no credit to a cardinal-duke.
[*All the actors press eagerly forward.* SAVERNY *enters, and watches the scene with curiosity.*

GRACIEUX (*aside, counting his money*).
Twelve only !　He said twenty.　The old scamp !
He 's robbed me !

LAFFEMAS.
　　　　　　Let each one repeat some scene,
That I may know your talents and may choose.
[*Aside.*]　If he gets out of that, this Didier 's sharp.
[*Aloud.*]　Are you all here ?
[MARION *stealthily approaches* DIDIER *and tries to lead him off.*

GRACIEUX (*going up to them*).
　　　　　　　Come with the others — you !

MARION.

Oh, heaven !

[DIDIER *leaves her and joins the actors ; she follows him.*

GRACIEUX.

You 're in luck to be with us.
To have new clothes, get every day a feast,
To speak the Cardinal's verses every night,
A happy lot !

[*All the actors take their places before* LAFFEMAS.
MARION *and* DIDIER *among them.* DIDIER *does not
look at* MARION ; *his eyes are bent on the ground ; his
arms are folded underneath his cloak.* MARION *watches
him anxiously.*

GRACIEUX (*at head of troupe, aside*).

Who would have thought this crow
Recruited actors for the Cardinal ?

LAFFEMAS (*to* GRACIEUX).

First you.   What do you play ?

GRACIEUX (*with a low bow and a pirouette which shows off
his hump*).

I 'm called the Sylph
Among the troupe.   This piece I know the best.

[*He sings.*

"On the bald heads of magistrates,
   Enormous wigs are spread.
Out of that fleece, in due time, come
   Chains, gallows, tortures dread.
Whenever one called president
   Shall shake his bigger head.

"Let any barber, strolling fool,
   Wash, powder, and pomade

" The hair which bald heads steal from beards,
    Let them be combed and frayed
    In shape of a right gorgeous wig, —
    Your magistrate is made.

" The lawyer is a sea of words
    Hurled wildly at the bench.
    A killing kind of mixing up
    Of Latin and bad French — "

        LAFFEMAS (*interrupting him*).

You sing so false, you'd make an eagle sick.
Be still!

        GRACIEUX (*laughing*).

  I may sing false — the song is true!

        LAFFEMAS (*to* SCARAMOUCHE).

It's your turn now.

        SCARAMOUCHE (*bowing*).

          I'm Scaramouche, my lord!
" The Lady of Honour," sir, I open thus.   [*Declaiming.*
" 'Naught is so fine,' said once a Queen of Spain,
' As bishop at the altar, soldier in
The field, unless it is a girl in bed,
Or robber on the gallows — ' "
[LAFFEMAS *interrupts* SCARAMOUCHE *with a gesture and*
    signs to TAILLEBRAS *to speak.* TAILLEBRAS *makes a*
    profound obeisance, then draws himself up.

        TAILLEBRAS (*with emphasis*).

          As for me,
Sir, I am Taillebras. From Thibet, sir,
I come; I've punished the great Khan, I've captured
The Mogul —

LAFFEMAS.

Choose something else —
[*Low to* SAVERNY, *who stands beside him.*
A beauty,
Eh, this Marion!

TAILLEBRAS.

It is one of our best.
If you prefer, I will be Charlemagne,
The Emperor of the West.   [*Declaiming with emphasis.*
"Strange destiny!
O Heaven, I appeal to you!   Bear witness
Unto my woe.   I must despoil myself,
Surrender my beloved one to another.
I must endow my rival, fill his heart
With joy, while my poor stomach stings with grief.
Thus, birds, you can no more perch in the woods;
Thus, flies, you can no more buzz in the fields;
Thus, sheep, you can no longer wear your wool.
Thus, bulls, you can no longer raze the plains."

LAFFEMAS.

Good!
[*To* SAVERNY.]   Listen, the fine verses!   "Bradamante"
By Garnier; what a poet!
[*To* MARION.]   'T is your turn,
My beauty.   First, your name.

MARION (*trembling*).

I am Chimène!

LAFFEMAS.

Indeed!   Chimène?   Then you must have a lover.
He has killed a man in duel —

MARION (*terrified*).

LAFFEMAS (*maliciously*).

I 've a good memory.   If one escapes —

MARION (*aside*).

Great heaven!

LAFFEMAS.

Come!   Now let us hear your scene.

MARION (*half turned towards* DIDIER).

" Since to arrest you in this fatal course
Your life and honour are of no avail,
If ever I have loved you, Roderick,
Defend yourself to save me from Don Sancho.
Fight valiantly against the fearful fate
Which must surrender me to one I hate.
Shall I say more ?   Go ; your defence shall be
Your right to force my duty, seal my lips !
If love for me still in your brave heart lies,
Go win this combat, for Chimène is prize."
[LAFFEMAS *rises gallantly and kisses her hand.* MARION
is pale ; she looks at DIDIER, *who remains motionless
with eyes on the ground.*

LAFFEMAS.

No voice but yours could take so firm a hold
Upon the secret fibres of our heart.
You are adorable.
    [*To* SAVERNY.]   You can't deny
Corneille is not worth Garnier, after all.
'T is true, his verses have a finer ring
Since he 's belonged unto the Cardinal-Duke.
[*To* MARION.]   What a complexion !   What fine eyes !
    Good God !
This is no place for you !   You 're buried here.
Sit down !

[*He sits and makes sign to* MARION *to sit beside him ; she draws back.*

MARION (*low to* DIDIER, *with anguish*).
For God's sake, let me stay with you !

LAFFEMAS (*smiling*).
Come sit by me, I say !
[DIDIER *repulses* MARION, *who staggers terrified to the bench where* LAFFEMAS *sits, and falls upon it.*

MARION (*aside*).
'T is horrible !

LAFFEMAS (*smiling at* MARION, *with an air of reproach*).
At last !
[*To* DIDIER.]   Now, sir, your turn.   What is your name ?

DIDIER (*with gravity*).
My name is Didier !

MARION, LAFFEMAS, SAVERNY.
Didier !

DIDIER (*to* LAFFEMAS, *who laughs triumphantly*).
                           Yes, you can
Send all of them away.   You 've got your prey.
Your prisoner himself takes up his chain.
This joy has cost you a great deal of work.

MARION (*running to him*).
Didier !

DIDIER (*with a freezing look*).
      Don't try to hinder me this time,
Madame !

[*She starts back and falls crushed upon the bank: to*
    LAFFEMAS.
                I've watched you creeping close to me,
You demon! In your eyes I've seen that glare
Of hell fire which illuminates your soul.
I might have 'scaped your trap, — a useless thing;
But to see cunning wasted thus grieved me.
Take me, and get well paid for treachery.

LAFFEMAS (*with concentrated rage, trying to laugh*).
You are not a comedian, it would seem!

DIDIER.

It's you who played the comedy.

LAFFEMAS.
                        Not well
But with the Cardinal I'll write a play.
It is a tragedy: you have a part.
[MARION *screams with horror.* DIDIER *turns from her
    with contempt.*
Don't turn your head in such a lordly way.
We will admire your acting, never fear!
Come, recommend your soul to God, my friend.

MARION.

Ah, God!
[*At this moment* MARQUIS DE NANGIS *passes across the
    back of the stage, in the same attitude, with his escort
    of Halberdiers.* MARION'S *cry arrests him; pale and
    silent he turns to the characters.*

LAFFEMAS (*to* MARQUIS DE NANGIS).
        Marquis, I claim your aid. Good news!
Lend me your escort. The murderer escaped
Our vigilance, but we've recaptured him.

MARION (*throwing herself at* LAFFEMAS'S *feet*).
Oh, pity for him!

LAFFEMAS (*with gallantry*).
At my feet, madame!
'T is I should kneel at yours.

MARION (*on her knees, clasping her hands*).
My lord the judge,
Have mercy upon others, if some day
You hope a jealous judge, more powerful
Than you are, will be merciful to you!

LAFFEMAS (*smiling*).
You 're preaching us a sermon, I believe!
Ah, madame, reign at balls and shine at fêtes,
But do not preach us sermons. For your sake,
I would do anything; but he has killed —
It is a murder.
DIDIER (*to* MARION).
Rise!   [MARION *rises, trembling.*
You lie! it was a duel.

LAFFEMAS.
Sir!

DIDIER.
I say, you lie!

LAFFEMAS.
Have done!
[*To* MARION.] Blood calls
For blood; this rigour troubles me — I wish —
But he has killed — killed whom? The young marquis
Gaspard de Saverny, [*Indicating* MARQUIS DE NANGIS.
Nephew to him,
That worthy old man there. A rare young lord;

The greatest loss for France and for the King.
Were he not dead, I do not say that I —
My heart is not of stone, and if —

SAVERNY (*taking a step forward*).
The man
You think is dead is living.   I am he !
[*General astonishment.*

LAFFEMAS (*starting*).
Gaspard de Saverny !   A miracle !
There is his coffin.

SAVERNY (*tearing off his false moustache, his plaster,
and black wig*).
But he is not dead !
Who recognizes me ?

MARQUIS DE NANGIS (*as if awakening from a dream,
starts, and with a great cry throws himself into his
nephew's arms*).
Gaspard !   My nephew !
It is my child !
[*They remain locked in each other's arms.*

MARION (*falling upon her knees and lifting her eyes to
heaven*).
Didier is saved !   Praise God !

DIDIER (*coldly, to* SAVERNY).
What is the use ?   I wished to die.

MARION (*still on her knees*).
Kind God,
You have protected him !
VOL. XIV. — 12

DIDIER (*continuing, without listening to her*).
                        How otherwise
Could he have caught me in his trap ?   Think you
My spur could not have crushed the spider's web
Which he had made to catch a gnat ?   Henceforth
I ask no other boon than death.   This is
No friendly gift from you, who owe me life !

MARION.
What does he say ?   You must live —

LAFFEMAS.
                                  All 's not over.
Is it certain that this is the Marquis ?

MARION.
It is.

LAFFEMAS.
We must have proof of it at once.

MARION (*indicating* MARQUIS DE NANGIS, *who is still
          holding* SAVERNY *in his arms*).
Look at that old man, how he smiles and weeps !

LAFFEMAS.
Is that Gaspard de Saverny ?

MARION.
                        What heart
Can question such a close embrace ?

MARQUIS DE NANGIS (*turning around*).
                              You ask
If it is he, — Gaspard, my son, my soul ?
[*To* MARION.]   Did he not ask if it was he, madame ?

LAFFEMAS (*to* MARQUIS DE NANGIS).

Then you affirm that this man is your nephew?
He is Gaspard de Saverny?

MARQUIS DE NANGIS (*with intensity*).
I do!

LAFFEMAS.

According to the law I do arrest
Gaspard de Saverny, in the King's name.
Your sword!
[*Surprise and consternation among the characters.*

MARQUIS DE NANGIS.
My son!

MARION.
Oh, heaven!

DIDIER.
Another head!
Yes, two were needed. 'T is the least, to bring
This Roman Cæsar one head in each hand.

MARQUIS DE NANGIS.
Speak! By what right —

LAFFEMAS.
Ask my lord cardinal.
All who survive a duel fall beneath
The ordinance. Give me your sword.

DIDIER (*looking at* SAVERNY).
Rash man!

SAVERNY (*drawing his sword and presenting it to*
               LAFFEMAS).
'T is here!

MARQUIS DE NANGIS (*stopping him*).
          A moment!   None is master here
Save me!   I mete out justice high and low.
Our sire the King would be no more than guest.
[*To* SAVERNY.]   Give up your sword to none but me.
[SAVERNY *hands him his sword, and clasps him in his arms.*

LAFFEMAS.
                                        In truth,
That is a feudal right quite out of date.
The Cardinal might blame me for it, but
I would not willingly annoy you —

DIDIER.
                     Wretch!

LAFFEMAS (*bowing to* MARQUIS DE NANGIS).
So I consent.   You can return the favour
By loaning me your guard and 'prison, sir.

MARQUIS DE NANGIS (*to his Guards*).
Not so!   Your sires were vassals to my sires.
I forbid any one to stir a step.

LAFFEMAS (*with voice of thunder*).
My masters, hark to me: I am the judge
Of the secret tribunal, Criminal-
Lieutenant to the Cardinal.   Conduct
These men to prison.   Four of you mount guard
Before each door.   You're all responsible.
It would be rash to disobey when I command

You to go here or there or do a deed.
If any hesitate, it is because
His head annoys him.
[*The Guards, terrified, drag the two prisoners off in silence.*
MARQUIS DE NANGIS turns away indignant and
buries his face in his hands.

MARION.
All is lost!
[*To* LAFFEMAS.] Have pity!
If in your heart —

LAFFEMAS (*low to* MARION).
If you will come to-night,
I 'll tell you something —

MARION (*aside*).
What is it he wants?
His smiles are terrible. He has a gloomy,
Treacherous soul. [*Turning with desperation to* DIDIER.
Didier!

DIDIER (*coldly*).
Farewell, madame!

MARION (*shuddering at the tone of his voice*).
What have I done? Oh, miserable woman!
[*She sinks upon the bank.*

DIDIER.
Miserable! Yes!

SAVERNY (*embraces* MARQUIS DE NANGIS, *then turns to*
LAFFEMAS).
Is your pay doubled
When you bring two heads?

LACKEY (*entering, to* MARQUIS DE NANGIS).
My lord,
The funeral preparations for the Marquis
Are now completed.   I am sent to you
To know what hour and day the ceremony
Will be performed.

LAFFEMAS.
Come back one month from now.
[*The Guards lead off* DIDIER *and* SAVERNY.

ACT IV.

THE KING.

SCENE. — *Chambord. The guard-room in the Castle of Chambord.*

SCENE I.

DUKE DE BELLEGARDE, *rich court costume covered with embroidery and lace, the order of the Holy Ghost around his neck, and the star upon his cloak.* MARQUIS DE NANGIS, *in deep mourning and followed by his escort of Guards. Both cross the back of the hall.*

DUKE DE BELLEGARDE.

Condemned ?

MARQUIS DE NANGIS.

Condemned !

DUKE DE BELLEGARDE.

E'en so !   The King can pardon.
It is his kingly right and royal duty.
Have no more fear.   In heart as well as name
He 's son of Henry IV.

MARQUIS DE NANGIS.

I was his comrade.

DUKE DE BELLEGARDE.

Indeed, we spoiled full many a coat of armour
For the proud sire !   Now go unto the son,
Show him your grey hairs, and in lieu of prayer
Cry out "Ventre Saint Gris !"   Let Richelieu

Himself give better reason!   Hide here now.
                              [*He opens a side door.*
He's coming soon.   Do you know, to be frank,
Your costume's of a style to make one laugh.

MARQUIS DE NANGIS.

Laugh at my mourning?

DUKE DE BELLEGARDE.

                              Ah, these coxcombs here!
Old friend, stay there; you'll not have long to wait.
I will dispose him 'gainst the Cardinal.
I'll stamp upon the ground for signal; then
Come out.

MARQUIS DE NANGIS (*grasping his hand*).

May God repay you!

DUKE DE BELLEGARDE (*to a* MUSKETEER *who walks up and down in front of a small gilt door*).

                              Monsieur, pray,
What does the King?

MUSKETEER.

                              He's working, my lord duke!
                              [*Lowering his voice.*
A man in black is with him.

DUKE DE BELLEGARDE (*aside*).

                              At this moment
He is signing a death-warrant, I believe.
                    [*To the old* MARQUIS, *grasping his hand.*
Be brave!   [*He conducts him to a neighbouring gallery.*
While waiting for the signal, look
At these new ceilings, they're by Primatice.
[*Both go out.* MARION, *in deep mourning, enters through the great door in the back, which opens on a staircase.*

SCENE II.

MARION, *the Guards.*

HALBERDIER (*to* MARION).
Madame, you cannot enter!

MARION (*advancing*).
Sir!

HALBERDIER (*placing his halberd against the door*).
I say,
No entrance!

MARION (*with contempt*).
Here you turn your lance against
A woman.   Elsewhere, 't is in her defence.

MUSKETEER (*laughing, to* HALBERDIER).
Well said!

MARION (*firmly*).
I must immediately have audience
With the Duke de Bellegarde.

HALBERDIER (*lowering his halberd, aside*).
Ah, these gallants!

MUSKETEER.
Enter, madame.   [*She enters with determined step.*

HALBERDIER (*aside, watching her from the corner of
his eye*).
Well, the old duke is not
As feeble as he looks.   This rendezvous

Would have cost him a sojourn in the Louvre,
In former times.

MUSKETEER (*making sign to* HALBERDIER *to keep still*).
The door is open.
[*The little gilt door is opened.* M. DE LAFFEMAS *comes
out, holding in his hand a parchment to which a red
seal hangs by strands of silk.*

———

SCENE III.

MARION, LAFFEMAS : *gesture of surprise from both.* MARION
turns away from him with horror.

LAFFEMAS (*low, advancing slowly towards* MARION).
You!
What is your errand here?

MARION.
What's yours?

LAFFEMAS (*unrolls the parchment and spreads it out before
her eyes*).
Signed by
The King!

MARION (*glances at it, then buries her face in her hands*).
Good God!

LAFFEMAS (*speaking in her ear*).
Will you?
[MARION *shivers and looks him in the face; he fixes his
eyes on hers: lowering his voice.*
Wilt thou?

MARION (*pushing him away*).

Away!

Foul tempter!

LAFFEMAS (*straightening himself up, sneeringly*).
You will not!

MARION.

I have no fear!
The King can pardon: 't is the King who reigns.

LAFFEMAS.
Go try him.   See what his good will is worth!
[*He turns away, then turns back: folds his arms and
    whispers to her.*
Beware of waiting until I refuse!
[*Exits.* DUKE DE BELLEGARDE *enters.*

SCENE IV.

MARION, DUKE DE BELLEGARDE.

MARION (*going towards* DUKE DE BELLEGARDE).
Here you are captain, my lord duke.

DUKE DE BELLEGARDE.
'T is you,
My beauty!   [*Bowing.*
        Speak!   What does my queen desire?

MARION.
To see the King.

DUKE DE BELLEGARDE.
When ?

MARION.
Now !

DUKE DE BELLEGARDE.
This is short notice !
Why ?
MARION.
For something !

DUKE DE BELLEGARDE (*bursting into a laugh*).
We will send for him !
How she goes on '
MARION.
Then you refuse me ?

DUKE DE BELLEGARDE.
Nay !
Am I not yours ?   Have we refused each other
Anything ?
MARION.
That 's very well, my lord !
When shall I see the King ?

DUKE DE BELLEGARDE.
After the Duke.
I promise you shall see him when he passes
Through this hall.   But while waiting, talk with me !
Ah, little woman, are we good ?   In black ?
Lady-in-waiting you might be.   You used
To laugh so much.
MARION.
I don't laugh now.

DUKE DE BELLEGARDE.
Indeed!
I think she's weeping!   Marion!   You?

MARION (*wiping her eyes : with firm tone*).
My lord,
I want to see his Majesty at once!

DUKE DE BELLEGARDE.
For what?

MARION.
Just Heaven!   For —

DUKE DE BELLEGARDE.
Is it against
The Cardinal?

MARION.
It is!

DUKE DE BELLEGARDE (*opening the gallery for her*).
Please enter here.
I put the discontented all in there;
Do not come out before the signal please.
[MARION *enters ; he shuts door.*
I would have run the risk for my old friend.
It costs no more to do it for them both.
[*The hall is gradually filled with Courtiers ; they talk to-
    gether.* DUKE DE BELLEGARDE *goes from one to the
    other.* L'ANGELY *enters.*

SCENE V.

The same. DUKE DE BEAUPRÉAU, LAFFEMAS, VISCOUNT
DE ROHAN, COUNT DE CHARNACÉ, ABBÉ DE GONDI,
and other courtiers.

DUKE DE BELLEGARDE (*to* DUKE DE BEAUPRÉAU).
Good-morning, Duke !

DUKE DE BEAUPRÉAU.
Good-morning !

DUKE DE BELLEGARDE.
Any news ?
DUKE DE BEAUPRÉAU.
There 's talk of a new cardinal.

DUKE DE BELLEGARDE.
Which one ?
The Archbishop of Arle ?

DUKE DE BEAUPRÉAU.
No ! Bishop of Autun.
All Paris thinks he has obtained the hat.

ABBÉ DE GONDI.
'T is his by right.   He was commander of
Artillery at the siege of La Rochelle.

DUKE DE BELLEGARDE.
That 's true !
L'ANGELY.
The Holy See has my approval.
This one will be a cardinal according
To the canons.

ABBÉ DE GONDI (*laughing*).
L'Angely — the fool!

L'ANGELY (*bowing*).
My lord knows all my names.
[LAFFEMAS *enters; all the Courtiers vie with each other in
   paying court to him and surrounding him.* DUKE DE
   BELLEGARDE *watches them with vexation.*

DUKE DE BELLEGARDE (*to* L'ANGELY).
                              Fool, who 's that man
Who wears the ermine cloak ?

L'ANGELY.
                              Whom every one
Is paying court to ?

DUKE DE BELLEGARDE.
                    Yes. I know him not.
Is he a follower of Monsieur d'Orleans ?

L'ANGELY.
They would not fawn on him so much.

DUKE DE BELLEGARDE (*watching* LAFFEMAS, *who struts
                   about*).
                              What airs !
As if he were grandee of Spain !

L'ANGELY (*low*).
                              It is
Sir Laffemas, intendant of Champagne,
Lieutenant-Criminal —

DUKE DE BELLEGARDE (*low*).
                              Infernal, say !
He 's called the Cardinal's executioner ?

L'ANGELY (*still low*).
The same.

DUKE DE BELLEGARDE.
          That man at Court !

L'ANGELY.
                    Why not ?   One extra
Tiger-cat in the menagerie !
Shall I present him ?

DUKE DE BELLEGARDE (*haughtily*).
               Peace, you fool !

L'ANGELY.
                              I think
I 'd cultivate him if I were a lord.
Be friendly !   Unto each man comes his day.
If he takes not your hand, he may your head.
[*He seeks* LAFFEMAS, *presents him to* DUKE DE BELLE-
    GARDE, *who bows with ill-concealed displeasure.*

LAFFEMAS (*bowing*).
Sir Duke !

DUKE DE BELLEGARDE.
          Sir, I am charmed —
                    [*Aside.*]   Upon my life,
We 're fallen low, Monsieur de Richelieu !
                              [LAFFEMAS *walks away.*

VISCOUNT DE ROHAN (*bursting into laughter among a
          group of Courtiers in the back of the hall*).
Delightful !

L'ANGELY.
What?

VISCOUNT DE ROHAN.
That Marion is here.

L'ANGELY.
Here — Marion?

VISCOUNT DE ROHAN.
We were just saying this:
"Chaste Louis' guest is Marion." How rich!

L'ANGELY.
A charming piece of wit, indeed, my lord!

DUKE DE BELLEGARDE (*to* COUNT DE CHARNACÉ).
Sir wolf-hunter, have you found any prey?
Is hunting good?

COUNT DE CHARNACÉ.
There 's nothing! Yesterday
I had great expectations, for three peasants
Had been devoured by wolves. At first I thought
We would find several at Chambord. I beat
The woods, but not a wolf, nor trace of one!
[*To* L'ANGELY.] Fool, know you anything that 's gay?

L'ANGELY.
Nothing,
My lord, except two men will soon be hung
At Beaugency for duelling.

ABBÉ DE GONDI.
So little!
Bah! [*The small gilt door is opened.*

AN USHER.

The King!

[THE KING *enters; he is in black, his eyes are cast down.*
The order of the Holy Ghost is on his doublet and his
cloak. Hat on his head. The Courtiers all uncover
and range themselves, silently, in two rows. The
Guards lower their pikes and present muskets.

SCENE VI.

The same. THE KING. THE KING *enters slowly, passes*
through the crowd of Courtiers without lifting his head,
stops at front of stage, and stands for several instants
absorbed and silent. The Courtiers retire to the back
of the hall.

THE KING.

All things move on from bad to worse.   Yes, all!

                [*To Courtiers, nodding his head.*

God keep you, gentlemen!

[*He throws himself into a large arm-chair and sighs*
profoundly.

                I have slept ill!

                [*To* DUKE DE BELLEGARDE.

My lord!

DUKE DE BELLEGARDE (advancing with three profound
salutations).

The time for sleeping, sire, is past.

THE KING (eagerly).

True, Duke!   The State is rushing to destruction
With giant strides!

DUKE DE BELLEGARDE.
                    'T is guided by a hand
Both strong and wise.

                    THE KING.
                    He bears a heavy burden,
Our good lord cardinal!

            DUKE DE BELLEGARDE.
                    Sire!

                    THE KING.
                              He is old.
I ought to spare him, but I have enough
To do with living, without reigning!

            DUKE DE BELLEGARDE.
                              Sire,
The Cardinal's not old !

                    THE KING.
                    Pray, tell me frankly, —
No one is watching or is listening here, —
What do you think of him ?

            DUKE DE BELLEGARDE.
                    Of whom, sire ?

                    THE KING.
                                    Him !

            DUKE DE BELLEGARDE.
His Eminence ?

                    THE KING.
            Of course!

DUKE DE BELLEGARDE.
My dazzled eyes
Can hardly fix themselves —

THE KING.
Is that your frankness?
There is no cardinal here, nor red, nor grey!
No spies! Speak! Why are you afraid? The King
Wants your opinion of the Cardinal.

DUKE DE BELLEGARDE.
Entirely frank, sire?

THE KING.
Yes, entirely frank.

DUKE DE BELLEGARDE (*boldly*).
Well then, I think him a great man!

THE KING.
If needful
You would proclaim it on the house-tops? Good!
Can you not understand? The State, mark me,
Is suffering, because he does it all
And I am nothing!

DUKE DE BELLEGARDE.
Ah!

THE KING.
Rules he not war
And peace, finances, states? Makes he not laws,
Edicts, mandates, and ordinances too?
Through treachery he broke the Catholic league;
He strikes the house of Austria, — friendly
To me, — to which the Queen belongs.

DUKE DE BELLEGARDE.
                                    Ah, sire,
He lets you keep a vivary within
The Louvre.   You have your share.

THE KING.
                              Then he intrigues
With Denmark.

DUKE DE BELLEGARDE.
            But he let you fix the marc
Among the jewellers.

THE KING (*whose ill-humour increases*).
            He fights with Rome!

DUKE DE BELLEGARDE.
He let you issue an edict, alone,
By which a citizen was not allowed
To eat more than a crown's worth at a tavern,
E'en though he wished to.

THE KING.
                        All the treaties he
Concludes in secret.

DUKE DE BELLEGARDE.
            Yes; but then you have
Your hunting mansion at Planchette.

THE KING.
                              All — all!
He does it all!   All with petitions rush
To him!   I 'm but a shadow to the French!
Is there a single one who comes to me
For help?

DUKE DE BELLEGARDE.

Those who have the king's evil come.

[*The anger of* THE KING *increases.*

THE KING.

He means to give my order to his brother!
I will not have it!   I rebel.

DUKE DE BELLEGARDE.

But, sire —

THE KING.

I am disgusted with his people!

DUKE DE BELLEGARDE.

Sire!

THE KING.

His niece, Combalet, leads a model life.

DUKE DE BELLEGARDE.

'T is slander, sire!

THE KING.

Two hundred foot-guards!

DUKE DE BELLEGARDE.

But

Only a hundred horse-guards!

THE KING.

What a shame!

DUKE DE BELLEGARDE.

He saves France, sire.

THE KING.

     Does he ?   He damns my soul!
With one arm fights the heathen, with the other
He signs a compact with the Huguenots.
    [*Whispering to* DUKE DE BELLEGARDE.
Then, if I dared to count upon my hand
The heads — the heads that fall for him at Grève !
All friends of mine !   His purple robes are made
Of their hearts' blood !   'T is he who forces me
To wear eternal mourning.

DUKE DE BELLEGARDE.

     Treats he his own
More kindly ?   Did he spare Saint Preuil ?

THE KING.

       He has
A bitter tenderness, they say, for those
He loves.   He must love me tremendously !
   [*Abruptly, after a pause, folding his arms.*
He has exiled my mother !

DUKE DE BELLEGARDE.

     But he thinks
He does your will.   He 's faithful.   He is firm
And sure.

THE KING.

   I hate him !   He is in my way.
He crushes me !   I am not master here —
Not free !   And yet I might be something.   Ah,
When he walks o'er me with such heavy tread,
Does he not fear to rouse a slumbering king ?
For trembling near me, be it ne'er so high,
His fortune vacillates with every breath

I draw, and all would crumble at a word,
Did I wish loud, what I wish in my heart!   [*A pause.*
That man makes good men bad, and bad men vile!
The kingdom, like the king, already sick,
Grows worse.   Without is cardinal, within
Is cardinal; no king is anywhere!
He torments Austria, lets any one
Capture my vessels in Gascony's Bay.
Allies me with Gustavus Adolphus!
What more? I do not know.   He's everywhere.
As if he were soul of the king, he fills
My kingdom, and my family, and me.
I am much to be pitied.   [*Going to window.*
                Always rain!

                DUKE DE BELLEGARDE.
Your Majesty is suffering?

                    THE KING.
                I am bored.   [*A pause.*
I am the first in France and yet the last!
I'd change my lot to lead a poacher's life, —
To hunt all day; to have no cares to fret
The pleasures of the chase; to sleep 'neath trees;
To laugh at the King's officers, to sing
During the storm; to live as freely in the woods
As birds live in the air.   The peasant in
His hut, at least, is master and is king;
But with that scarlet man forever there,
Forever stern and cold, and speaking thus,
" This must be your good pleasure, sire! "   Oh, outrage!
This man conceals me from my people's gaze.
As with young children, he hides me beneath
His robe; and when a passer-by asks, " Who
Is that behind the Cardinal? " they say,

"The King!" Then there are new lists every day.
Last week the Huguenots; the duellists
To-day! He wants their heads. Such a great crime,—
A duel! But the heads; what does he do
With them?
[DUKE DE BELLEGARDE *stamps his foot.* *Enter* MARQUIS
  DE NANGIS *and* MARION.

SCENE VII.

The same. MARION, MARQUIS DE NANGIS. MARQUIS
  DE NANGIS *advances with his escort to within a few
  steps of* THE KING; *he kneels there.* MARION *falls on
  her knees at the door.*

MARQUIS DE NANGIS.
Justice, my sire.

THE KING.
Against whom? Speak!

MARQUIS DE NANGIS.
Against a cruel tyrant, — against Armand,
Called here the cardinal-minister!

MARION.
Mercy.

My sire!
THE KING.
For whom?

MARION.
For Didier!

MARQUIS DE NANGIS.
                              And for him,
Gaspard de Saverny !

THE KING.
        I 've heard those names.

MARQUIS DE NANGIS.
Justice and mercy, sire !

THE KING.
        What title ?

MARQUIS DE NANGIS.
                              Sire,
I am uncle of one.

THE KING.
        And you ?

MARION.
                      I 'm sister
Unto the other !

THE KING.
        Why do you come here,
Sister and uncle ?

MARQUIS DE NANGIS (*indicating first one of* THE KING'S
        hands, then the other).

            To entreat mercy
From this hand, and justice from that !   My sire,
I, William, Marquis de Nangis, Captain
Of Hundred Lances, Baron of Mountain
And Field, do make appeal to my two lords, —
The King of France and God, for justice 'gainst
Armand du Plessis, Cardinal Richelieu.
Gaspard de Saverny, for whom I make
This prayer, is my nephew —

MARION (*low to* MARQUIS DE NANGIS).
                              Oh, speak for both,
My lord !

MARQUIS DE NANGIS (*continuing*).
        Last month he had a duel with
A captain, a young nobleman, Didier.
Of parentage uncertain.   'T was a fault.
They were too rash and brave.   The minister
Had stationed sergeants —

THE KING.
                              Yes, I know the story.
Well, what have you to say ?

MARQUIS DE NANGIS.
                              That 't is high time
You thought about these things !   The Cardinal-Duke
Has more than one disastrous scheme afoot.
He drinks the best blood of your subjects, sire !
Your father, Henry IV., of royal heart,
Would not have sacrificed his nobles thus !
He never struck them down without dire need !
Well served by them, he sought to guard them well.
He knew good soldiers had more use in them
Than trunkless heads.   He knew their worth in war,
This soldier-king whose doublet smelled of battle !
Great days were those.   I shared, I honour them !
A few of the old race are living yet.
Never could priest have touched one of those lords.
There was no selling of a great head cheap !
Sire, in these treacherous days to which we 've come,
Trust an old man, keep a few nobles by.   ·
Perhaps, in your turn, you will need their help.
The time may come when you will groan to think

Of all the honours lavished on La Grève!
Then, sadly, your regretful eyes will seek
Those lords indomitably brave and true,
Who, dead so long, had still been young to-day.
The country's heart yet pants with civil war;
The tocsin of past years re-echoes yet,
Be saving of the executioner's arm!
He is the one should sheathe his sword, not we!
Be miserly with scaffolds, O my sire!
'T will be a woful thing some later day
To mourn this great man's help, who hangs to-day
A whitening skeleton on gallows-tree!
For blood, my king, is no good, wholesome dew.
You 'll reap no crops from irrigated Grève!
The people will avoid the sight of kings.
That flattering voice which tells you all is well,
Tells you you 're son of Henry IV., and Bourbon, —
That voice, my sire, however high it soars,
Can never drown the thud of falling heads!
Take my advice : play not this costly game.
You, King, are bound to look God in the face,
Hark to the words of fate, ere it rebels!
War is a nobler thing than massacre!
'T is not a prosperous nor joyful State
When headsmen have more work than soldiers have!
He for our country is a pastor hard,
Who dares collect his tithes in slaughtered heads!
Look! this proud lord of inhumanity
Who holds your sceptre has blood-covered hands!

THE KING.

The Cardinal 's my friend!   Who loves me must
Love him!

MARQUIS DE NANGIS.

     Sire!

THE KING.

Silence ! He 's my second self.

MARQUIS DE NANGIS.

Sire !

THE KING.

Bring no more such griefs to trouble me !
[*Showing his hair, which is beginning to turn grey.*
Petitioners like you make these grey hairs !

MARQUIS DE NANGIS.

An old man, sire ; a woman, sire, who weeps !
A word from you is life or death for us !

THE KING.

What do you ask ?

MARQUIS DE NANGIS.

Pardon for my Gaspard !

MARION.

Pardon for Didier !

THE KING.

Pardons of a king
Are often thefts from justice !

MARION.

Oh, no, sire !
Since God himself is merciful, you need
Not fear ! Have pity ! Two young, thoughtless men,
Pushed by this duel o'er a precipice
To die ! Good God ! to die upon the gallows !
You will have pity, won't you ? I don't know
How people talk to kings, — I 'm but a woman ;
To weep so much perhaps is wrong. But oh,

A monster is that cardinal of yours.
Why does he hate them? They did naught to him.
He never saw my Didier. All who do
Must love him! They 're so young — these two! To
    die
For just a duel! Think about their mothers.
Oh, it is horrible! You will not do it, sire!
We women cannot talk as well as men.
We 've only cries and tears and knees, which bend
And totter as kings turn their eyes on us.
They were in fault, of course! But if they broke
Your law, you can forgive it! What is youth?
Young people are so heedless! For a look,
A word, a trifle, anything or nothing,
They always lose their heads like that! Such things
Are happening every day. Each noble, here,
He knows it. Ask them, sire! Is it not true,
My lords? Oh, frightful hour of agony!
To know with one word you can save two lives!
I 'd love you all my life, sire, if you would
Have mercy — mercy, God! If I knew how,
I 'd talk so that you 'd have to say that word.
You 'd pardon them; you 'd say, " I must console
That woman, for her Didier is her soul."
I suffocate, sire. Pity, pity me!

THE KING.

Who is this woman?

MARION.

She 's a sister, sire,
Who trembles at your feet. You owe something
Unto your people!

THE KING.

Yes! I owe myself
To them, and duelling does grievous harm.

MARION.

You should have pity !

THE KING.

And obedience, too !

MARQUIS DE NANGIS.

Two boys of twenty years !   Think of it well !
Their years together are but half of mine !

MARION.

Your Majesty, you have a mother, wife,
A son, — some one at least who's dear to you !
A brother ?   Then have pity for a sister !

THE KING.

No, I have not a brother !   [*Reflects a moment.*
                    Yes, *Monsieur!*
          [*Perceiving the escort of* MARQUIS DE NANGIS.
Well, my lord marquis, what is this brigade ?
Are we besieged, or off to the Crusades ?
To bring your guards thus boldly in my sight,
Are you a duke and peer ?

MARQUIS DE NANGIS.

                    I 'm better, sire,
Than any duke and peer, created for mere show !
I 'm Breton baron of four baronies.

DUKE DE BELLEGARDE (*aside*).

His pride is great, and here, unfortunate !

THE KING.

Good !   To your manors carry back your rights,
And leave us ours within our own domain.
We are justiciary !

MARQUIS DE NANGIS (*shuddering*).
Sire, reflect!
Think of their age, their expiated fault!
[*Falling on his knees.*
The pride of an old man, who, prostrate, kneels!
Have mercy!
[THE KING *makes an abrupt sign of anger and refusal.*
I was comrade to Henry!
Your father and our father! I was there
When he — that monster — struck the fatal blow.
'Til night I watched beside my royal dead:
It was my duty. I have seen my father
And my six brothers fall 'neath rival factions;
I have lost the wife who loved me. Now
The old man standing here is like a victim
Whom a hard executioner, for sport,
Has bound unto the wheel the whole long day.
My master, God has broken every limb
With his great iron rod! 'T is night-time now,
And I 've received the final blow! Farewell,
My king! God keep you!
[*He makes a profound obeisance, and exits.* MARION *lifts
  herself with difficulty and, staggering, falls on the
  threshold of the gilt door of* THE KING'S *private room.*

THE KING (*to* DUKE DE BELLEGARDE, *wiping his eyes and
  watching the retreating figure of* MARQUIS DE NANGIS).
A sad interview!
Ah, not to weaken, kings must watch themselves!
To do right is not easy. I was touched.
[*Reflects for a moment, then interrupts himself suddenly.*
No pardoning to-day, for yesterday
I sinned too much! [*Approaching* DUKE DE BELLEGARDE.
Before he came, my lord,
You said bold things, which may be bad for you

When I report to my lord cardinal
The conversation we have had.   I'm sorry
For you, Duke.   In the future, have more care!
I slept so wretchedly, my poor Bellegarde.
      [*With a gesture dismissing Courtiers and Guards.*
Pray leave us, gentlemen!
         [*To* L'ANGELY.]   Stay, you!
[*All go out except* MARION, *whom* THE KING *does not see.*
   DUKE DE BELLEGARDE *sees her crouching on the thresh-*
   old of the door and goes to her.

         DUKE DE BELLEGARDE (*low to* MARION).
                              My child,
You can't remain here, crouching by this door;
What are you doing like a statue there?
Get up and go away!
                  MARION.
                  I'm waiting here
For them to kill me!

      L'ANGELY (*low to* DUKE DE BELLEGARDE).
                  Leave her there, my lord!
[*Low to* MARION.]   Remain!
[*He returns to* THE KING, *who is seated in the great arm-*
   chair and is in a profound reverie.

                 ———

             SCENE VIII.

           THE KING, L'ANGELY.

         THE KING (*sighing deeply*).
                  Ah! L'Angely, my heart is sick.
'T is full of bitterness.   I cannot smile.

You, only, have the power to cheer me.   Come !
You stand in no awe of my majesty.
Come, throw a glint of pleasure in my soul.   [*A pause.*

L'ANGELY.

Life is a bitter thing, your Majesty.

THE KING.

Alas !

L'ANGELY.

Man is a breath ephemeral !

THE KING.

A breath, and nothing more !

L'ANGELY.

Unfortunate
Is any one who is both man and king.
Is it not true ?

THE KING.

A double burden — yes.

L'ANGELY.

And better far than life, sire, is the tomb,
If but its gloom is deep enough !

THE KING.

I 've thought
That always !

L'ANGELY.

To be dead or unborn is
The only happiness.   Yes, man 's condemned !

THE KING.

You give me pleasure when you talk like this !
                                              [*A silence.*

L'ANGELY.

Once in the tomb, think you one e'er gets out?

THE KING (*whose sadness has increased with the Fool's words*).

We 'll know that later. I wish I were there! [*Silence.*
Fool, I 'm unhappy! Do you comprehend?

L'ANGELY.

I see it in your face so thin and worn,
And in your mourning —

THE KING.

Ah, why should I laugh?
Your tricks are lost on me! What use is life
To you? The fine profession! Jester to the King!
Bell out of tune, a jumping-jack to play with,
Whose half-cracked laugh is but a poor grimace!
What is there in the world for you, poor toy.
Why do you live?

L'ANGELY.

For curiosity.
But you — why should you live? I pity you!
I 'd sooner be a woman than a king
Like you. I 'm but a jumping-jack whose string
You hold; but underneath your royal coat
There 's hid a taughter string, a strong arm holds.
Better a jumping-jack in a king's hands
Than in a priest's, my sire.   [*Silence.*

THE KING (*thinking, growing more and more sad*).

You speak the truth,
Although you laugh. He is a fearful man!
Has Satan made himself a cardinal?
What if 't were Satan who possessed my soul!
What say you?

L'ANGELY.

I have often had that thought

Myself!

THE KING.

We must not speak thus.   'T is a sin !
Behold, how dire misfortune follows me !
I had some Spanish cormorants.   I come
To this place, — not a drop of water here
For fishing !   In the country !   Not a pond
In this accursed Chambord large enough
To drown a flesh-worm !   When I wish to hunt —
The sea !   And when I wish to fish — the fields !
Am I unfortunate enough ?

L'ANGELY.

Your life

Is full of woe

THE KING.

How will you comfort me ?

L'ANGELY.

Another grief !   You hold in high esteem,
And justly too, the art of training hawks
For hunting partridges.   A good huntsman —
You 're one — ought to respect the falconer.

THE KING.

The falconer !   A god !

L'ANGELY.

Well ! there are two

Who are at point of death !

THE KING.

Two falconers ?

L'ANGELY.

Yes!

THE KING.

Who are they ?

L'ANGELY.

Two famous ones !

THE KING.

But who ?

L'ANGELY.

Those two young men whose lives were begged of you !

THE KING.

Gaspard and Didier ?

L'ANGELY.

Yes ; they are the last.

THE KING.

What a calamity !   Two falconers !
Now that the art is very nearly lost.
Unhappy duel !   When I'm dead, this art
Will go from earth, as all things go at last !
Why did they fight this duel ?

L'ANGELY.

One declared
That hawks upon the wing were not as swift
As falcons.

THE KING.

He was wrong.   But yet that seems
Scarcely a hanging matter —   [*Silence.*
And my right
Of pardon is inviolable — though
I am too lenient, says the Cardinal !   [*Silence.*
[*To* L'ANGELY.]   The Cardinal desires their death ?

L'ANGELY.

He does !

THE KING (*after pausing and reflecting*).
Then they shall die !

L'ANGELY.
They shall !

THE KING.

Poor falconry !

L'ANGELY (*going to window*).
Sire, look !

THE KING (*turns around suddenly*).
At what !

L'ANGELY.
Just look, I beg of you !

THE KING (*rising and going to the window*).
What is it ?

L'ANGELY (*indicating something outside*).
They have changed the sentinel !

THE KING.
Well, is that all ?

L'ANGELY.
Who is that fellow with
The yellow lace ?

THE KING.
No one — the corporal !

L'ANGELY.
He puts a new man there. What says he, low ?

THE KING.

The password! Fool! What are you driving at?

L'ANGELY.

At this: Kings act the part of sentinels.
Instead of pikes, a sceptre they must bear.
When they have strutted 'round their little day,
Death comes, — the corpqral of kings, — and puts
Another sceptre-bearer in their place,
Speaking the password which God sends, and which
Is clemency.

THE KING.

No, it is justice. Ah,
Two falconers! It is a frightful loss!
Still, they must die.

L'ANGELY.

As you must die, and I.
Or big or little, death has appetite
For all. But though they 've not much room,
The dead sleep well. The Cardinal annoys
And wearies you. Wait, sire! A day, a month,
A year; when we have played as long as needful, —
I, my own part of fool; you, king; and he,
The master, — we will go to sleep. No matter
How proud or great we are, no one shall have
More than six feet of territory there.
Look! how they bear his lordly litter now!

THE KING.

Yes, life is dark; the tomb alone is bright.
If you were not at hand to cheer me up —

L'ANGELY.

Alas! I came to-day to say farewell.

THE KING.

What 's that ?

L'ANGELY.

I leave you !

THE KING.

You 're a crazy fool !
Death, only, frees from royal service.

L'ANGELY.

Well,

I am about to die !

THE KING.

Have you gone mad ?

L'ANGELY.

You have condemned me, — you, the King of France !

THE KING.

If you are joking, fool, explain yourself.

L'ANGELY.

I shared the duel of those two young men, —
At least, my sword did, sire, if I did not.
I here surrender it.
[*Draws his sword and, kneeling, presents it to* THE KING.

THE KING (*takes it and examines it*).

Indeed, a sword !
Where does it come from, friend ?

L'ANGELY.

We 're noble, sire !
The guilty are not pardoned.   I am one.

THE KING (*sombre and stern*).

Good-night, then! Let me kiss your neck, poor fool,
Before they cut it off.   [*Embraces* L'ANGELY.

L'ANGELY (*aside*).
He 's in dead earnest!

THE KING (*after a pause*).

For never does a worthy king oppose
The course of justice. But you claim too much,
Lord Cardinal, — two falconers and my fool!
All for one duel!
[*Greatly agitated, he walks up and down with his hand
    on his forehead. Then he turns to* L'ANGELY, *who is
    most anxious.*
                Go! console yourself!
Life is but bitterness, the tomb means rest.
Man is a breath ephemeral.

L'ANGELY (*aside*).
                The devil!
[THE KING *continues to pace the floor and appears vio-
    lently agitated.*
                THE KING.
And so, you think you 'll have to hang, poor fool!

L'ANGELY (*aside*).

He means it! God! I feel cold perspiration
Starting upon my brow.
                [*Aloud.*]   Unless a word
From you —
                THE KING.
                Whom shall I have to make me laugh?
If you should rise from out the tomb, come back
And tell me all about it. 'T is a chance!

L'ANGELY.

The errand is a pleasant one !
[THE KING *continues to walk rapidly, speaking to* L'ANGELY *now and then.*

THE KING.

What triumph
For my lord cardinal — my fool !   [*Folding his arms.*
Think you
I could be master if I wished to be ?

L'ANGELY.

Montaigne would say, " Who knows ? "   And Rabelais,
" Perhaps."

THE KING (*with gesture of determination*).

Give me a parchment, fool.
[L'ANGELY *eagerly hands a parchment which he finds on the table near the writing-desk.* THE KING *hastily writes a few words, then gives the parchment back to* L'ANGELY.

Behold !
I pardon all.

L'ANGELY.

All three ?

THE KING.

Yes.

L'ANGELY (*running to* MARION).

Come, madame,
Come, kneel, and thank the King.

MARION (*falling on her knees*).

We have the pardon ?

L'ANGELY.

Yes! It was I —

MARION.

Whose knees must I embrace, —
His Majesty's or yours?

THE KING (*astonished, examining* MARION: *aside*).

What does this mean?
Is this a trap?

L'ANGELY (*giving parchment to* MARION).

Here is the pardon. Take it!
[MARION *kisses it, and puts it in her bosom.*

THE KING (*aside*).

Have I been duped?
[*To* MARION.] One instant! Give it back!

MARION.

Good God!
[*To* THE KING, *with courage, touching her breast.*
Come here and take it, and tear out
My heart as well!
[THE KING *stops and steps backward, much embarrassed.*

L'ANGELY (*low to* MARION).

Good! Keep it, and be firm!
His Majesty wont take it, there!

THE KING (*to* MARION).

Give it
To me!

MARION.

Take it, my sire!

THE KING (*casting down his eyes*).
               Who is this siren ?

L'ANGELY (*low to* MARION).
He would n't touch the corset of the Queen !

THE KING (*after a moment's hesitation, dismisses* MARION
        with a gesture without looking at her).
Well, go !

        MARION (*bowing profoundly to* THE KING).
        I 'll fly to save the prisoners !   [*Exits.*

        L'ANGELY (*to* THE KING).
She 's sister to Didier, the falconer.

          THE KING.
She can be what she will. It 's very strange,
The way she made me drop my eyes ! Made me,
A man —   [*Silence.*
        Fool, you have played a trick on me !
I 'll have to pardon you a second time.

          L'ANGELY.
Yes, do it ! Every time they grant a pardon,
Kings lift a dreary weight from off their hearts.

          THE KING.
You speak the truth. I always suffer when
La Grève holds court. Nangis was right: the dead
Serve nobody. To fill Montfaucon
I make a desert of the Louvre !   [*Walking rapidly.*
                 'T is treason
To strike my right of pardon out, before
My face. What can I do ? Disarmed, dethroned,

And fallen: in this man absorbed, as in
A sepulchre! His cloak becomes my shroud:
My people mourn for me as for the dead.
I am resolved: those two boys shall not die!
The joy of living is a heavenly gift.   [*After reflection.*
God, who knows where we go, can ope the tomb;
A king cannot.   Back to their families
I give them; that old man, that fair young girl,
Will bless me.   It is said: I've signed it, — I,
The King.   The Cardinal will be furious,
But it will please Bellegarde.

L'ANGELY.

                    One can, sometimes,
Be kingly by mistake.

ACT V.

THE CARDINAL.

SCENE. — *Beaugency. The Tower of Beaugency. A courtyard; the tower in the background, all around a high wall. To the left, a tall arched door; to the right, a small rounded door in the wall; near the door a stone table and stone bench.*

SCENE I.

Some Workmen. They are pulling down a corner of the back wall on the left. The demolition is almost completed.

FIRST WORKMAN (*working with his pickaxe*).
It 's very hard!

SECOND WORKMAN (*working*).
Deuce take this heavy wall we 're pulling down!

THIRD WORKMAN (*working*).
Saw you the scaffold, Peter?

FIRST WORKMAN.
Yes, I did.
[*He goes to the large door and measures it.*
The door is narrow; never will the litter
Of the Lord Cardinal go through it.

THIRD WORKMAN.
Bah!
Is it a house?

FIRST WORKMAN (*with affirmative gesture*).
      With great long curtains.   Yes.
It takes some four and twenty men on foot
To carry it.
          SECOND WORKMAN.
         I saw the great machine,
One night when it was very dark.   It looked
Just like Leviathan in shadow-land.

          THIRD WORKMAN.
What does he come here with his sergeants for?

          FIRST WORKMAN.
To see the execution of those two young men.
He's sick.   He needs to be amused.

          SECOND WORKMAN.
               To work!
  [*They resume work; the wall is about torn down.*
Saw you the scaffold, all in black?   That comes
Of being noble!
          FIRST WORKMAN.
      They have everything.

          SECOND WORKMAN.
               I wonder
If they would build a black scaffold for us.

          FIRST WORKMAN.
What have those young men done that they should die?
Hein?   Do you understand, Maurice?

          THIRD WORKMAN.
               I don't.
It's justice.

[They continue their work. LAFFEMAS *enters;* THE WORK-
MEN *are silent. He comes from the back as though he
were coming from an inside court of the prison; stops
beside* THE WORKMEN, *appears to examine the breach,
and gives them some directions. When the space is
opened, he orders them to hang black cloth across it,
which covers it entirely; then he dismisses them. At
almost the same moment* MARION *appears, dressed in
white, and veiled; she enters through the great door,
crosses the court rapidly, and runs to the grating of
the small door, at which she knocks.* LAFFEMAS *follows slowly in the same direction. The grating is
opened;* THE TURNKEY *appears.*

SCENE II.

MARION, LAFFEMAS.

MARION (*showing a parchment to* THE TURNKEY).
  Order of the King!

     THE TURNKEY.
         You can't
Enter, madame.
      MARION.
  What!

LAFFEMAS (*presenting a paper to* THE TURNKEY).
  Signed, the Cardinal!

     THE TURNKEY.
Enter.
[When about to enter, LAFFEMAS *turns, looks at* MARION *a
moment, then approaches her.* THE TURNKEY *shuts
the door.*

LAFFEMAS (*to* MARION).
You here? This questionable place!

MARION.
I am. [*Triumphantly showing the parchment.*
I have the pardon!

LAFFEMAS (*showing his*).
Yes? I have
The revocation!

MARION (*with a cry of horror*).
Mine was yesterday, —
The morning!

LAFFEMAS.
Mine, last night!

MARION (*with hands over her eyes*).
My God! No hope!

LAFFEMAS.
Hope is a flash of lightning which deceives.
The clemency of kings is a frail thing;
It comes with lagging steps and goes with wings.

MARION.
The King was moved with pity for their fate!

LAFFEMAS.
What can the King against the Cardinal?

MARION.
Oh, Didier, our last hope's extinguished now!

LAFFEMAS (*low*).
Not — not the last!

MARION.

Just Heaven!

LAFFEMAS (*drawing near to her*).

There is here
A man whom one short word from you could make
Happier than any king, and mightier too!

MARION.

Away!

LAFFEMAS.

Is that your answer?

MARION (*haughtily*).

I beg you!

LAFFEMAS.

How fleeting are the whims of the fair sex!
You were not always, madame, so severe!
Now that 't is question of your lover's life —

MARION (*without looking at him, turning to the small door,
her hands clasped*).

If it would save your life, I could not go
Back to that infamy. My soul 's grown pure
At touch of you, my Didier; sin is shamed.
Your love gives back my lost virginity.

LAFFEMAS.

Well, love him!

MARION.

Ah, he pushes me from crime
To vice! Oh, monster go! Let me keep pure!

LAFFEMAS.

There is but one thing left for me to do!

MARION.

What is it ?

LAFFEMAS.

I can show you — let you see.
It is to-night.

MARION (*trembling all over*).
Oh, heaven ! this night !

LAFFEMAS.

This night
The Cardinal, in litter, will attend.
[MARION *is buried in a deep and painful reverie. Suddenly she passes her two hands over her brow and
turns, as if wild, towards* LAFFEMAS.

MARION.

How could you manage their escape ?

LAFFEMAS (*low*).
You mean ?
Two of my men could guard this place, by which
The Cardinal passes —   [*He listens at the small door.*
I think some one comes !

MARION (*wringing her hands*).
You 'll save him ?

LAFFEMAS.

Yes.
[*Low.*]   To tell you in this place —
The walls have echoes — elsewhere.

MARION (*with despair*).
Come !
[LAFFEMAS *goes towards the large door and signs to her to
follow. She falls on her knees, turned towards the*

grating of the prison ; then she arises with a convul-
sive effort and disappears through the great door after
LAFFEMAS. SAVERNY *and* DIDIER *enter, surrounded*
by Guards.

SCENE III.

DIDIER, SAVERNY. SAVERNY, *dressed in the latest fashion,*
enters gaily and petulantly. DIDIER *is in black, walks*
slowly, is very pale. A jailer accompanied by Halber-
diers conducts them. THE JAILER *places the two Hal-*
berdiers as sentinels beside the black curtain. DIDIER
sits, silently, on the stone bench.

SAVERNY (*to* THE JAILER, *who opens the door for him*).
                                                    Thank you.
The air is very good !

THE JAILER (*low, and drawing him aside*).
                              My lord, two words with you.

SAVERNY.
Four, if you like.

THE JAILER (*lowering his voice still more*).
                              Will you escape ?

SAVERNY (*eagerly*).
                                        Speak ! How ?
THE JAILER.
That's my affair.
SAVERNY.
                    Truly ?   [THE JAILER *nods his head.*
                    Lord Cardinal,
You meant to keep me from attending balls,

But it appears I am to dance again.
The pleasant thing that life is!
              [*To* THE JAILER.]   When, my friend?

THE JAILER.
To-night, as soon as it is dark.

SAVERNY.
                    My faith!
I shall be charmed to leave these quarters.   Whence
Comes this assistance?

THE JAILER.
                    Marquis de Nangis.

SAVERNY.
My good old uncle!
    [*To* THE JAILER.]   'T is for both, I hope!

THE JAILER.
I can save only one!

SAVERNY.
              For twice as much?

THE JAILER.
I can save only one!

SAVERNY (*tossing his head*).
                    Just one?
        [*Low to* THE JAILER.]   Then listen;
Good jailer, that's the one to save!   [*Indicating* DIDIER.

THE JAILER.
                    You jest!

SAVERNY.
I do not!   He's the one!

THE JAILER.
What an idea!
Your uncle wants to save you, not save him.

SAVERNY.

It's settled?   Then prepare two shrouds at once.
[*Turns his back on* THE JAILER *who goes out, astonished.*
   A REGISTRAR *enters.*
We can't be left alone an instant — strange!

REGISTRAR (*saluting the prisoners*).
The royal councillor of the Great Chamber
Is close at hand.   [*Salutes them again and exits.*

SAVERNY.
'T is well!   [*Laughing.*
               Annoying luck!
Twenty years old — September — and to die
Before October!

DIDIER (*motionless at front of stage, holding the portrait
   in his hand, and as if absorbed in a deep study of it*).
               Come, look at me well!
Eyes in my eyes: thus.   You are beautiful!
What radiant grace!   Hardly a woman, you!
No: much more like an angel.   God himself
When he formed that divinely honest look
Put much fire in it but more chastity.
That childish mouth, pushed open by sweet hopes,
Throbs with its innocence.
          [*Throwing the portrait violently to the ground.*
               Why did that peasant
Take me unto her breast?   Why not have dashed
My head against the stones?   What did I do

Unto my mother to be cursed with birth ?
Why, in that misery, it may be crime,
Which forced her to abandon her own blood,
Had she not motherhood enough to choke
Me in her arms ?

SAVERNY (*returning from back of court*).
    The swallows fly quite low ;
'T will rain to-night.

DIDIER (*without hearing him*).
    A faithless, a mad thing,
A woman is : inconstant, cruel, deep,
And turbulent as is the ocean. Ah,
Upon that sea I trusted all my fortune !
In all the vast horizon saw one star !
Well ! I am ship-wrecked ! Nothing 's left but death.
Yet I was born good-hearted : might have found
The spark divine within me by-and-by.
Fair looked the future ! O remorseless woman,
Did you not shrink in face of such a lie,
Since to your mercy I trusted my soul ?

SAVERNY.
Forever Marion ! You 've strange ideas
About her !

DIDIER (*without heeding him, picks up the picture and
fixes his eyes upon it*).
    Down 'mongst the degraded things
I must throw you, oh, woman who betrays !
A demon, with eyes touched by angels' wings.
      [*Puts it back into his breast.*
Come back ; here is your place !

[*Approaching* SAVERNY.]   A curious thing !
That portrait is alive ; I do not jest.
While you were sleeping there so peacefully
It gnawed my heart all night.

SAVERNY.

Alas ! poor friend.
We 'll talk of death.
[*Aside.*]   It comforts him, although
I find it rather sad.

DIDIER.

What did you say ?
I have not listened.   Since I heard that name
I have been stupefied.   I cannot think :
I can't remember, cannot hear nor see !

SAVERNY (*taking hold of his arm*).

Death, friend !
DIDIER (*joyfully*).
Oh, yes !

SAVERNY.

Let 's talk about it.

DIDIER.

Yes !
SAVERNY.

What is it, after all ?

DIDIER.

Did you sleep well
Last night ?

SAVERNY.

No, badly, for my bed was hard.

DIDIER.

When you are dead, your bed will be much harder,
But you will sleep extremely well, — that's all.
They 've made hell splendidly ; but by the side
Of life, it's nothing.

SAVERNY.

                                     Good !   My fears are gone !
But to be hung !   That certainly is bad.

DIDIER.

You 're getting death ; don't be an egotist.

SAVERNY.

You can be satisfied ; but I am not.
I 'm not afraid of death, — that is no boast, —
When death is death, but on the gallows !

DIDIER.

                                                 Well,
Death has a thousand forms, — gallows are one.
That moment is not pleasant when the rope
Puts out your life as one puts out a flame,
Choking your throat to let your soul fly up ;
But, after all, what matter ?   If all's dark,
If only all this earth is hidden well,
What matter if a tomb lies on one's breast ?
What matter if the night-winds howl and blow
About the strings of flesh crows tore from you
When you were on the gibbet ?   What care you ?

SAVERNY.

You 're a philosopher.

DIDIER.

                              Yes, let them rave.
Let vultures tear my flesh, let worms consume,

As they consume all, even kings; my body
Is what's concerned, not I.   What do I care?
When sepulchres shut down our mortal eye,
The soul lifts up the mighty mass of stone
And flies away —

[*A Councillor enters, preceded and followed by Halberdiers in black.*

SCENE IV.

The same.   COUNCILLOR OF THE GREAT CHAMBER,
in full dress, THE JAILER, *Guards.*

THE JAILER (*announcing*).
The Councillor of the King!

COUNCILLOR (*saluting* SAVERNY *and* DIDIER *in turn*).
My mission's painful and the law severe —

SAVERNY.
I understand: there is no hope!   Speak, sir!

COUNCILLOR (*unfolds a parchment and reads*).
"We, Louis, King of France and of Navarre,
Reject appeals made by these men condemned,
But moved by pity, change the punishment
And order them beheaded."

SAVERNY (*joyfully*).
God be praised!

COUNCILLOR (*saluting them once more*).
You are to hold yourselves in readiness;
It will take place to-day.
[*He salutes and prepares to exit.*

DIDIER (*who has remained in the same thoughtful
attitude, to* SAVERNY).

As I was saying,
After this death, although the corpse be mangled,
Though every limb be stamped with hideous wounds,
Though arms be twisted, broken every bone,
Though through the mire the body has been dragged,
From out that putrid, bleeding, awful flesh
The soul shall rise, unstained, untouched, and pure.

COUNCILLOR (*coming back, to* DIDIER).
'T is well to occupy yourselves with such
Great thoughts.

DIDIER (*gently*).

Please do not interrupt me, sir.

SAVERNY (*gaily to* DIDIER).
No gallows !

DIDIER.

Order of the *féte* is changed,
I know. The Cardinal travels with his headsman,
And he must be employed; the axe will rust.

SAVERNY.
You 're cool about it, yet the stake is great.
[*To* THE COUNCILLOR.] Thank you for such good news.

COUNCILLOR.

I wish 't were better !
Good sir, my zeal —

SAVERNY.

Excuse me. What 's the hour ?

COUNCILLOR.

At nine o'clock to-night.

DIDIER.

I hope the sky
Will be as dark as is my soul.

SAVERNY.

The place?

COUNCILLOR (*indicating the neighbouring court*).
Here in the court.   The Cardinal will come.
[COUNCILLOR *exits with his escort.   The two prisoners remain alone.   Day begins to fade.   The halberds of
   the two sentinels, who silently promenade before the
   breach, are all that can be seen.*

DIDIER (*solemnly, after a pause*).
At this portentous hour we must reflect
Upon the fate awaiting us.   Our years
Are equal, though I 'm older far than you.
It is but just, therefore, that mine should be
The voice to cheer and to exhort you, since
I am the cause of all your misery.
'T was I who challenged you.   You were content
And happy: 't was enough for me to pass
Across your life to ruin it.   My fate
Pressed down upon yours 'til it crushed it.   Now,
Together, we are soon to face the tomb.
We 'll take each other's hand —   [*Sound of hammering.*

SAVERNY.
What is that noise?
DIDIER.
It is our scaffold which they 're building, or
Our coffins they are nailing.
                    [SAVERNY *sits on the stone bench.*
                    When the hour

Has tolled, sometimes the heart of man gives way.
Life holds us in a thousand secret ways.   [*A bell strikes.*
I think a voice is calling to us.   Hark !   [*Another bell.*

SAVERNY.

The hour is striking.   [*A third bell.*

DIDIER.

Yes, the hour !   [*A fourth bell.*

SAVERNY.

In chapel !
[*Four more bells.*

DIDIER.

It is a voice that calls us, just the same.

SAVERNY.

Another hour !
[*He leans his elbows on the stone table and drops his head
   on his hands.   The Guard is changed.*

DIDIER.

My friend, do not give way !
Don't falter on this threshold we must cross.
The tomb they 're fitting up for us is low,
And won't permit the entrance of a head.
Let 's go to meet them with a fearless tread.
The scaffold can afford to shake, not we.
They claim our heads; and since no fault is ours,
We 'll bear them proudly to the fatal block.
                [*Approaches* SAVERNY, *who is motionless.*
Courage !   [*Touches his arm and finds he is asleep.*
        Asleep !   While I 've been preaching courage
This man has slept !   What is my bravery
Compared to his ?   Sleep on, you who can sleep.
My turn will come, — provided all things die,

That nothing of the heart survives within
The tomb, to hate what it has loved too much.

[*It is night.   While* DIDIER *has become absorbed in his
thoughts,* MARION *and* THE JAILER *enter through the
opening in the wall;* THE JAILER *precedes her.   He
carries a dark-lantern and a bundle, both of which
he places on the ground, then advances cautiously
towards* MARION *who has remained standing on the
threshold, pale, motionless, half-wild.*

SCENE VI.

The same.   MARION, THE JAILER.

THE JAILER (*to* MARION).

Be sure to come at the appointed hour.

[*Goes up stage; during the rest of this scene he continues
to walk up and down at the back.*

MARION (*advances with tottering steps as if absorbed in
some desperate thought.   Every now and then she
draws her hand across her face as if to rub off something*).

His lips, like red-hot iron, have branded me!

[*Suddenly she discovers* DIDIER, *gives a cry, runs and
throws herself breathless at his feet.*

Didier — Didier!

DIDIER (*roused with a start*).

          Here, Marion!   My God!

[*Coldly.*]   'T is you?

MARION.

          Who should it be?   Oh, leave me here —
Here at your feet!   It is the place I love!

Your hands, your dear loved hands, give them — your
    hands!
Oh, they are wounded! Those harsh chains did that.
The wretched creatures! But I'm here — you know —
Oh, it is terrible!   [*She weeps; her sobs are audible.*

DIDIER.

Why do you weep?

MARION.

Why? Didier, I'm not weeping! No, I laugh!
                              [*She laughs.*
We'll soon escape from here! I laugh. I'm happy.
You will live; the danger's passed.
              [*She falls again at* DIDIER's *feet and sobs.*
                              My God!
All this is killing me! I'm broken — crushed.

DIDIER.

Madame —

MARION (*rises, without hearing him, and gets the bundle
              and brings it to him*).
              Now hurry! We have not much time!
Take this disguise. I've bribed the sentinels.
We'll leave Beaugency without being seen.
Go down that street, at the wall's end, out there!
The Cardinal will come to see them execute
His orders; we can't lose an instant now.
The cannon will be fired when he arrives,
And we'll be lost if we should still be here.

DIDIER.

'T is well!

MARION.

Quick ! hurry ! Didier, you are saved !
To be free !   Didier, how I love you — God !

DIDIER.

You say a street where the wall ends

MARION.

I do.
I saw it.   I've been there.   It is quite safe.
I saw them close up the last window, too.
It may be we shall meet some women, but
They 'll think you 're just a passer-by.   Come, love ;
When you are far off — please put on these things —
We 'll laugh to see you thus disguised.   Come, dear !

DIDIER (*pushing the clothes aside with his foot*).
There is no hurry.

MARION.

Death waits at the door.
Fly ! Didier ! Since I 've come !

DIDIER.

Why did you come ?

MARION.

To save you !   What a question to ask me !
Why such a freezing tone ?

DIDIER (*with a sad smile*).

Ah, well !   We men
Are often senseless.

MARION.

We are losing time.
The horses wait.   What you have in your mind,
You 'll tell me afterwards.   We must fly now.

DIDIER.

Who is that man there watching us?

MARION.
                                    The jailer.
He 's safe; I bribed him, as I did the guard.
Do you suspect them? You have such an air.

DIDIER.

It 's nothing.   We 're so easily deceived.

MARION.

Come!   Each lost moment chills me to the heart.
I seem to hear the tread of that great crowd.
Hasten, my Didier — on my knees — oh, fly!

DIDIER (*indicating* SAVERNY, *asleep*).
Tell me which one of us you want to save.

MARION (*overcome for a moment*).
[*Aside.*]   Gaspard is generous: he would not tell.
[*Aloud.*]   Does Didier speak to his beloved thus?
My Didier, what have you against me?

DIDIER.
                                    Naught.
Lift up your face and look me in the eyes.
                [MARION, *trembling, fixes her eyes on him.*
It is a perfect likeness!   Yes.

MARION.
                        My love,
I worship you, but come!

DIDIER.
                        Don't turn away!
[*He looks at her fixedly.*

MARION (*terrified at his look*).

[*Aside.*]   The kisses of that man, he sees them ! God !
[*Aloud.*]   You have a secret, something against me !
It hurts you !   Tell me all about it, dear.
You know we often make things worse by thinking,
And too late find it out ; then we regret.
I had my share in all your thoughts, love, once !
Speak, are those days for evermore gone by ?
Do you not love me now ?   Have you forgot
My little room at Blois ?   Forgotten how
We loved each other, till the world was lost ?
Sometimes you grew uneasy ; then I said,
" If any one should see him ! "   Oh, 't was fine !
But one day has destroyed it all.   You 've said
A thousand times, in words that burned my soul,
I was your love, I knew your secrets, I
Could make you anything I chose.   What have
I ever asked ?   I 've always thought witn you !
This time, oh, yield to me !   It is your life
I 'm pleading for.   My Didier, hark to me.
Alive or dead, I swear to follow you.
All things with you, love, will be sweet to me, —
To fly, or die upon the scaffold.   What !
You push me back ?   You shall not !   Leave your hand —
I want it.   My poor brow, it does no harm
To rest it on your knees.   I am so tired ;
I ran so fast to come !   What would they say,
The people I knew once, to see me now ?
I was so gay, so merry ; now I weep !
What is it that you have against me ?   Speak !
Oh, shame !   You must let me lie at your feet.
It 's very cruel of you not to say
One single word.   When we have thoughts, we speak !
'T would be more merciful to stab me, love !
See, I have dried my tears, and I am smiling.

You smile too.   Oh, if you don't smile at me,
I will not love you!   I have always done
Just what you wanted ; now it is your turn.
These chains are what have chilled your soul.   Love smile
And speak to me, and say " Marie."

DIDIER.

" Marie "

Or " Marion " ?

MARION (*falls annihilated at his feet*).
Didier, be merciful !

DIDIER (*with terrible tone*).
Here, no one finds an entrance easily.
Prisons of state are guarded night and day,
The doors are iron, walls twenty cubits high ;
To open these remorseless doors, madame,
To whom here did you prostitute yourself ?

MARION.

Who told you ?

DIDIER.

No one ; but I understand.

MARION.

Didier, I swear by every hope divine
It was to save you, tear you from this place ;
To melt the executioner — to save you —
Don't you hear ?

DIDIER (*folding his arms*).
I thank you !   To descend
As low as that !   To have no shame, no soul !

Oh, madame! can one be so infamous?
       [*Crossing the court with a great cry of rage.*
Who is this trader in disgrace and vice,
Who puts a price like that upon my head?
Where is the jailer, where the judge, the man? —
That I may crush him as I crush this thing.
[*He is about to break the portrait in his hands, but he stops,
    and beside himself, continues.*
The judge? Yes, gentlemen, make laws and judge!
What matters it to me if the false weight
Which swings your vile scales to this side or that
Be made of woman's honour or man's life?
[*To* MARION.] Go to your lover!

MARION.

                       Do not treat me thus!
Another word of scorn and I fall dead
Here at your feet. If ever love was true
And strong and pure, mine was. If any man
Was ever worshipped by a woman, you
Have been by me.

DIDIER.

             Hush! Do not speak! I might,
For sorrow, have been born a woman too.
I might have been as infamous as you.
I might have sold myself, have given my breast
To any passer-by, as place for rest.
But if there came to me, in his frank way,
An honest man, filled with the love of truth,
If I had met a heart insane enough
To keep its vain illusions all these years,
Oh, sooner than not tell that honest man
" I'm this," sooner than charm and dazzle him,
Sooner than fail to warn him that my eyes
So candid and my lips so pure were lies,

Sooner than be perfidious and base like that,
I 'd want to dig my grave with my own hands.

MARION.

O God !

DIDIER.

How you would laugh if you could see
The picture that my heart painted of you !
How wise you were to shatter it, madame !
There you were chaste and beautiful and pure !
What injury has this poor man done you,
Who loved you on his bended knees ?
                              [*Presenting portrait to her.*
                              Perhaps
This is a fitting time to give you back
This pledge of love ardent and true.

MARION (*turning away with a cry*).

                              Oh, shame !

DIDIER.

Did you not have it painted just for me ?
          [*He laughs, and dashes the locket to the ground.*

MARION.

Will some one, out of pity, kill me now ?

THE JAILER.

Time 's passing.

MARION.

                    Yes, it flies ; and we are lost.
Didier, I 've not the right to say a single word.
I am a woman to whom naught is due.
You have rebuked and cursed me : you did well !
I merit still more hate and shame.   You 've been
Too kind ; my broken, bruisèd heart is grateful.

But the remorseless hour draws near.   Away!
The headsman you forget, remembers you.
I've planned it all.   You can escape.   Now, listen —
My God! do not refuse.   You know how much
It costs me.   Hate me, strike me, curse me, leave
Me to my shame, disown me, walk upon
My bleeding heart — but fly!

DIDIER.

>   Fly where?   From whom?
There's naught but you to fly from in this world;
And I escape you, for the grave is deep.

THE JAILER.

The hour is passing.

MARION.

>   O my Didier, fly!

DIDIER.

I will not!

MARION.

>   Just for pity!

DIDIER.

>   Pity! why?

MARION.

To see you taken, bound!   To see you — *there!*
Only to think it makes me die of horror!
Come!   I will be a servant unto you.
Come!   Take me, when I have redeemed myself,
Just to have something underneath your feet.
The one you called " a wife " in times of trial —

DIDIER.

A wife!   [*Cannon sounds in the distance.*
>   This makes of you a widow, then!

MARION.

Didier !

THE JAILER.

The hour is past.

[*Rolling of drums. Enter* COUNCILLOR OF THE GREAT CHAMBER, *accompanied by penitents bearing torches, and by* EXECUTIONER. *A crowd of soldiers and people follow.*

MARION.

Ah, Christ !

SCENE VII.

The same. COUNCILLOR, EXECUTIONER, *Populace, Soldiers.*

COUNCILLOR.

I 'm ready,

Gentlemen !

MARION (*to* DIDIER).

I told you that he 'd come !

DIDIER (*to* COUNCILLOR).

We 're ready also.

COUNCILLOR.

Which is named Gaspard,

Marquis de Saverny ?

[DIDIER *points to* SAVERNY, *who is asleep.*

[*To* EXECUTIONER.] Awaken him !

EXECUTIONER (*shaking him*).

How well he sleeps, my lord !

SAVERNY (*rubbing his eyes*).
                          Ah, how could you
Break in on such a pleasant sleep !

DIDIER.
                          'T is only
Interrupted, friend !

SAVERNY (*half awake : sees* MARION *and salutes her*).
                          Oh, I was dreaming
About you, my beauty !

COUNCILLOR.
                          Have you made
Your peace with God ?

SAVERNY.
                I have, sir.

COUNCILLOR.
                          It is well.
Please sign this paper !

SAVERNY (*takes the parchment, runs over it*).
                          'T is the *procès-verbal*
Good !   This is a most curious thing, — account
Of my own death, signed with my autograph !
          [*Signs, and reads the paper again : to* COUNCILLOR.
You have made three mistakes in spelling, sir.
          [*Takes the pen and corrects them.   To* EXECUTIONER.
You have awakened me ; put me to sleep !

COUNCILLOR (*to* DIDIER).
Didier !
          [DIDIER *approaches :* COUNCILLOR *gives pen to him.*
          Your name is there.

MARION (*hiding her eyes*).
The gruesome thing !

DIDIER.

I could sign nothing with intenser joy !
[*The Guards form themselves into a line to lead them away.*

SAVERNY (*to some one in the crowd*).

Sir, step aside and let that young child see !

DIDIER (*to* SAVERNY).

My brother, 't is for me you suffer death ;
Let us embrace each other !   [*He embraces* SAVERNY.

MARION (*running to him*).
And for me

No kisses, Didier !

DIDIER (*indicating* SAVERNY).
This is my friend, madame !

MARION (*clasping her hands*).

How hard you are upon me, a poor thing,
Who always on my knees to king or judge
Have begged mercy for you from every one !
Pardon of them for you ; pardon of you for me !

DIDIER (*rushes to* MARION, *trembling, and bursting
into tears*).

No, I cannot !   The torture 's horrible !
No, I have loved too much to leave her so !
It is too hard to keep a cold, impassive face
When underneath the heart is breaking down.
Come to my arms, oh, woman, come !
[*Presses her convulsively to his heart.*
I love you !

I 'm about to die.   Before them all,

It is my loftiest joy to tell you this:
I love you!

MARION.

Didier! [*Embraces her again with rapture.*

DIDIER.

To my heart, oh, come!
You who behold this direful tragedy,
I wonder if there's one of you who would
Refuse love unto one who'd given herself
Entirely and unceasingly to him?
Oh, I was wrong! Say, would you have me face
Eternity without a pardon from
Her lips? No! Stand by me and listen, love:
Among all womankind — and those who hear
Will prove me right by their own hearts — the one
I love, the one in whom I trust, the one
I venerate is you, — is always you!
For you were kind, devoted, loving, good.
My life is almost ended. When death's near
A clearer light illuminates all things.
If you deceived me, 't was excess of love;
And if you fell, have you not cruelly atoned?
Perhaps your mother — life's so hard — forgot
You in your cradle, as my mother did;
When you were young and helpless, perhaps they sold
Your innocence. Ah, lift up your white brow!
And listen, all of you. At such an hour
The earth is a mere shadow and the heart
Speaks true. Well, at this moment, from the height
Of the dread scaffold, — and there's naught so high
When guiltless souls ascend it, — here,
I say to you, Marie, angel of light,
Whose lustre earth has dimmed, my love, my wife,
In God's name, before whom I soon shall stand,
I pardon you.

MARION (*suffocated with tears*).
  Ah, Christ!

DIDIER.
              It is your turn.
Speak now, and pardon me!   [*He kneels before her.*

MARION.
  Didier!

DIDIER.
                        Your pardon,
Love! I was the most at fault, the most
Unkind. God has chastised you much through me.
Weep for me when I'm gone, because to have
Hurt you is such a burden to take hence
Into eternity. Don't leave it on me;
Pardon me!
            MARION (*inaudibly*).
Have mercy on me — God!

DIDIER.
Just speak one word; put your sweet hands upon
My forehead. If your heart is full and you
Can't speak, please make a sign. I'm dying; you
Must comfort me.
[MARION *places her hand on his forehead; he rises, em-
    braces her tenderly, with a smile of celestial joy.*
                  Farewell! Come, gentlemen!
Let us move on!

    MARION (*throws herself wildly between him and the
                Soldiers*).
            Oh, no! Stop! This is madness!
If you think you can behead him easily,

You have forgotten I am here.   Spare us!
Oh, men! oh, soldiers, judge, people!   Spare us!
How do you want me to ask you?   Upon
My knees?   Well, here I am!   Now if
In you there's anything that quivers at
A woman's voice, if God has thrown no curse
On you — don't kill him!
          [*To the spectators.*]   Men and women — you!
When you go back into your homes to-night,
You'll find your mothers and your daughters; they
Will say to you, "It was a wicked crime.
You might have saved him, and you did not.   Shame!"
Didier, they ought to know that I must follow
You!   They will not kill you if they want
To keep me living!

DIDIER.

Let me die, Marie.
'T is better, dear one, for my wound is deep;
It would have taken too much time to heal.
Better for me to go; but if, sometime —
You see I'm weeping too — another comes,
A happier man, more fortunate than I,
Think of your old friend sleeping in the tomb.

MARION.

You shall not die!   Are these men all inhuman?
You must live!

DIDIER.

Don't ask things impossible.
No; with your bright eyes, turn, illuminate
My grave for me.   Embrace me.   You will love
Me better, dead.   I'll hold a sacred place
In your dear memory.   But if I lived,
Lived near you with my lacerated soul, —
I, who have loved no one but you, — you see

It would be painful. I would make you weep.
I 'd have a thousand thoughts I could not speak.
I 'd seem to doubt you, watch you, worry you.
You would be most unhappy. Let me die !

COUNCILLOR (*to* MARION).

The Cardinal will pass by soon, madame !
You can ask pardon for him then.

MARION.

Oh, yes !

The Cardinal is coming, — that is true.
You 'll see then, gentlemen, that he will hear !
My Didier, you shall hear me talk to him !
The Cardinal ! Indeed, you must be all insane,
To think such an old man — a Christian too,
The gracious cardinal — will not be glad
To pardon you. Have you not pardoned me ?
[*Nine o'clock strikes.* DIDIER *makes sign to all to hush.*
MARION *listens with terror. After the nine strokes
have sounded,* DIDIER *goes and stands close to* SAVERNY.

DIDIER (*to the spectators*).

You who have come to see the last of us,
If any speak of us, bear witness all,
That without faltering we have heard the hour
Bring us its summons to eternity.
[*The cannon sounds at the door of the tower; the black
veil which concealed the opening in the wall, falls:
the gigantic litter of* THE CARDINAL *appears, borne by
twenty-four foot-guards, surrounded by twenty other
guards bearing halberds and torches. The litter is
scarlet and ornamented with the arms of the House of
Richelieu. It crosses the back of the stage slowly.
Great agitation among the crowd.*

MARION (*dragging herself up to the litter on her knees
              and wringing her hands*).

In your Christ's name ! In name of all your race,
Mercy for them, my lord !

A VOICE (*from the litter*).
                    No mercy !
[MARION *falls to the ground. The litter passes and the
    procession of the condemned men follows it. The crowd
    rush madly after them.*

MARION (*alone, lifts herself half way up, and drags herself
              along by her hands : looking around*).
                                        Ah !
What did he say ? Where are they gone ? My love !
My Didier ! No one ! Not a sound ! Is it
A dream, — this place ? the crowd ? — or am I mad ?
[*The people rush back in disorder. The litter reappears
    in the background on the side where it went off.
    MARION rises and gives a terrible cry.*
He's coming back !

GUARDS (*pushing the people aside*).
                Make way !

MARION (*erect and half-wild, pointing to the litter*).
                        Look, all of you !
It is the red man who goes by !
                                [*She falls senseless.*

THE END.

LUCRETIA BORGIA.

DRAMATIS PERSONÆ.

DON ALPHONSO D'ESTE, *Duke of Ferrara.*
GENNARO, *a young soldier of fortune.*
GUBETTA, *the poisoner, under the assumed name of the Count de Belverana, a Spaniard.*
MAFFIO ORSINI,
JEPPO LIVERETTO,
DON APOSTOLO GAZELLO, *Cavaliers of Venice.*
OLOFERNO VETILLOZZO,
ASCANIO PETRUCCA,
RUSTIGHELLO, *an officer and spy of the Duke's.*
ASTOLFO, *a servant of the Duchess.*
BAPTISTE, *Captain of the Guard.*
PIETRO.
LUCRETIA BORGIA, *Duchess of Ferrara.*
PRINCESS NEGRONI.

Monks, Maskers, Lords, Pages, Ladies, etc.

LUCRETIA BORGIA.

———•———

ACT I.

SCENE. — *The palace of Barbarigo, at Venice, splendidly illumi-*
nated. Grand entrance, with three steps to ascend. A terrace in
front, extending from the first wing to the U. E. *The terrace is fes-*
tooned with flowers, etc. Back is a magnificent view of Venice by
moonlight, with the canal of Jucca in front, with handsome gondo-
las passing and re-passing, from which music is heard, gay and
sad alternately, which gradually dies away in the distance.
Time, night. A carnival. Maskers of all kinds pass and repass to
appropriate music. Several of the maskers come forward and per-
form an appropriate dance, and exeunt L. *and* R. U. E.

Enter, L. U. E., GENNARO, MAFFIO ORSINI, DON APOSTOLO
GAZELLA, ASCANIO PETRUCCA, OLOFERNO VITELLOZZO,
JEPPO LIVERETTO, *come down, and* GUBETTA, *who
rather conceals himself from observation, up stage,* L.
2 E. *All have masks in their hands, and all very
richly dressed.*

JEPPO.

Now, signors, I am best acquainted with this story.

MAFFIO.

Well, then, give us the full particulars.

OLOFERNO.

There never was a tale more full of horror! There
never was a deed more black and damning!

ASCANIO.

Ay, a dark and bloody deed, perpetrated by some malicious demon who revels in blood and crime.

JEPPO.

I know all the particulars, gentlemen; I have them from his Excellency, my cousin, the Cardinal Carriale. You all know the Cardinal Carriale, who —

GENNARO (*throwing himself on a bench,* R., *and yawning*).

Ah, me! I see how it is: Jeppo is going to tell us one of his long stories. Good-bye: I can't stand it; I am already sufficiently worn out.

MAFFIO.

These things, Gennaro, are of too trifling and domestic a nature for your bold and daring spirit. You have no kindred, no father or mother, to whose safety you must look. We have. You are the child of chance; but that you are *noble*, your look, your words, your conduct fully proves, and stamp your greatness on your brow.

GENNARO (*yawning*).

Thank you, worthy friend.

MAFFIO.

But still you cannot claim a right to these honours yet.

GENNARO (*starting up*).

Maffio, I make no boast of the purity of my blood, of the nobleness of my rank, or of claims to honours, only as I win them. God is the only parent I have ever known; and the proudest potentate that ever reared his haughty crest to awe us into reverence by his birth and rank can vaunt no higher lineage, or feel more noble than I do now, when I acknowledge that to Him alone I address the holy name of Father!

MAFFIO.

Believe me, I meant not offence. We are brothers in arms. You saved my life at Romana; and we have sworn to aid each other in war and in love, and to revenge each other's wrongs, when required. Our very fates are allied; for, by the predictions of an astrologer, all of us, friends and companions in arms, now together here, are doomed to perish on the self-same day. You say truly, no earthly parent has yet called you son. What, then, are the histories of families to you, who have none? We have an interest in these secret murders: our fathers, mothers, and relatives are concerned. No one of us, except yourself, but has felt the deadly malice of this invisible fiend in the death of some near relative. Our hearts have quivered from the secret stabs of these midnight murderers.

GENNARO (*giving his hand*).

My friend, pardon my ill-timed rashness.

MAFFIO.

From my heart. Come, Jeppo, tell us what you know.

GENNARO (*throwing himself again on bench*, R., *in a sleeping position*).

Pray wake me when Jeppo finishes his story.

JEPPO.

Well, well, fear not our care. And now for my story, which, on my life, is a marvellous one. It was in the year 1480 —

GUBETTA (L., *against column*).

Ninety-seven.

JEPPO.

Ninety-seven! Yes, yes, you are right. In the year 1497, on a certain Sunday —

GUBETTA.

Friday.

JEPPO.

Well, Friday, in November —

GUBETTA.

December.

JEPPO.

Well, you may be right, Count, but it does not matter; November or December, it is all the same. But on a certain Friday night, a waterman of the Tiber, who was sleeping in his boat just below the church Santo Hieronimo, at Ripetta, was awakened by the tramp of footsteps, and raising his head, he perceived through the mists of the night (or, rather, *morning*, I should say, for it was two hours past midnight) two men coming down the street on the left of the church, who walked cautiously about, hither and thither, along the quay. In a few moments two others appeared on the street at the right of the church, who, at a signal from the first, advanced to the river; these were joined by three others, one of whom was mounted on a large white horse, and attended by a comrade on either side, — making, in all, seven men.

GENNARO.

What! the *white horse* made the seventh *man*, Jeppo?

JEPPO.

The quay was silent and deserted. The houses around were shrouded in gloom and darkness, save one, from which gleamed a lonely light. The seven men and the white horse drew nigh to the water's edge, and then the boatman, to his horror and surprise, distinctly perceived a corpse hanging across the pommel of the saddle. Two of the men watched at the corners of the streets, while the others hastily disencumbered the horse of its burden, and, with a violent swing, committed the body to the stream. The man upon the horse then asked, "Is all safe?" to which one of the men replied, "Yes, yes, my lord; no fear of that." They then departed, taking the road to Saint Jacques. This is the boatman's story.

MAFFIO.

Mysterious, indeed! Doubtless a man of rank who had been murdered, and the rider was the assassin.

GUBETTA (*down* L.).

Mysterious, indeed! for on that white horse were two brothers!

JEPPO.

You are right, De Belverana. The horseman was no other than Cæsar Borgia, and the corpse was that of his only brother, John Borgia!

MAFFIO.

A house of demons is that of Borgia. But tell us, Jeppo, why a brother thus assassinated his brother.

JEPPO.

That is almost too horrible to repeat. I cannot tell you now; this is nor time nor place.

GUBETTA (*crossing to* MAFFIO, C.).

I will tell you, signor. Cæsar Borgia, Cardinal of Valence, assassinated John Borgia, Duke of Candia, his brother, with his own hand, at his own altar, because they both loved the same woman.

MAFFIO.

And the woman? Who was the woman?

GUBETTA.

Their cousin. She yet lives, and her name is —

JEPPO.

Enough, enough, Belverana! Do not insult our ears even with the name of that fiend in an angel's form. There is not one of us but has experienced the effects of her infernal power.

MAFFIO.

Methinks I have heard of a child connected with this affair. Is it not so?

JEPPO.

Yes, there was a child, and I have heard his father named.

GUBETTA.

Yes; John Borgia.

MAFFIO.

The child, if living, would be now a man.

OLOFERNO.

Ay, but he has disappeared long since; and whether Cæsar Borgia conceals him from the mother, or the mother from him, no one can tell.

APOSTOLO.

She does wisely, if it be the mother; for this Cæsar Borgia, since he has become Duke of Valence, has slain besides his brother John, his two nephews, sons of Godfrey Borgia, and his cousin the cardinal, Francois Borgia, and has even attempted the life of the Pope. He riots in human blood!

JEPPO.

He aims to become the sole male of the name, and then his wealth would be enormous.

GUBETTA.

That cousin, whom you [*to* JEPPO] are so loath to name, made a secret pilgrimage to the nunnery of St. Sixtus, at the time of the assassination of John Borgia, and secluded herself for many months, no one exactly knowing why.

JEPPO.

I have heard a cause assigned. It was to separate herself from her second husband, John Sforza.

MAFFIO.

What was the boatman's name who saw the act related by you? Know you who he was?

JEPPO.

I do not know.

GUBETTA.

His name was Georgio Schiavone; his business was to trade in provisions and fuel down the Tiber, to Ripetta. He is dead, — died some time since; died *rather* suddenly, some say by poison. It is very likely.

[*Crosses to* R., *and goes up the stage.*

MAFFIO (*in a low tone, to his companions*).

This Spaniard knows more of our affairs than we do ourselves. 'T is strange.

ASCANIO (*low, to* MAFFIO).

I distrust him, as well as yourself. Say nothing, but let us keep an eye upon his movements. Despite that smooth tongue of his, there is danger in him, or I greatly err.

JEPPO.

Ah, gentlemen, what an age we live in! What with war, pestilence, love, intrigue, murder, poison, and the Borgias, show me the man in Italy sure of life for a single day.

APOSTOLO.

Well, comrades, we are, as you are doubtless aware, all attached to the embassy, which the republic of Venice sends to the Duke of Ferrara, to congratulate him on the recapture of Rimni, upon the Maltesta. When do we leave Venice?

OLOFERNO.

The day after to-morrow, certain. The two ambassadors are already appointed, — the Senator Tripolo, and Grimani, the captain of the galleys.

ASCANIO.

Does Captain Gennaro accompany us?

MAFFIO.

Yes, if *I* do. We never separate; we are more than brothers in heart.

ASCANIO (*in a low voice*).

Gentlemen, one word — an important suggestion. For the present, let none of us drink *Spanish* wine.

[*Looking towards* GUBETTA.

JEPPO.

I have another important word: Have you taken care to see that we have any other wine? I have no partiality for Spain; but if the choice is between Spanish wine or no wine at all, I shall embrace Spain decidedly.

MAFFIO.

Let us in. Halloa, Gennaro! Faith! Jeppo, your story had its effect; he sleeps soundly.

JEPPO.

Let him sleep, then. I'll drink his share with my own, for I am devilish thirsty.

[Exeunt all, R. U. E., *except* GUBETTA.

GUBETTA *(comes forward,* L. C.*).*

"This Spaniard knows more of our affairs than we do ourselves," said they. I heard their words, low as they spoke them. Ha, ha, ha! They are right; I *do* know more than they themselves; but Donna Lucretia knows more than I, and my Lord of Valentenois knows more than Donna Lucretia; the devil knows more than my Lord of Valentenois, and Pope Alexander the Sixth knows more, I believe, than the devil himself! *[Looks on* GENNARO.*]* How these young men sleep! *[Goes down to* L. H. *corner and leans against a pillar.]* Ha! she comes!
[Enter LUCRETIA, L. U. E., *magnificently dressed, with her face masked. She looks hurriedly round, does not see* GUBETTA, *approaches* GENNARO, *and gazes fondly and earnestly on his face for some moments, then speaks.*

LUCRETIA.

He sleeps! The *fête* has wearied him! How beautiful! That pale forehead, those jetty locks, those long silken lashes, those proud lips, that noble form! *[Looking up, starts on seeing* GUBETTA, L. LUCRETIA *goes down* C.*]* Ha, Gubetta!

GUBETTA (L. C.).

Hush! *[Looking warily round.]* Speak lower, if you please, signora. I am not known as Gubetta here, but as the Count of Belverana, a Castilian noble. And you, madame, do not forget that you are the Countess of Pontequadrato, a Neapolitan lady. We must appear as strangers to each other; such was your Highness's command. Remember, you are not in Ferrara, but in Venice !

LUCRETIA (R. C.).

Right; you are quite right. But there are none within sound of our voices now, save this young soldier, who calmly and soundly sleeps. I wish a moment's converse.   [*About to remove mask.*

GUBETTA.

Might I presume to urge your Highness *not* to remove your mask. Some one will recognize you.

LUCRETIA.

Well, and if I *am* recognized, what then ?   What have I to fear ?   Let him who makes the discovery tremble; he has most cause.

GUBETTA.

We are in Venice, signora, where you have many foes, and they are free !   The Republic will guard your person from violence, but it cannot shield you from insult.

LUCRETIA (*sadly*).

True; alas, too true !   My very name excites horror, wherever heard.

GUBETTA.

Besides, it is the middle of the carnival, and the city is filled with Romans, Neapolitans, Tuscans, Genoese, Lombards, Romagnols, — Italians of all Italy.

LUCRETIA (*mournfully*).

And all Italy hates me !   Ah, me ! how sad my fate ! But it must not, shall not longer be. I was not born to be the thing I have been and am; and I realize it now, alas! more than I ever did. The example of my family has made me what I am. [*Crosses to* L. *She paces the stage hurriedly a moment.*] It shall be so! Gubetta!

GUBETTA (R. C.).

Your Highness!

LUCRETIA.

Issue immediate orders that all be in readiness for me to visit Spoleto.

GUBETTA.

Your commands have been anticipated; all is now prepared for your instant departure.

LUCRETIA.

What has been done with Galeas Accailoi?

GUBETTA.

In prison, only awaiting your order to be hanged.

LUCRETIA.

And Godfrey Buondelmonte?

GUBETTA.

Is in his dungeon. The sentence is not yet signed for his execution.

LUCRETIA.

And Manfredi de Carsola?

GUBETTA.

Is not yet strangled.

LUCRETIA.

And Spadacappa?

GUBETTA.

According to your orders, he will receive poison on Easter day. It is now carnival; it will be Easter in six weeks.

LUCRETIA.

And Pierre Copra ?

GUBETTA.

Is still Bishop of Pesaro, and Regent of Chancery; but ere one month is over he will be but a lump of cold clay. Your father, Saint Peter, the Pope, has at your request given the order for his arrest, and he will be retained in the chambers of the Vatican until beheaded.

LUCRETIA (*calmly and quietly*).

Gubetta, write in haste to the Pope, and say I crave pardon for Pierre Copra, and then let no time be lost ere Accailoi, Manfredi de Carsola, Buondelmonte, and Spadacappa are set at liberty !

GUBETTA (*astonished*).

Pray, your Highness, let me breathe! By heavens, it hails mercy and rains pardons! I'm drowned in them! I fear I shall never recover from this terrible flood of good actions.

LUCRETIA.

Be my actions good or bad, indifferent or otherwise, what care you ? What does it signify to you, so long as I reward your service ?

GUBETTA.

Ah, signora, much! A good action is far more repugnant to my nature than a bad or even indifferent one. I like ease.

LUCRETIA (*solemnly*).

Attend to me. I am tired of this feast of blood. I'll no more of it. You have long been my firm and faithful confidant.

GUBETTA (R.).

For fifteen years have I had the honour of being your Highness's faithful coadjutor.

LUCRETIA (L.).

Gubetta, my old friend, my faithful accomplice, do you not feel a desire to change this kind of life? Have you no wish to be blessed? We two have drawn down curses which, like a mountain's crushing weight, now press upon my heart. Have you not had enough of crime?

GUBETTA (*coolly*).

I perceive plainly that you are about becoming the most virtuous lady in Italy!

LUCRETIA.

Are not our names the synonymes of death, of murder? And does not that sometimes trouble you, as it does me?

GUBETTA.

Not at all, lady. Often, as I pass through the streets of Spoleto or Ferrara, I catch the suppressed execrations of the citizens near me. "There goes Gubetta!" "Gubetta!" cries a second, "the poisoner!" "Gubetta, poniard! Gubetta, gibbet!" exclaims a third; and "Cutthroat! assassin!" with other delicate and complimentary terms pass around; while others, who dare not wag their vile tongues, speak quite as emphatically with their eyes. But what care I for this? I laugh at them, and with a look can make even the boldest tremble. It is my reputation, and as useful to me in my calling as is bravery to a soldier, or devotion to priest.

LUCRETIA.

But see you not that this reputation might excite *hatred* and *horror* in some heart where you might wish for *love?*

GUBETTA.

There are but few in the world whom one *can* love, and they are not always those whom one *should* love.

LUCRETIA.

Gubetta, Gubetta, be silent; you do not comprehend this heart. There is even now in Italy, this fated Italy, *one* pure and noble heart — a heart throbbing with high and holy feelings, brave, noble, daring, though of unknown origin — for whom (God knows its truth!) I would resign all, — life, fame, everything! Oh, to inspire his breast with one gleam of tenderness, one ray of love for me, — a miserable, guilty woman; hated, abhorred, cursed of man and spurned by Heaven; a very *slave*, though the proud mistress of thousands! Oh, could I but hope one day to feel that pure heart throb free and joyously against my own, I would welcome torture, chains, or death to win it! Do you now comprehend me? Can you *now* conceive my anxiety to efface the past, to remove the plague-spot from my name, and in place of the infamy which all Italy now associates with my character, win one of penitence, virtue, and glory?

[LUCRETIA *crosses to* R.

GUBETTA (L.).

Madame! madame! upon what strange herb has your Highness trodden to-day, thus to change your very nature? 'T is droll, in sooth!

LUCRETIA.

Beware! beware, sir! Jest not with me! This is no new fancy; it is not evanescent. But when a weak mortal is hurried on in a current of crime, it is not easy for her to stop when and where she would. Two spirits have for years been struggling here, within this bosom,

a good and an evil one.   God grant the good one triumph
at last!

> [*She crosses to* L., *turns up stage, and down again.*

GUBETTA.

All is now explained.   All is now clear that before
puzzled me.   One month ago your Highness left your
husband, my Lord Don Alphonso D'Este, with an appar-
ent intention of visiting Spoleto; but under a Neapolitan name you came direct to Venice, and I, your faithful
servitor, am directed to take the garb and name of a
Spaniard; to this is added a strict injunction neither to
speak *to* nor *of* you, or give sign of recognition, should we
meet.   You visit *fêtes*, operas, balls, and, availing yourself of the privilege of the carnival, go ever masked,
while it is but seldom you speak to *any* one, and but a
word at a time even to *me*, and that hurriedly and in
secret.   And now, lo! all this mummery ends in a sermon !   A homily, madame, — from *you* to *me !*   Is 't not
strange ?   You have changed name, dress, rank, residence,
bearing, and now it seems your very *nature* is also
changed.   This is carrying the carnival to an extreme !

> [*Crossing to* L.

LUCRETIA (*on his right.   She grasps his arm, and draws
him towards* GENNARO, *and points to him*).

Do you see that youth ?

GUBETTA (L. C.).

He is no stranger to me!   He sleeps soundly now, but
could sleep still sounder.

LUCRETIA (C.).

Is he not strangely beautiful ?

GUBETTA.

He looks well enough for a soldier, and would look better were his eyes not closed. A face like that without eyes is like a palace without windows. [*They come down.*

LUCRETIA (R.).

Ah, you cannot dream, Gubetta, how tenderly I love him!

GUBETTA (L.).

No; that is a *dream* better suited for your royal husband! But your Highness loses time. That young soldier is reported to be in love with a fair young girl called Fiametta.

LUCRETIA (*eagerly*).

And the girl — does she return his love? Speak!

GUBETTA.

Most truly, it is said.

LUCRETIA.

Thank Heaven! Oh, how I pray for his happiness!
[*She goes up to* GENNARO.

GUBETTA.

Stranger still! Another change! I imagined those who loved to be jealous, and I never had cause to consider your Highness an exception to the rule, to say the least.

LUCRETIA (*gazing on* GENNARO).

What a noble figure! and his countenance, so proud, and yet so melancholy! Leave me, Gubetta.

GUBETTA (*crossing to* R.).

I obey your Highness's wishes. She's metamorphosed so strangely that I scarcely know her; and it will puzzle even her holy father the Pope, or his own brother the devil, to recognize her now, I fancy!

[*Exit* GUBETTA, R. 1 E. LUCRETIA *remains gazing a moment; then, perceiving the absence of* GUBETTA, *she looks around to see if she is alone, then speaks.*

LUCRETIA.

This, then, is he. At last I am so blest as to be permitted to gaze on his dear face without peril. Dear — oh, how dear thou art to me!

[*Pause. Enter* DUKE D'ESTE, L. U. E., *accompanied by* RUSTIGHELLO, *both masked and cloaked. They watch her motions, unseen by her.*

Oh, Heaven! spare me the anguish of ever being scorned or hated by him, for thou knowest he is all under heaven that I love! I dare not remove my mask, yet I must wipe away these flowing tears.

[*She takes off her mask, kisses* GENNARO'S *hand, and bends over him; then kneeling, clasps her hands as if in prayer.*

DUKE D'ESTE (*at back* L. U. E.).

That is sufficient. My visit to Venice was to satisfy myself of her infidelity, and I have this night beheld enough to convince me that my suspicions are just. I will now return to Ferrara. That young man is her lover! Who is he, Rustighello?

RUSTIGHELLO.

He is called Captain Gennaro, a soldier of fortune, brave and generous; a man, too, without parents or kin, so far as *he* knows. He is at present in the service of the republic of Venice.

DUKE D'ESTE.

He must be brought to Ferrara.

RUSTIGHELLO.

He will proceed there of his own accord the day after
to-morrow, with several of his comrades, who are members of the embassy of Tripolo and Grimani.

DUKE D'ESTE.

'T is well, 't is well; he falls easily into the toils.　We
can now return.　[*Exeunt* D'ESTE *and* RUSTIGHELLO, L. U. E.

LUCRETIA.

Oh, Heaven ! may there be as much of happiness in
store for him as there has been of misery endured by me !
[*She rises, looks anxiously round, kneels, and bends over*
GENNARO, parts the hair from his forehead, and fondly
presses her lips to it.　GENNARO starts and grasps her
hand before she can rise, and partly rising, exclaims:

GENNARO.

A woman ! a kiss ! by my faith, an adventure !　[*They*
come down stage.]　Happy indeed must those slumbers be
which beauty guards.　On my honour, were you a queen
and I a poet this would be an adventure for Alain Char-
tier, the troubadour of Provence.　You have the grace,
the bearing of a queen, but I, alas ! am no poet; I am but
a soldier.

LUCRETIA (L. C., *with dignity*).

Captain Gennaro, leave me, leave me.　Some one
approaches.　In Heaven's name, do not — do not follow !

GENNARO (C.).

Any command but that, and I am your slave.

LUCRETIA (L. C.).

Do not let your wild companions see me, I entreat;
and as you hope to see me more, follow me not now.
[*Exit*, L. 2 E.

GENNARO.

" As I hope to see her more," I 'll not lose sight of her
now.   [*Exit* GENNARO, *following*, L. 2 E.
[*Enter* JEPPO, R. U. E., *as they exeunt. Catches a glimpse
of them.*

JEPPO.

Halloa! Gennaro! What form is that which he pur-
sues? Can it be she? It is — it is, by heavens! *That*
woman at Venice! What does she here? [*Enter* MAFFIO.
R. U. E.] Ha, Maffio!

MAFFIO (*down* R. C.).

How now? What is the matter?

JEPPO (L. C.).

She is here, — that woman of whom we were speaking!
she that —

MAFFIO.

Ha! are you sure?

JEPPO.

Quite; as I am that this is the palace of Barbarigo,
and not that of Labia.

MAFFIO.

She has an affair of gallantry with Gennaro, then! He
must be saved. It is imperiously necessary to draw my
brother from the spider's web which that dangerous
woman is weaving round him. Quick! let us seek and
inform our friends.   [*Exeunt*, R. U. E.
[*Gondolas pass at back; music plays from them. Re-
enter* GENNARO, *holding the hand of* LUCRETIA, L. 3 E.
She is now closely masked again.

LUCRETIA (R.).

The terrace is now deserted, and I can unmask with
safety. I wish you to see my face, Gennaro. [*Unmasks.*

GENNARO (L., *with rapture*).

Beautiful! Ah, signora, you are *very* beautiful!

LUCRETIA.

Look, Gennaro, and look earnestly; then tell me you
do not regard my features with horror.

GENNARO.

Horror, lady? On the contrary, my heart involun-
tarily draws me towards you.

[*Attempts to clasp her. She avoids him.*

LUCRETIA.

Tell me, — oh, tell me truly ! — could you *love* me ?

GENNARO.

Why should I not love you, beautiful as thou art?
But, frankly, my heart is not my own ; I love another.

LUCRETIA.

I know who she is, — the fair Fiametta.

GENNARO.

No, lady ; oh, no!

LUCRETIA.

Ah ! who, then ?

GENNARO.

My mother.

LUCRETIA.

Your mother ! your mother ! Can it be that you love
her above all others ?

GENNARO.

Ay, 't is true ; next my God, I adore my mother! And yet I have never seen her face, nor heard her voice, nor felt her soft embrace, nor the warmth of her holy kiss upon my lips. How strange is the feeling that impels me towards you, and makes me speak of that which I never yet imparted even to my foster brother, Maffio Orsini ! But it seems as if we had met before — I know not when or where. It is as a dream to me. But listen to me, lady. Of my origin I nothing know. I was reared to the age of seven years by a fisherman of Calabria, whom I had ever looked upon as my father. It was at that period he informed me he was not my sire, — that he could not claim that sacred title. Some time after this, a cavalier, with visor closed, brought me a letter, and then, without disclosing his face or name, departed. That letter was from my mother. Ah, how full of love and tenderness was that letter ! It apprised me that I was of noble birth, of ancient family, but no more. She said that she herself was unhappy. Alas, my dear mother !

LUCRETIA (*with great emotion*).

Dear, dear Gennaro !

GENNARO.

Since that day I have been an adventurer, because, being noble by birth, I wished to make myself truly so by my sword. I have roved over all Italy, to discover the secret of my birth, but in vain. Yet, no matter where I am, the first of every month the same messenger brings me a letter from my mother, receives my answer, and departs. We cannot even converse together, for he is deaf and dumb.

LUCRETIA.

And you know nothing of your family ?

GENNARO.

I only know I have a mother that loves me, and is herself unhappy.

LUCRETIA.

And her letters, what have you done with *them ?*

GENNARO.

Here! [*Laying his hand upon his breast.*] Here I have them, next my heart! The letters of my mother are the only breastplate I ever wear. Here is her last letter, lady.

[GENNARO *takes a letter from his bosom, kisses it and hands it to* LUCRETIA. *She opens and reads it.*

LUCRETIA (*reads*).

"Seek not to know me, my dear Gennaro, until the day which I shall appoint. I am ever surrounded by those who would destroy me, as they have your poor father. The secret of your birth, my child, must for the present be confined to myself. I fear your daring spirit would start forth and blazon to the world an origin so illustrious as yours. You cannot understand the perils by which you are surrounded. Oh, be content, then, for a little time, to know that you have a mother who adores you, and who watches night and day, unceasingly, over your safety. The time will come, dearest, when you may, without danger, know all ; until then, as you regard your own life, and the life of her who gave you existence, seek not to know more. My son, my own Gennaro, — *adieu !* My heart beats wildly when I think of thee ! my eyes fill with unrestrained tears of tenderness, and my hand falters as I trace these lines for thy dear eyes to gaze upon, while language fails to express the depth, the fathomless depth, of my love for — "

[*She pauses, overcome with emotion, hands the letter back to him, which he again kisses, and places in his bosom.*

GENNARO.

Ah, madame, how tenderly you have read my poor mother's words! You weep, too. Bless you, bless you, lady, for this kind sympathy. You can understand now why I do not yield myself up to pleasure, like my gay comrades. It is because my heart is always full; one thought alone possesses it, — *my mother !* Give me her — to console, to avenge, to serve — and then I can think of love. I am a soldier of fortune, it is true, but I fight no cause but a just one, for I live in the faith and cheering hope of one day laying at my mother's feet a sword bright, unsullied by a single breath. I have ever refused the princely offers proffered me to enter the service of the infamous Lucretia Borgia, but —

LUCRETIA.

Gennaro, Gennaro, hold! You know not what you say. Oh, you should pity the bad, though you condemn their deeds.

GENNARO.

Should we, then, pity those who are themselves so pitiless ? But let us speak no more of her. I have told you *my* history ; tell me, lady, who *you* are.

LUCRETIA.

An unhappy woman who loves you purely, truly, holily.

GENNARO.

And your name, lady ?

LUCRETIA.

Ask me no more now ; I must not, dare not answer.

MAFFIO (*outside*, R. U. E.).

Nay, Jeppo, follow me ; I insist.

LUCRETIA (*crossing to* L. H.).

Great Heaven ! what is this ?   I cannot avoid them ; it is too late !

GENNARO.

Fear not, lady ; I will defend you with my life.

[*She hastily resumes her mask ; then enter,* R. 3 E., MAFFIO, JEPPO, ASCANIO, OLOFERNO, APOSTOLO, *Attendants with torches, Lords, Ladies, pages, etc., as from the palace within.* MAFFIO *and friends range down on* R., LUCRETIA, L., GENNARO, L. C. *Others group above and around, intently observing all.*

MAFFIO.

Gennaro, know you to whom you are speaking of love ?

LUCRETIA (*aside*).

Just Heaven, spare him and me !

MAFFIO.

Behold her face, and then —   [*Advancing.*

GENNARO (*drawing his sword*).

Maffio Orsini, stand back !   You are my friend ; you are all friends of mine ; but, by heaven ! who touches that mask, or lays finger upon this lady, save in kindness, dies.   Be she what she may, she is a woman, and my sword and life are pledged to her defence.

MAFFIO.

We wish not to wrong her.   Permit us to introduce ourselves.

GENNARO (*pausing a moment*).

Well, be it so.   [*Retires up a little,* C.

" Know you to whom you are speaking of love?"

Etched by L. Flameng — From Drawing by
François Flameng.

MAFFIO (*crossing to* LUCRETIA).

Madame, I am Maffio Orsini, brother to the Duke of Gravina, whom you caused to be stabbed in his dungeon.

JEPPO (*crossing to her*).

Madame, I am Jeppo Liveretto, brother of Liveretto Vittelli, whom your ruffians strangled while he slept.

ASCANIO (*crossing to her*).

Madame, I am Ascanio Petrucca, cousin of Pandolpho Petrucca, Lord of Sienne, who was assassinated by your order, that you might seize his fair city.

GENNARO (*in* C., *a little up*).

Gracious heavens! what means all this?

OLOFERNO (*crossing to her*).

Madame, I am called Oloferno Vitellozzo, nephew of Iago D'Appiani, whom you poisoned at a *fête*, to pillage his lordly castle of Piombino.

APOSTOLO (*crossing to her*).

Madame, you beheaded Don Francisco Gazella, maternal uncle of Don Alphonse of Arragon, your third husband, whom you caused to be murdered on the grand staircase of St. Peter's. I am cousin of one victim, and son of the other.

[*Each gentleman, after addressing* LUCRETIA, *passes up the stage, and falls down to his former situation on* R., *excepting* JEPPO, *who remains* L. C., *near* GENNARO.

LUCRETIA (L., *aside*).

Oh, patience, patience! Must I bear all this?

GENNARO (C.).

In Heaven's name, who is this woman ?

MAFFIO (R. C.).

And now that we have proclaimed our names and titles, and stated our claims to your regard, permit us to reveal *your* name.

LUCRETIA.

No, no, no ! [*Crossing to* C., *and falling on her knees.*] Have pity ! Spare me ! Have compassion, though *I* merit none ; but oh, do not speak ! Plunge me into your deepest dungeon, and proclaim it there ! shriek it among howling fiends — anywhere — but not before Gennaro !

MAFFIO (*drawing off her mask*).

Let us see if you can yet blush at your crimes.

[*She starts up.*

GENNARO (*enraged, and drawing his sword*).

Maffio Orsini ! thus to insult a woman ! No more, but draw !

JEPPO (L. H. *of* GENNARO).

Gennaro [*laying his hand on his arm*], you know not what you do ! This woman, for whom you would risk your life, is an assassin and an adulteress !

MAFFIO.

And her name —

LUCRETIA.

Spare me ! Oh, spare me this ! As *you* hope for mercy, spare me !

MAFFIO.

Her name, I say — 't is a spell to empty hell withal, and people earth with devils ! Her name is —

LUCRETIA (*turning to him*).

Gennaro, do not — do not listen ! I entreat, on my knees, as thou dost revere thy *mother*, dear Gennaro !
[GENNARO *drops his sword at the word "Mother," and clasps his hands.*

MAFFIO.

Her name is Lucretia Borgia !

GENNARO.

Lucretia Borgia ! horror !
[*He casts her from him with horror, while she, with a shriek of despair, starts up, advances towards him a step, and falls fainting at his feet.*

ACT II.

SCENE. — *Grand square in Ferrara. On the* R. *a palace, with a latticed balcony, and a grand escutcheon of stone, and with armorial bearings, over which, in bold relief, on a white surface of marble, is the word "* BORGIA," *in large gold letters. On the* L. H. *is a handsome edifice, opening upon the Square. Streets beyond, with domes, towers, steeples, etc. A large and small door to palace.*

SCENE I.

Enter from U. D. *of palace,* LUCRETIA *and* GUBETTA.

LUCRETIA (L.).

Is all prepared for the night, Gubetta?

GUBETTA (R.).

All is quite ready, your Highness.

LUCRETIA.

All five of them will be present?

GUBETTA.

They are all invited, madame.

LUCRETIA (*with bitterness*).

They have most cruelly outraged my feelings!

GUBETTA (*coolly*).

I was not present. Did all proclaim your name?

LUCRETIA.

They insulted me, mocked my sufferings, vilified my character, publicly tore off my mask, and exposed my face, denounced my name with every epithet of ignominy, — and all before him, of all others in this wide world; before Gennaro! Let me remember that! [*Crosses to* R.

GUBETTA (L. H.).

Fools, fools, to come to Ferrara, then, I trow! But I forgot they could not do otherwise, having been appointed by the senate members of the embassy, which, by the way, arrived here yesterday.

LUCRETIA.

Anything but that I would have borne. But that he — Gennaro — my life's last hope — he now hates, despises me! And they have caused it all! Let me not forget it! O God, revenge shall yet be mine, be sure it shall! [*Crosses to* L. H.

GUBETTA (R.).

I rejoice to hear it; I shall again be busy; I like it.

LUCRETIA (L.).

My very nature seemed changed; my resolves were pure, my aspirations holy. I could have borne all, ay, all but that, — his hate! They should have wrung my heart, and I would have bowed submissively before Heaven, so *he* had still thought kindly of me. But to poison him against me more deeply than ever! O Heaven! the very thought calls from the centre of my heart, and my swelling brain throbs with anguish, while the dark spirit of despair shrieks in my ear, "Revenge!" and it shall have it! [*Crosses to* R.

GUBETTA (L.).

Good! good! I like this! You are yourself again! Your fantasies of mercy have left you, and you act naturally once more. I am now at ease with your Highness. As fire opposes water; light, darkness; and black differs from white, — so stand *I* opposed to the so-styled good and virtuous.

LUCRETIA (R.).

Did Gennaro come here with the others?

GUBETTA.

He did, your Highness.

LUCRETIA (*sternly*).

Gubetta, on your life, see, I charge you, that no harm comes to him! If a hair of his is touched, if he stands in peril, and you avert it not, beware the waked wrath of Lucretia Borgia! Would, would I could but see him once more!

GUBETTA.

That you can do at any hour. I induced his valet to take that house (*points to* L. H.) for his master. Your balcony commands a view of it, and, concealed from sight, you can see him go in and out as often as you choose to enjoy that ineffable delight.

LUCRETIA.

Nay, I would speak with him.

GUBETTA.

Nothing is easier, signora. Send Astolfo with a message that your Highness, to-day, at a certain hour, would see him at the palace, on business of high import.

LUCRETIA (*thoughtfully*).

Yes, I could do that; but would he come?

GUBETTA.

He could be *caused* to obey. But go in, your Highness, for I momentarily expect them to pass this way. It were better that they saw you not. I will meet them.

LUCRETIA.

They still consider you the Count of Belverana?

GUBETTA.

Ay; I have convinced them on that point past doubt. I have borrowed their money.

LUCRETIA.

Borrowed their money! and why?

GUBETTA.

To have them in my power. Nothing binds friends so fast as money borrowed or lent; and it is so decidedly Spanish, as an air of poverty, while at the same time we seize the devil by the tail.

LUCRETIA.

Silence, sir! This is no time for jests. But see, they are coming down yonder street, and Gennaro is with them. Gubetta, I charge you, guard from harm or danger *Gennaro!* [*Exit* LUCRETIA *into palace,* U. D.

GUBETTA.

Who the devil *is* this Gennaro, in whom she takes such an interest? and what the devil does she design doing with him? It is quite plain I am not in *all* the secrets of this fair lady. It touches my curiosity. In faith, she has not reposed her usual confidence in me in this matter. Madame Lucretia is becoming platonic. Well, I am astonished at nothing. But here are the young bloods of Venice. They are not over wise, to leave the free state of Venice and come to Ferrara after having offended the Duchess of Ferrara. Were *I* they, I should have stayed away. But young people *will* be rash. The throat of a tigress is of all sublunary places that into which they precipitate themselves most eagerly. Well, let the fools have their way.

[*Retires behind a pillar of the balcony.*
[*Enter*, L. U. E., MAFFIO, APOSTOLO, JEPPO, ASCANIO, OLO-
FERNO, *and* GENNARO. *They converse in a low tone, and with inquietude.*

MAFFIO.

Say what you please, friends, but we are not very safe here in Ferrara, after having insulted the Duchess, Lucretia Borgia.

APOSTOLO.

But what could we do? The signory of Venice appointed us, and their fiat is imperative, were it to exterminate one's own family. There is no disguising it, however, that Lucretia Borgia is to be dreaded, and she is supreme in Ferrara.

JEPPO.

She dare not harm us; we are in the service of the republic of Venice, and form a part of her embassy. Let this duchess touch a hair of our heads, and the doge would instantly declare war; and Ferrara would not willingly rub against Venice now.

MAFFIO.

Ah, you may be stretched at full length in your sepulchre without touching a *hair* of your head. It is

by *poison* the Borgia family effect their purposes, — a
poison of so subtle a nature that no medicine on earth
can remedy. It is sure and deadly, noiseless, and better than the axe or the poniard. These Borgias have
poisons which kill in a day, a month, or year, as they
please. It is by it they impart a more pleasing flavour
to their wines, so that the drinker more eagerly drains
his cup, and, with joy and rapture in his face, falls dead.
Sometimes a foe of the Borgias falls into a state of melancholy, his skin wrinkles, his eyes sink deep in the
head, his hair turns white, the teeth fall out, his knees
are weak, and while he breathes, you hear the death-
rattle in his throat. Sleep forsakes him; he shivers in
the noonday sun with cold, and youth puts on the appearance of old age. He dies, and then it is recollected
that he drank a cup of Cypress wine at the palace of a
Borgia !

ASCANIO.

This is horrible ! It were well that we quit Ferrara.
Our ambassadors have an audience of the Duke to-day,
and we shall then be at liberty to leave. I would we
had never come.

JEPPO.

Well, to-morrow we can go. I am invited to sup with
the Princess Negroni, with whom I am almost in love,
and I would not fly from the prettiest woman in all
Ferrara.

OLOFERNO.

The Princess Negroni ? I am invited too !

MAFFIO.

And I !

APOSTOLO.

And I !

ASCANIO.

And I !

GUBETTA.

And so am I, gentlemen.

[*Coming forward from behind pillar.*

JEPPO.

Aha! the Count of Belverana!   [*Shaking his hand.*
Good! we 'll all go together, and a merry night we 'll
make it!

GUBETTA (*crossing to* JEPPO).

May his holiness have you in sacred keeping many
years, Signor Jeppo.

MAFFIO (*in a low tone, to* JEPPO).

Let us not go to this feast to-night. I have a pre-
sentiment of ill; and, besides, I distrust this amiable
count.

JEPPO.

Pooh! he was my father's companion in arms! But
do as you please; I shall go.

[LUCRETIA *appears on the balcony,* R., *listening.*

ASCANIO (*to* GENNARO, *who is musing,* L. H.).

Speak! Are you not invited, Captain?

GENNARO.

No; the Princess would not notice a poor soldier like
myself. But she would have found me bad company at
the best.

MAFFIO (*crossing to* GENNARO).

Ah! I suspect you have a rendezvous *d'amour;* is it
not so?

JEPPO.

Apropos! tell us what said the fair Lucretia to you the other evening. She is in love with you, 't is clear. Masked face, but a naked heart!

MAFFIO.

And, my brother, you have taken lodgings directly opposite to hers. Ah, Gennaro, Gennaro!

JEPPO.

Take care, Gennaro, for they do say the Duke is not a little jealous of his beautiful wife. Come, enlighten us poor devils about her — do!

ALL.

Ay, do! Signor Gennaro in love! Ha, ha, ha!

GENNARO.

Gentlemen, I have borne your raillery thus long, because we are sworn friends; but if you couple my name again with that of the infamous Lucretia Borgia, you will see swords flashing in the sun! I respect you all, but I respect my honour more!

LUCRETIA (*aside*).

Alas! alas! they have accomplished it! He hates my very name!

MAFFIO.

Why, Gennaro, brother, we are only indulging in a little pleasantry, and we have good right to do so when a gallant cavalier wears a lady's colours on his bosom.

GENNARO.

I! What mean you?

MAFFIO (*pointing to his scarf*).

That scarf.

JEPPO.

Yes, my friend, that scarf. Is it not the colours of the Duchess?

GENNARO.

This scarf was sent me by Fiametta Berano, in Venice.

MAFFIO.

You may believe so, if you like, but 't was from the hands of the fair Lucretia, I 'll be sworn.

GENNARO.

Gentlemen, I 'm in no mood for jesting now. Are you sure of what you say?

JEPPO.

Sure! Why, every child knows the colours of the Duchess; and, to be plain, your own valet was bribed to tell you this tale, as from Fiametta; he acknowledged it to me.

GENNARO.

Damnation! [*Tears off the scarf, and tramples it under foot.*] Thus do I tread upon her gifts, and thus do I scorn the terrible Borgia! [*Crosses to* R. C.

LUCRETIA (*with great feeling, pressing her hands to her forehead*).

'T is past! Farewell all my bright visions of happiness! Oh, farewell to peace! He tramples on my very heart! It is not *him* I blame; but let those who have caused this, and planted in his heart this horror, beware of a greater one! Let them now, if they can, escape from the awakened wrath of the scorned Lucretia Borgia! [*She retires from the balcony.*

MAFFIO.

How bright and beautiful she is — this Lucretia — notwithstanding her fiendish nature! I am told she was not always so.

GENNARO.

Name her not again! I scorn — detest her! Love her, said you? Love the woman who murdered your brother, whose place I now fill in your heart! Let us think only of that! See, here is the accursed palace of luxury, and seat of festering crime, — the home of a Borgia! The mark of infamy which I cannot stamp upon the forehead of this woman I will leave at least on the front of her palace!

[*He leaps on to a stone step, and with his dagger erases the first letter of the word* BORGIA *on the wall, so that there remains but the word* ORGIA.

MAFFIO.

For God's sake, Gennaro, what have you done? Your life is now in deadly peril every coming moment!

GUBETTA (R. *corner*).

Signor, you have but shortened the lady's name by a letter; when next she meets you, she'll shorten your body by a head, at least! Half the city will to-morrow be questioned for that pun, signor.

GENNARO.

Let the other half, then, say it was I, and be you the first!

MAFFIO.

Gentlemen, let us leave this place. I like it not; and have you not observed those two men, who seem to have been watching us?

JEPPO.

I have. They are, no doubt, a couple of amiable cut-throats.

MAFFIO.

Gennaro, as you value the safety of your friends, no more bravado! If you are in peril, I have sworn to share it, remember!

GENNARO.

Your hand, brother. Fear me not. Gentlemen, good-night.   [*Exit into house on* L. H.

JEPPO (*going up with the others*).

Good-night. The very devil is in our friend to-night. Gentlemen, pause. A last look! [*All turn round ; pointing at the word.*] Orgia! That is indeed a joke!
            [*All exeunt,* L. U. E., *laughing, except* GUBETTA.

GUBETTA.

A joke, is it? Ha, ha! I'm a little afraid, my friends, that you'll find it a serious one before the Duchess and myself have got over it. And Gennaro, too! Ha, ha, ha! Good, good! very good! I like that! The lady will not relish such a joke, even from him. I shall soon be wanted, I see plainly. The devil never deserts his friends, and I am a favoured subject. I thank him.
                        [*Exit into palace through* U. D.

SCENE II.

A street in Ferrara. *Enter* RUSTIGHELLO, R., *and*
ASTOLFO, L. H.

ASTOLFO.

Good-day.   What movement brought you this way ?

RUSTIGHELLO.

The usual one, I believe.

ASTOLFO.

Well, what are you doing here ?

RUSTIGHELLO.

Watching and waiting for you to be gone.   And what
are you doing ?

ASTOLFO.

Watching and waiting for *you* to be gone.

RUSTIGHELLO.

Indeed !   Whom are you looking for ?

ASTOLFO.

The young Venetian, Captain Gennaro.

RUSTIGHELLO.

And so am I — with an invitation from the Duke.

ASTOLFO.

And I bear an invitation from the Duchess.

RUSTIGHELLO.

What awaits him from the Duchess, think you ?

ASTOLFO.

Love, no doubt.   What from the Duke?

RUSTIGHELLO.

Death, no doubt.

ASTOLFO.

What's to be done?   He can't wait on both these invitations very well at once.   He can't be a lover and a corpse at the same time.

RUSTIGHELLO.

Stay, I have an idea how we can settle this.   Here's a ducat.   I'll toss it up, and let the side which turns up determine which of us shall have the guest.   I choose the Duke's head; the cross shall be yours.

ASTOLFO.

So be it.   If I lose, I'll tell the Duchess the bird had flown; and if you lose, you must say the same to the Duke.

RUSTIGHELLO.

Certainly.   It matters little to me which of us wins; so here goes.   I say, "head's up!"   [*Tosses up the coin.*

ASTOLFO.

And "head" it is.   He is yours, and will die.   The man was born to be hanged, it seems.   So be it.   Fate settles it, not I.   There's his lodging.   (L. H.).   Now I'll return to the Duchess.   [*Exit*, R. H.

RUSTIGHELLO.

Now for the Captain!   The Duke invites!   [*Exit*, L. H.

Don Alphonso D'Este.

Photogravure by Goupil et Cie— From Painting
by Gaston Mélingue.

SCENE III.

[*A splendid apartment in the ducal palace. Hangings of tapestry of Hungarian leather, elaborately stamped with arabesque and grotesque figures of gold, in the style of the fifteenth century (the latter part). A large door in* C., *and two small doors* R. *and* L. H. *The one on* L. H. *is a secret door, and looks like the panelling, until it is opened. On* R. H., *state chair, embroidered with arms of the house of* D'Este. *On* R. C. *an elegant table, covered with a rich cloth of scarlet, with books, papers, rich inkstand, pens, etc. A Gothic chair beside the table.* DON ALPHONSO D'ESTE, DUKE OF FERRARA, *in splendid attire, in his robe of rank, is discovered at table writing. Enter* RUSTI- GHELLO, L. H. D., 1 E.

RUSTIGHELLO.

My lord duke, your first orders are executed. The prisoner is in the palace. I await your further order.

DUKE D'ESTE (*taking a small key from bosom*).

Take this key and go to the Numa Gallery; count all the panels of the wainscot, commencing at the figure of Hercules, till you come to the twenty-third. Search carefully, and in the mouth of one of the painted dragons you will find a small opening. Insert this key, then press upon it, and the panel will turn, as upon pivots. In this secret recess you will find a small salver of gold, and near it a golden flagon, and a flagon of silver, with two enamel cups. Take them, without disturbing their contents in any way, to my private cabinet. I need not warn you not to taste their contents.

RUSTIGHELLO.

Is that all, my lord?

DUKE D'ESTE.

No; when you have executed my order, do you take
your station in my cabinet, there (R. D. F.), where you
may hear all that passes. If I ring this silver bell, immediately enter with your drawn sword; but if I call you
by name, enter with the salver and wine. Go!

[RUSTIGHELLO *bows and exits by the small* D. R. H. *in* F.
THE DUKE *rises, paces the chamber with an agitated
air a moment, and then throws himself into his
chair, and leans his head upon his hands.* Enter
ASTOLFO, C. D.

ASTOLFO.

My lady the Duchess demands an audience with your
Highness.

DUKE D'ESTE.

We await the Duchess.

[*Exit* ASTOLFO, C. D.   *Enter* THE DUCHESS LUCRETIA, C. D.,
impetuously.

LUCRETIA.

My lord duke, some one has mutilated the name of
your wife, engraved over the armorial bearings of our
house, in front of this palace; some one of your people, I
fear it is. This is an indignity too infamous patiently to
bear. It has been done in public, in the broad face of
day. Do you hear it, sir? I know not the offender's
name; but, by the Virgin! I will not tamely tolerate this
insult. I would rather a thousand times die by the
poniard than have my name made the vile jest, the quib-
ble and sarcasm of the rabble. I demand justice! Can
you calmly sit there and hear of this insult to your wife?
Or is it because it is not against yourself that you bear it
thus? You say you love me; show that you love my

fair fame. You are jealous, too; show that it is for my reputation. I demand justice! You are the Duke, and can give it. You are my husband, and *shall* protect me! You have given me your hand, and I now demand the strength of your strong arm.

DUKE D'ESTE (*calmly*).

Madame, what you complain of was known to me.

LUCRETIA.

Known, sir, and the criminal not discovered!

DUKE D'ESTE.

The criminal *is* discovered.

LUCRETIA.

Let him be instantly arrested.

DUKE D'ESTE.

He *is* arrested.

LUCRETIA.

Then why is he not punished?

DUKE D'ESTE.

I awaited your counsel, madame.

LUCRETIA.

I thank you. Where is the miscreant?

DUKE D'ESTE.

Here, in the palace.

LUCRETIA.

Here! He shall be made an example of. It is high treason, my lord. It is fitting that the head which conceives and the hand that executes should be forfeited. I will pass sentence with my own lips.

DUKE D'ESTE.

You shall do so.   Baptiste!   [*Enter* BAPTISTE, L. H. D.,
1 E.]   Show in the prisoner.
    [*Exit* BAPTISTE, L. H. D., 1 E.   THE DUKE *rises.*

LUCRETIA.

A word yet, my lord.   Be this man who he may, — one
of your own family, an officer of your household, even a
subject of Venice, — swear by your ducal crown he shall
not depart alive!

DUKE D'ESTE.

Mark me well.   I swear, by my sacred honour and by
my ducal crown, he *dies,* be he who he may!

LUCRETIA.

My lord, I am content; now I would see the prisoner.
[*Enter,* L. H. D. 1 E., GENNARO, *disarmed, and four Guards.*
THE DUKE *sits in state chair,* R. H.

LUCRETIA (*seated in chair,* L. *of table*).

Gennaro!   [*With agony.*]   My lord, what fatality is
this?

DUKE D'ESTE (*smiling, and in an undertone*).

What! you know this man, then, Lucretia?
[*She gazes a moment on him, then sinks into the chair at
table.*

GENNARO.

My lord duke, I am a simple captain in the service of
Venice.   You have ordered my arrest; I address you
with that respect befitting your rank, and ask of what I
stand accused.

DUKE D'ESTE.

Signor, the crime of high treason!   The family name
of our much loved duchess, Lucretia Borgia, has been

shamefully mutilated on the façade of our own ducal palace. We seek the criminal.

LUCRETIA (*eagerly*).

It is not he, Alphonso! It is not this young man!

DUKE D'ESTE.

How know you that, Lucretia?

LUCRETIA.

It cannot be. He is of Venice, not of Ferrara. The act was committed this morning, and he was then, I'm told, with one named Fiametta.

GENNARO (L.).

Your pardon. It is not true, your Highness.

DUKE D'ESTE.

You see your Highness has been wrongly informed. Captain, on your honour, are you the man who committed this offence?

LUCRETIA (*rises in terror*).

Air! air! I suffocate! [*Crosses to* L., *and in passing whispers to* GENNARO, *rapidly.*] Oh, say it was not you!

DUKE D'ESTE (*aside*).

She whispered him as she passed!

GENNARO.

Duke Alphonso, the fisherman of Calabria who reared me, taught me this maxim: "Do what you promise, and honestly say what you have done." By acting thus, one may often hazard life, but he preserves his honour. Duke, I am the man!

DUKE D'ESTE.

Madame, you have my oath on my ducal crown !

LUCRETIA (*with effort*).

Guards, retire with your prisoner a moment.   My lord,
a word with you.   [THE DUKE *comes down.*
[*Exeunt* BAPTISTE *and Guards,* D. L. 1 E., *with* GENNARO.

DUKE D'ESTE (R.).

Madame, what would you with me ?

LUCRETIA (L.).

It is my will, Alphonso, that this young man should
live.

DUKE D'ESTE.

Indeed ! how very strange ! A few moments since,
you demanded, with tears and imprecations, justice
against one who had insulted you.   You made me pledge
my word, — nay, swear an oath, that the offender should
die. I did so. You have my oath. He is guilty, by
his own confession ; and again, mark me, by my soul he
dies ! You are at liberty to choose the manner of his
death ; but I have called God to witness an oath, and it
shall be sacred.

LUCRETIA (*laughing, and with great tenderness*).

Don Aphonso, I am a true woman, — wayward and
capricious, spoiled by foolish indulgence.   You know my
temper.   Let us reason, cordially, tenderly, like man and
wife.   Be seated.

[LUCRETIA *sits* R. *of table.* THE DUKE *kneels to her on
foot-stool on her left.*

DUKE D'ESTE (*with an air of gallantry*).

At your feet. I am ever happy to be here, for you are
queen of love, as well as of beauty.

LUCRETIA.

You know I love you, Alphonso. I am cold some-times, and it is natural to my character; but it does not proceed from want of affection for you. Whenever you have chid me mildly, have I not yielded? and I would do so ever, dear lord!

DUKE D'ESTE.

Nay, I bow to you. My fair wife. [*Putting his arm round her waist.*] You are brilliant as the star of evening, and your bright eyes, soft lips, and angel form would wake an anchorite to passion.

LUCRETIA.

Is it not ridiculous that we should quarrel — we who are seated on the first ducal throne in the world — about a Venetian adventurer, a mere soldier of fortune? We must put him away, and say no more about it. A silly braggart to annoy us thus! Let him depart. I will tell Baptiste to send this Gennaro out of Ferrara instantly, that he may no longer be the cause of discord.

DUKE D'ESTE.

Nay; why such haste? There is time enough.

LUCRETIA.

I wish to have it from our thoughts. Nay, you must let me have this affair my own way.

DUKE D'ESTE.

This must be *my* way Lucretia. The man must die!

LUCRETIA.

Why, what cause have you to wish for this young man's life?

DUKE D'ESTE (*rising*).

My word is given. The oath of a prince is sacred.

LUCRETIA.

That is well enough to tell the people; but between
you and me, Alphonso, we know what it is. You gave
your oath to Petrucci to render Sienne; you have not
done it, nor ought you to do it. The history of nations
is full of this.

DUKE D'ESTE (L.).

But, Lucretia, an oath!

LUCRETIA (R.).

Give me no more of such reasoning; I am no fool.
Come, give me his life as readily as you gave me his
death, unless you have a reason to give instead. You
are silent. It is I who am insulted, not you.

DUKE D'ESTE.

That is precisely why I will not accord him grace.

LUCRETIA.

My lord, if you love me, you will no longer deny this
trivial boon. Let us be merciful. Mercy, Alphonso, is
that quality alone in which man may imitate his Maker.

DUKE D'ESTE.

Mark me, for the last time! I cannot, *will not!* He
dies!

LUCRETIA.

" Will not" and " cannot"! Why will you not?

DUKE D'ESTE.

I will tell you why. This adventurer is your lover!
[*She starts.*] You sought him in Venice, and met him

there. I was on your track; I followed you; saw you,
masked and breathless, bending over his sleeping form,
while the burning kiss was fastened on his lips. It is
time to avenge my honour; and if in no other way I'll
trench round my nuptial couch a rivulet of blood!
Watch well your lovers hereafter, for the door by which
they enter you may guard as you please; but at the
door by which they depart shall be but one porter, and
he the headsman!   [*Crosses to* R.

LUCRETIA (L.).

My lord, I swear to you solemnly, you wrong him and
me.

DUKE D'ESTE (R.).

Nay, it is useless. "Oaths are well enough for the
people. Give me no more such reasoning. I am no
fool."

LUCRETIA.

Oh, Alphonso! if you knew —

DUKE D'ESTE.

Hold, madame! Hear, once for all! I hate the whole
bloodthirsty race of Borgia; and you, whom I have so
fondly, fervently loved, I now cast from my heart forever! I know your whole race to be polluted by every
crime.

LUCRETIA (*kneeling*).

My lord! my lord! use me as you will; heap upon
me every epithet of reproach; but, in the name of the
holy Mother, spare, oh spare this Gennaro!

DUKE D'ESTE.

Within one hour you may have his corpse! He *dies,*
by my soul!

LUCRETIA (*starting up, and with great emphasis, folding her arms on her bosom*).

Duke of Ferrara, beware! I am Lucretia Borgia ; and there does not breathe on earth the being who has scorned and yet escaped my vengeance! [*Crosses to* R.

DUKE D'ESTE (L.).

I fear you not. I am a man and a soldier! My duchy swarms with warriors good and true. I fear not the Pope with his Vatican thunders, for I have not, like the poor King of Naples, resigned my artillery into his hand, nor shall I do so.

LUCRETIA.

You may repent this language, my lord. You forget who I am.

DUKE D'ESTE.

You are Lucretia Borgia! You are the daughter of Saint Peter, but you are not at Rome. You are the wife, subject, and servant of Alphonso, Duke of Ferrara, who can command and will enforce obedience and respect. [*She gazes a moment at him, and then she sinks into the ducal chair, pale and trembling with rage and fear.*] Why, how is this? You tremble! You may well do so! I am no longer your slave, for, regardless of a censorious world, my future course is marked; and now this the first of your lovers whom I have put my hand upon, *dies!* The choice of his death is with you ; quick! decide!

LUCRETIA.

O my God! my God! Would I dare tell all! Oh, Alphonso, listen to me ! How can he be my lover who so grossly insults me ?

DUKE D'ESTE.

Do lovers never quarrel? His mode of death, — decide! No answer? Then the sword!

[About to raise the bell from table.

LUCRETIA *(seizing his hand).*

Stay! oh, stay!

DUKE D'ESTE.

Will you please to pour out for your lover a glass of Syracuse wine?

LUCRETIA.

Oh, Gennaro!

DUKE D'ESTE.

He must die!

LUCRETIA.

Not by the sword! not by the sword! I — I — choose the other mode.

DUKE D'ESTE.

You cannot deceive me! The wine must be poured out from the *gold* flagon! You know its superior qualities; and till he drinks, be sure I leave not your side. Baptiste! [*Enter* BAPTISTE, L. H. D. 1 E.] Bring in your prisoner! [BAPTISTE *exits and re-enters,* L. H. D. 1 E., *with* GENNARO, *guarded, as before.*] Captain Gennaro, we have reason to believe the offence of this morning was the thoughtless folly of youth, rather than malice and design of insult.' On this account the Duchess of Ferrara pardons you, on condition that you immediately depart for Venice. You are called brave and generous, and we desire not to deprive the Republic of a single faithful arm now, when Candia and Cyprus are threatened by the Saracen.

GENNARO (L.).

My lord duke, your clemency has my thanks, and doubly so, as I looked not for mercy at your hands. I thank you.

DUKE D'ESTE.

Well, that is past. How like you the service of Venice ? On what conditions are you engaged ?

GENNARO.

I command fifty mounted men, my lord, whom I feed,
clothe, and pay; for which I am allowed two thousand
sequins of gold a year.

DUKE D'ESTE.

Would you enter my service if I were to give you four
thousand sequins ?

GENNARO.

For two years I must still serve the republic of Venice,
for which term I am bound.

DUKE D'ESTE.

How "bound," Captain ?

GENNARO.

My lord, by oath.

DUKE D'ESTE (*low to* LUCRETIA, *with a smile*).

You hear, madame ; even a poor adventurer regards his
"oath." [*Aloud to* GENNARO.] Have you any favour to
ask, any boon to crave, before you leave Ferrara ?

GENNARO.

I have not ; but I will mention one thing before I depart, as an equivalent return for the life you have now
spared. As your clemency has been freely extended, I
name it, but should not have done so otherwise. Your
Highness may not have forgotten that at the storming of
Faenza, two years since, your brother, the Duke Hercules
d'Este, was in deadly peril from two halberdiers of the
enemy. His life was saved by a young soldier of Venice.

DUKE D'ESTE (*rising*).

'T is true, and I have sought that brave soldier in vain.

GENNARO.

He now stands before you, Duke!

DUKE D'ESTE.

Ah, is it so, indeed ? My gallant captain! [*Comes forward, and grasps his hand.* THE DUCHESS *starts up, and advances*, R. H.; *after a pause, returns to seat.* THE DUKE *observing the joy of* THE DUCHESS *drops* GENNARO'S *hand.*] Will you accept this purse of gold sequins ?

GENNARO (L.).

My lord duke, I am pledged to the Republic not to receive gold from any foreign prince. Yet though I may not take it for myself, I will, with your permission, present it to these brave soldiers here, — my guard.

DUKE D'ESTE (C.).

The purse is yours. But you will not refuse to join us in a glass of Syracusan wine ? [*Going up to table.*

GENNARO.

Most willingly, my lord.

DUKE D'ESTE (*at table*).

Rustighello! [*He enters*, R. D. F.] The wine! [*He exits.*] And to do honour to the brave soldier who saved my brother's life, the Duchess shall with her own fair hand pour out for you. [GENNARO *bows, and turns to the soldiers, to whom he gives the money. Enter* RUSTIGHELLO, *with the wine*, R. D. F.] 'T is well. [*Aside.*] Lucretia, listen to what I tell this man. [*To* RUSTIGHELLO.] Place yourself near that door; if I ring this bell, enter with your drawn sword. Now go! [*Exit* RUSTIGHELLO, R. D. F.] Captain Gennaro! Madame, pour out for our friend, from the *gold* flagon.

LUCRETIA (*seated* R. *of table. In a low tone to* THE DUKE).

Oh, must it be? Alphonso! husband! think, — he saved your brother's life! *Must* it be so? As there is a heaven above, I swear to you your suspicions are false? Did you but know what a horrible crime you are forcing me to commit, you would pause, my lord, — you would pause!

DUKE D'ESTE (L. *of table, carelessly*).

Take care, Lucretia; do not mistake the flagon. Pray, what may be your age, Captain?
[THE DUKE *fills for himself from the silver flagon, and raises it to his lips.*

GENNARO (L. C.).

Twenty years, your Highness.
[THE DUCHESS *is about to fill from the silver flagon the cup which* GENNARO *holds out as he replies.*

DUKE D'ESTE.

Lucretia, fill from the *gold* flagon, if you please, — or, shall I ring for the servant who waits my order at the door? It would, indeed, have been cruel, Lucretia, to have cut him off from life, from love, from the bright future that is before him, — on the very threshold of manhood, too, only twenty years of age, — from the gay *fêtes*, the masks, and carnivals of Venice, and the fair ones who love him, and whom he doubtless loves, would it not?

LUCRETIA (*aside*).

Oh, heaven! if he would but meet my eye, I might warn him with a glance.

GENNARO.

My lord duke, I value not life; but for the sake of my poor mother, I thank you for preserving it.

LUCRETIA.

Oh, horror! *[Aside.   Sinks into chair.*

DUKE D'ESTE.

Your health, Captain Gennaro.   May you live a thousand years.

GENNARO.

God bless you, my lord duke. *[Both drink.*

DUKE D'ESTE.

Farewell, Captain; you are free to depart, and I wish you a safe and a speedy journey.   I must leave you now. [THE DUKE *rises.   Aside, to* LUCRETIA.] I leave you with your lover, Lucretia.   He is now all your own, — yours while he lives; and if you choose to share his fate, you are at liberty to be his in death.   Thus perish all your paramours, madame! *[Exit,* C. D.

LUCRETIA.

Guards, you may withdraw. *[Exit Guards,* L. 1 E.   LU-CRETIA *watches them off, then starts up wildly from her seat, goes to* C. D., R. H. D. F., *and* D. L. 1 C; *fastens them; then rushes to* GENNARO, *and exclaims:]*   Gennaro, Gennaro, you are poisoned!

GENNARO.

Poisoned, madame!

LUCRETIA.

Yes, yes, Gennaro.   Oh, my God, you are poisoned!

GENNARO.

The wine was poured out by your own hand. True, true, I might have suspected it. You are Lucretia Borgia!

LUCRETIA.

Gennaro, Gennaro, you will drive me mad! Do not, oh, do not *you* reproach me, or my senses will forsake me! Listen to me. The Duke is mad with jealousy, believes you to be my lover, and left me no alternative but to see you poniarded by Rustighello (who is even now there) or pour out for you that wine with my own hands. It is a sure and deadly poison, — a poison the very mention of which makes every Italian turn pale who knows the history of the last twenty years; it is the poison —

GENNARO.

Of the Borgias

LUCRETIA.

Yes, and you have it in your veins! I can and must save you! [*Producing a small and elegant gold phial from her bosom.*] Here, here is an antidote, known but to two persons in the wide world, — my father and myself. Quick! one drop on your lip, and you are saved!
[*She approaches with the phial; he recoils from her, and gazes fixedly upon her face.*

GENNARO.

Madame, is not *this* the poison?

LUCRETIA.

Oh, misery! misery!

GENNARO.

I have not forgotten the fate of the brother of Bajazet. He was persuaded that he was poisoned, and took the proffered antidote; it caused his death.

LUCRETIA.

Great Heaven ! must he perish by my hand ? Oh, wretched, wretched woman that I am ! Gennaro, hear me ! [*On her knees.*] By the dread name of Him who readest the hearts of all, by the sacred love you bear your mother, I swear you are poisoned ! Drink, drink this, ere I go mad ! Your reproaches crush me, warp my reason ; but I have but one thought, hope, wish, prayer, — to save you ! Curse me, heap on my head your maledictions, crush me with contempt and scorn, but, as you ever hope to know your mother, drink this !

GENNARO.

Madame, I saved the life of the Duke's brother ; he is loyal and noble. You I have offended, and I have reason to dread your vengeance.

LUCRETIA.

Gennaro, if to give up my whole life would add one hour to yours ; if to spill the last drop of my blood could hinder you from shedding one tear ; if by torture I could seat you on a throne, — I would not hesitate, murmur ; I would do it, and die happy, too happy, to be your slave ! The Duke may soon return ; he thinks you already dead ; in a few moments it will be too late to save ! It is a choice of life or death ! Gennaro, drink this, and live !

GENNARO.

Lucretia Borgia, give me the phial ! I am a friendless orphan, a lone being on earth. It may be that you speak truly ; if not, be sure the God of the fatherless will avenge me. [*He drinks, and hands it to her.*

LUCRETIA (*falls on her knees in thankfulness*).

He 's saved ! he 's saved ! thank God, he 's saved ! [*Rising.*] Now lose not a moment, but mount a fleet steed, and begone! I have already sent one to your house; he waits your coming. Escape to Venice, and Heaven guard you! Have you money?

GENNARO.

I have, madame.

[*She takes him up to secret door,* L. F., *and opens it.*

LUCRETIA.

Stay one instant. Here, take this phial; keep it ever near you, for poison is in every cup! Now fly for your life! Yet one word more, and then farewell forever!

GENNARO.

Speak! I trust you now; I listen.

LUCRETIA (*with great emotion*).

We are parting forever. I had hoped to have seen you during your bright career, — to have marked your rising greatness. It cannot be; it puts your life in peril. We are parting, then, forever in this life! Gennaro, Gennaro, one word; have you not one kind word for me at parting, — only one, for the being who loves you better than her own soul; only one, ere we separate for eternity?

GENNARO.

You have saved my life, you say. I will believe it; I will forget all I ever heard, — ay, I will leave you with Heaven's blessing, if you but swear, by all that is sacred (by my own life, since I am dear to you), that your crimes have not caused misery to my dear but unknown mother.

LUCRETIA.

Gennaro, all I ever utter to you is truth; I will not be false in word or deed to you, and I cannot swear that oath.

GENNARO.

Oh, heavens! my mother! This, then, is the being who caused you a life of misery!

LUCRETIA.

Gennaro, hold! No; I am —

GENNARO.

You have avowed it! Adieu, Lucretia Borgia! adieu forever! Be thou accursed! [*Exit*, L. D. F.

LUCRETIA.

And be thou blessed forever!
[*Noise*, C. D. *She rushes up to* L. D. F., *closes the door, and comes down* R., *just as* THE DUKE *bursts open* C. D., *and rushes in.*
DUKE D'ESTE (*comes down* L.).

Now, where is Gennaro, madame?

LUCRETIA.

Seek him.

DUKE D'ESTE.

Guards! [*Rushes to* L. D. 1 E.; *finds it fast.*] Ah, closed! Rustighello! [*Rushes up to* R. D. F.] All closed! Where, where is Gennaro?

LUCRETIA.

With a drug I preserved his life! He is now on his road to Venice, and out of your power forever! Ha, ha, ha! *I* triumph now! He's safe! he's safe! thank God, he's safe! [*Falls fainting on the stage.*

DUKE D'ESTE.

Escaped! Furies seize thee! [*Rushes out*, C. D.

ACT III.

SCENE. — *A magnificent chamber in the Negroni Palace. On the*
R. *a* D. *In* C., *very large curtain, size of half the flat, to draw*
aside each way. Splendid chandeliers and candelabra. Magnifi-
cent banquet, with wines, fruit, and all kinds of eatables, served up
in the costly style of the fifteenth century. Pages attending. Music,
soft, but gay, is heard as the curtain rises. All the guests are seated,
ASCANIO, OLOFERNO, APOSTOLO, JEPPO, *and* GUBETTA, *and*
several ladies, elegantly dressed. At the head of the table is the
PRINCESS NEGRONI.

OLOFERNO.

Here's the wine of Xeres! Xeres de la Frontera is a
city of Paradise.

JEPPO.

Bravo, Signor Oloferno! you improve. But this wine
is of great power and unequalled flavour. The last time
we cavaliers drank together, 't was in Venice, at the
palace of his serene Highness, Doge Barbarigo; now we
are at Ferrara, and in the palace of the divine Princess
of Negroni. We drink to your health and your beauty.

[*All rise, and raising their glasses, bow to her. Enter,*
R. D. 1 E., MAFFIO *and* GENNARO, *the latter very re-*
luctantly.

MAFFIO.

Why, brother, what unaccountable dullness is this?
and why am I obliged to go to your lodgings ere I can
get you here? Egad! 't was devilish lucky I went when
I did, or you would have escaped us. When I saw your
horse at the door I suspected your trick, my friend.

GENNARO.

I know not why I have consented to delay my departure for Venice, and I regret that I have done so, even now. Had you not convinced me that I had been the dupe of that artful woman, I should have been already far on my way.

MAFFIO.

Ha, ha, ha! it was excellent, i' faith! The Duke poisons you, and the Duchess gives you a counter poison! Why, what a farce! The fair Lucretia is desperately in love, and she pretends to save your life, so that from gratitude you may at last reciprocate her regard.

GENNARO (R.).

But the Duke?

MAFFIO (L.).

Oh, he's a good-natured, easy fellow, a little jealous of his fair rib, — and he has cause, I fear, you rogue! — but utterly incapable of poisoning. Besides, you saved his brother's life.

GENNARO.

But why is the Duchess so anxious for my absence from Ferrara, if, as you say, she loves me?

MAFFIO.

For obvious reasons. You see her husband is in the way here, and she can easily seek you in Venice.

GENNARO.

True, very true; it must be so.   [*Crosses to* L.

MAFFIO (R.).

Come now, Gennaro! In pity's name, rouse up! Be either a child or a man; go to your nurse again, or join us at the table.

[MAFFIO *and* GENNARO *seat themselves at table.*

JEPPO (*down* L. C.).

Aha, Sir Truant, you have been found at last! Why, Maffio, where was he concealed? We thank you for executing your mission so faithfully, and bringing the poor wight before us. Ha, ha!

MAFFIO.

Come, Jeppo, give us a merry tale. The last time we met in Venice you gave us a serious story. Now give us its opposite, if you can.

PRINCESS (*coming forward*).

Signor Maffio [*he rises*], your friend seems not to participate in the general merriment. I trust he is not ill. He seems depressed and abstracted.

MAFFIO.

Madame, he is ever thus. You must pardon me for having brought him here without your invitation. He is my brother in arms, and we never separate. A Bohemian predicted that we should both die on the same day.

PRINCESS (*laughing*).

Did he say you would die in the morning or the evening?

MAFFIO.

In the morning, I think.

PRINCESS.

Then he knew nothing about it, I can tell you! So you love this young soldier?

MAFFIO.

Ay, madame, as much as one man *can* love another.

PRINCESS.

Then in friendship you must be happy.

MAFFIO.

Friendship does not occupy the entire heart, madame.

PRINCESS.

Indeed, Count, what then ?

MAFFIO.

Love, lady.

PRINCESS.

Ah, Count, you always have love on your lips.

MAFFIO.

And you in your eyes, dear lady.   [*Kissing her hand.*

PRINCESS.

You are a bold man, Count Orsini.

MAFFIO.

And you — you are a charming woman, Princess.
            [*Puts his arm round her.*

PRINCESS.

Count, release me !   I shall be stifled, sir !

MAFFIO.

One kiss of this fair hand !

PRINCESS.

No, no !   [*She escapes from him ; goes to her seat again.*

GUBETTA (*coming forward,* R.).

You seem in a fine train with the Princess.

MAFFIO. (L.).

And yet she always tell me " No."

GUBETTA.

Well, "no" on a woman's lips is the twin brother to
"yes."

JEPPO (*comes forward*, L.).

Well, how do you get on? How do you find the
Princess?

MAFFIO (C.).

Adorable!

JEPPO.

And her supper?

MAFFIO.

A feast for the gods! By the way, the Princess is a
widow.

JEPPO.

I should have known that by her gaiety. Count Belverana, you'd hardly believe that Maffio was almost
afraid to come here to-night.

GUBETTA (*crossing to* C.).

Afraid, was he? And of what?

JEPPO.

Of poison! and all because the palace of the Negroni
touches the palace of the Borgia.

GUBETTA.

Devil take the Borgias! Let us drink, and think of
them no more.   [*Crosses behind to table*, L.

JEPPO (*low to* MAFFIO).

I like the Count for one thing, — he hates the Borgias.

MAFFIO.

Yes, he never lets a chance escape of sending them to the devil, without grace; and yet, Jeppo, I have observed that this Spaniard to-night has drunk nothing but water.

JEPPO.

Suspicious again!

GUBETTA (*coming forward*, L.).

Do you know, Signor Maffio, you resemble my grandfather, named Gil-Basieo Fernan-Ireno Filipe Frasco Frasqueto, Count of Belverana?

JEPPO (*low, to* MAFFIO, R.).

I hope and trust you 'll never doubt his Spanish origin after that! [*Aloud.*] A good name, that of yours, Count; I hope you keep 'em catalogued!

GUBETTA.

My name was all my father had to give, and he gave me plenty of that. [*They laugh, and go up to table*, R. *Aside.*] I must try some way to get the ladies from the room, or I can never go to work. I have it! Signor Oloferno is drunk; I 'll draw him into a quarrel: that 'll do it. [*Goes to table*, R. H.

OLOFERNO (*partially drunk*).

Ladies, taste this wine! It is sweeter than the wine of Lachryma Christi, and more ardent than the wine of Cyprus. Drink; it is the wine of Syracuse, gentlemen!

GUBETTA.

It is evident that our friend is tipsy.

OLOFERNO.

Ladies, I will recite you some verses I have composed for this occasion. I wish I were a better poet ; I would raise myself to heaven. I wish I had two wings.

GUBETTA.

Of the pheasant on my plate. Devil take your verses! More wine !

ALL.

More wine !

OLOFERNO.

Oh, you 're no poet ! Silence, for my song !

GUBETTA.

Spare us, Marquis of Oloferno. We beg leave to drink to your departed reason. I dispense you from your song.

OLOFERNO.

You dispense me from my song ! You dispense !

GUBETTA.

Ay, as I would dispense a barking dog, or the devil from blessing me.

OLOFERNO.

You mean to insult me, Sir *Spaniard !*

GUBETTA.

I merely decline listening to your song, Signor *Italian !* I had rather taste the Cyprus wine in my throat than have your song in my ears.

OLOFERNO.

Your ears, you miserable Castilian refugee! I 'll shave them off close to your dog's head !

GUBETTA.

You are an absurd and ridiculous dunce! Didst ever
see the like? He gets drunk with Syracuse wine, and
has the demeanour of a man intoxicated with beer. I
can't stop to carve such poultry as you now; it is too
troublesome.

OLOFERNO.

I'll carve you to pieces!

GUBETTA.

As I do this pheasant now. Ladies, shall I help you?

OLOFERNO (*seizing a knife*).

By the Virgin! I'd stab the miscreant, were he in a
church.

[*The Lords and Ladies rise in alarm, and exclaiming,
"They are going to fight!" rush out of the room* R.
and L. *The friends hold* OLOFERNO, *and disarm him.*

OLOFERNO.

Set me free!

GUBETTA.

My worthy friend, your poetry has put the ladies to
flight. On my word, you are a gay troubadour, Signor
Vitellozzo!

JEPPO.

The ladies have gone indeed!

MAFFIO.

Let a knife glitter, and a woman flies

OLOFERNO.

Count, keep your valour warm till morning, and I'll
meet you then.

GUBETTA.

If you do, I'm your man! Ha, ha, ha! You have
put to flight the fairest ladies of Ferrara with a carving-
knife and a song. You should have wings, for in truth
you are a perfect goose of a man.

JEPPO.

Come, cease this quarrel. It is enough that we have
lost the ladies. Cut one another's throats in the morning at your leisure, and fight like gentlemen, with swords,
and not like cooks, with carving-knives.

ASCANIO.

Apropos! where are our swords?

APOSTOLO.

You forget they obliged us to leave them in the ante-
room, as we came in.

GENNARO (*who has not moved*).

It was a wise precaution, too, it seems.

MAFFIO.

Egad, brother Gennaro, that is the first thing you
have uttered to-night. And you have not drunk. You
are dreaming of the fair Lucretia; do not deny it.

GENNARO.

No more of that, Maffio! Come, fill me to drink. I'll
meet my friend with good wine with the same courage as
I would a foe in the field with weapons of death.

MAFFIO.

Fill me with the wine of Syracuse!

ALL.

The wine of Syracuse!

JEPPO.

A pest on all brawls. The ladies have gone, and will not return, it seems. [*Tries all the doors.*] And every door is fastened on the other side, too!

GUBETTA.

Rather a wise movement, I think, from past experience. Come, the wine!

[*Enter* ASTOLFO, 1 E., L. H., *with salver, one bottle of wine, and seven glasses.*

GENNARO.

Gentlemen, let us drink.

MAFFIO.

Ay, to the health, long life, and happiness of Gennaro; and may you soon find your mother.

GENNARO.

May Heaven grant it!

[*All drink, except* GUBETTA, *who throws his wine over his shoulder.*

MAFFIO (*aside, to* JEPPO).

Ha! did you see that?

JEPPO.

See what?

MAFFIO.

The Spaniard did not drink.

JEPPO.

Well.

MAFFIO.

He has thrown it over his shoulder!

JEPPO.

Pooh! the Count is drunk, and so are you, I think.

MAFFIO (*carelessly*).

Very like, very like!

GUBETTA (*aside*).

I must feign to be drunk. [*Aloud.*] A drinking-song, gentlemen! I will give you a bacchanalian song worth more than the love sonnet of our amiable friend, the Marquis of Oloferno. But first let me swear, by the old skull of my old father, that this same song is none of my making. I'm not a poet, and never could jingle two lines into rhyme in any way. So here goes. It is addressed to Monsieur Saint Peter, the famous doorkeeper of paradise, — a jolly lover of wine, like ourselves.

JEPPO.

He's drunk as Bacchus! He's more than drunk; he's a drunkard!

ALL (*except* GENNARO).

The song! the song!

GUBETTA (*rising and reeling*).

"Saint Peter, I pray you, quick open your gates,
    And let in some topers you know;
With voice full and strong, and thick fuddled pates,
    In chorus to chant 'Domino'!"

ALL (*except* GENNARO).

Gloria Domino!

[*General laughing, clinking of glasses, etc.; cries of "Bravo!" Amid the uproar, distant voices are heard without, chanting in a slow and solemn strain from the Roman ritual.*

CHORUS OF MONKS.

" De profundis clamavi ad te, Domine !   Conquassibat capita in terra multorum ! "   [*Lights gradually down.*

JEPPO (*roaring with laughter*).

Do you hear that ?   By the rubicund visage of jolly old Bacchus, while we sing bacchanalian songs, echo chants the vespers !   A full church chorus !

MAFFIO.

Some procession is passing, I think.

GENNARO (*who is seated in* L., *apart from the others*).

A procession at midnight !   No, no ; that is rather too late !

JEPPO.

Oh, nonsense !   On with your song, Count !

ALL.

Ay ! the song, the song !
[*Beat table.*   GUBETTA *rises, reeling.*

MONKS (*chant without, nearer*).

" De profundis clamavi ad te, Domine !   Conquassibat capita in terra multorum ! "
[*All the cavaliers laugh again vociferously.*

JEPPO.

How these monks bellow !   They are regular night brawlers !   [*Lights half down.*

ASCANIO.

Ay, but they are kicking up a riot in the streets ; we in doors !   [*Lights down.*

MAFFIO.

Halloa ! the lamps are going out !   We shall be in the dark presently !

GENNARO.

They seemed to be near at hand, and I think it is the service for the dead.

MAFFIO.

Very likely, very likely.

JEPPO.

Let us drink to the poor defunct, — poor devil!

GUBETTA (*meaningly*).

I should n't wonder if it were for four or five, instead of one.

JEPPO.

Well, more or less, here 's to all their healths, and a safe journey through purgatory. [*All laugh.*] Go on, Count, with your song, — your invocation to Saint Peter.

GUBETTA.

Speak civilly of Monsieur Saint Peter, the grand usher and patent turnkey of paradise. We may need his good offices soon.

ALL.

The song! the song!　　　　　　　　　　　　　　（

GUBETTA.

" To the songster so joyous, glass filled to the brim,
　　And belly so large, ripe for fun,
　When he enters your portals, at first glimpse of him,
　　You would swear it a butt or a tun ! "

ALL.

Gloria Domino !

[*Chant: solemn music. All touch glasses, with peals of laughter, which is continued, while the large curtains slowly open, discovering a large hall hung with black. A large altar in* C., *lighted, covered with black, with*

a large silver crucifix in C. *of it.* Six *monks slowly
enter, in cowl and scapulars of black, with their faces
all concealed, except by the apertures of their vizards,
for them to see through.* Each *bears a torch ; and as
they range down stage on* R., *they chant in a loud and
solemn tone.*

MONKS.

"De profundis clamavi ad te, Domine! Conquassibat," etc.

[*All the cavaliers stare with astonishment at them and
each other.*

MAFFIO.

What — what does this mean!

JEPPO (*laughing*).

Ha, ha, ha! a capital joke! I see it now! These are
our charming countesses, disguised thus to try our
courage. If we raise their masks we shall find them
the visages of mischievous, laughing, and beautiful
women. Just see!

[*He lifts the mask of one of the monks, and it reveals the
pale and ghastly countenance of an aged man, calm,
silent, motionless.* JEPPO *and others stand horror-
struck.*

MAFFIO.

Great heavens! what means this? My blood con-
geals with horror round my heart!

JEPPO.

This is too awful! We are ensnared! Our swords!
our swords!

MAFFIO.

Quick, or we are lost! This is the house of fiends!

[LUCRETIA, *dressed in black, appears at* C. D.

LUCRETIA.

Yes, you are in my palace!

[*Close curtains, and lights up gradually.*

ALL (*except* GENNARO, *who is unseen, on* L. H.).

Lucretia Borgia! -

LUCRETIA.

Ay, Lucretia Borgia! [*She slowly advances, with a sarcastic smile, and gazes on them.*] Yes, gallant Venetians you are the guests of the Duchess of Ferrara, — of Lucretia Borgia! There was a time — I have not forgotten it — when in Venice you spoke that name with scorn, contempt, and withering hatred; now it comes from the trembling lips of terror. Look on me, and listen. When last we met, my heart was softened, my feelings changed, my nature humanized, and sorrow and repentance for the past had bowed me to the earth. I had resolved never more to terrify Italy with frightful deeds. One feeling of nature still filled my bosom; it was love, — a pure and holy love for one whose fate for years I had in secret and in silence watched. You met me before him, and your eyes feasted on my wretchedness with exultation and triumph. You scorned my anguish, you mocked my sufferings, laughed at my misery, insulted my despair, tore from my face the mask, while my supplications for mercy were met with shouts of derision, and every epithet of ignominy and shame heaped upon my head. I could have borne all, had you not spoken it before him! It was but that I begged for; but you were merciless! I rose from that spot with the spirit of a demon in my heart; I swore to have revenge, — awful and fearful revenge. I have kept my oath! Ay, look at me once more! You are all poisoned! Ha, ha, ha!

ALL.

Poisoned!

LUCRETIA.

Ay, do not stir; the room without is full of armed men, and, my good friends, your deaths are sealed beyond the power of fate itself to change. Now, hear me; it is my turn. I think I have returned your civilities to me. You entertained me at a ball in Venice, I you with a supper at Ferrara, — *fête* for *fête*, feast for feast!

JEPPO.

This is a horrible waking from a wild dream of mirth!

MAFFIO.

Ay, my friend. We are dying! I feel it even now; but let us meet death unshrinkingly, and like men!

LUCRETIA.

Remember me at the carnival of Venice, and tell me, have I not, for a woman, well avenged myself for all the agony you then forced me to endure? Do you understand the word "vengeance" now? Holy fathers, conduct these men into the adjoining room, and shrive them; and do it quickly, for their time is short! For you, sirs, fear not; these are real monks of St. Sixtus; and I will also comfort you with the assurance that, while I thought of your souls, I have not neglected your bodies. [*Stamps.*] Open! Behold! [*Music, ending with chord. Curtains open, and ranged round the altar are five coffins, covered with black, on which are painted, in large white letters, the names of the five cavaliers. All start with horror.*] The exact number, — five! Maffio, Jeppo, Oloferno, Ascanio, and Apostolo, — exactly five!

GENNARO (*coming forward*).

And mine, madame, — where is the sixth?

LUCRETIA (*starting back*).

Powers of mercy !   Gennaro !

GENNARO.

Yes, I am Gennaro.

LUCRETIA.

I *am* accursed and helpless !   [*Sees* GUBETTA *on* R.].
Traitor ! villain ! accursed fiend !   Did I not bid thee
shield him as thine own eye ?

GUBETTA.

I knew not thy motive ; thy secret was too great for
me, and he drank what I prepared, with the others, —
his potion the same.

LUCRETIA (*stabbing him*).

And this be thine, thrice damned villain !

GUBETTA.

I die, but he dies also, mistress !   I — oh —   [*Dies.*

LUCRETIA.

Cast that carrion into the streets !   [*The body is carried
off*, R., *by the Guards.*]   Monks, accompany your charges
to the altar !   All, all leave me, except Gennaro ; and
whatever may be heard or conjectured of what passes
here, let no one dare to enter !   Begone !
[*She sinks into a chair*, R.   *Solemn music is heard behind.
    Monks go off*, C., *each with a cavalier, chanting, "De
    profundis clamavi ad te, Domine !" etc.   Curtains
    close.*   LUCRETIA *comes down* R., *and gazes a moment
    with agony on* GENNARO, *who returns it sternly.*

LUCRETIA.

Oh, Gennaro !

GENNARO.

Well, madame.

LUCRETIA.

Gennaro! Gennaro! how do I find you here, when I thought you leagues away? By what strange fatality does every blow from my hand fall on thy devoted head? Father of mercy! why are you here?

GENNARO.

It is my destiny.

LUCRETIA.

Gennaro! Oh, my God! Gennaro, you are dying,—again poisoned!

GENNARO.

Well, madame. And yet I still have your gift,—*this!*

LUCRETIA (*with a scream of joy*).

Thank Heaven! The antidote! You are saved! Drink!

GENNARO.

One word first: is there enough in this phial to save my friends?

LUCRETIA (*examines it*).

Barely enough for thee, Gennaro! Oh, quick! take it!

GENNARO.

Can you obtain more in time to save them?

LUCRETIA.

All that I possessed you have. Ere I could get more, it would be too late.

GENNARO.

It is very well.   [*Putting phial into his bosom.*

LUCRETIA (*alarmed*).

What is well? Nothing can be well till you have
taken that. I implore you, do not play with your life!
Trifle not now: a few moments longer, and it will be too
late. Quick! you can yet escape, and ere the dawn be far
from Ferrara! I will furnish the means. Drink that
antidote, and let us part! Oh, you *must*, you *shall* take
it, and *live*, Gennaro, *live!*

GENNARO (*seizing knife from table, and speaking sternly*).

And you, madame, must die!

LUCRETIA (*incredulously*).

How? What say you, Gennaro?

GENNARO.

You have, through your hellish agent, infamously,
treacherously, poisoned five men, my dear friends, — men
of rank and name; and among them Maffio Orsini, my
brother in heart, my companion in arms, he who twice
saved my life in battle; and between us all, vengeance is
common. I am his and their avenger! You must die!

LUCRETIA.

Die! and by your hand, Gennaro? No; that is impossible! It cannot be!

GENNARO.

It *will* be, madame, and quickly, too, for I am dying
also; I feel it here! So, while I address my prayers on
high for mercy, do you the same, with clasped hands and
bended knees, before that God you have so terribly outraged!

LUCRETIA.

This is some awful dream! *Thou* take *my* life? It is
too fearful! No, no; I 'll not believe it! I say again, it

is impossible! Amid my most frightful conceptions, *that* is the most agonizing that ever swept across my brain! No, no; He who knows all will not permit it!

[*Crosses to* L. H.

GENNARO (*seizing her arm*).

My throbbing brain and beating heart cry out for haste; I must obey their voice! [*Raises his arm.*

LUCRETIA (*winding about him, and falling before him on her knees*).

Gennaro, cast aside that knife, as you hope for Heaven's mercy! [*He raises knife.*] Hold, oh, hold, one moment, and listen to me! Did you but know all! But cast that knife aside; I cannot speak while that flashes in my sight! Stay! know you who I am or who you are? The time has come when you must know all. The same blood flows in our veins, Gennaro! you are a Borgia, son of the Duke of Candia, and I —

GENNARO.

I, then, am a Borgia! — nephew of Lucretia Borgia! Oh, horror! My mother, then, was the Duchess of Candia, she whom the Borgias have made wretched! It is you of whom my poor mother spoke in her letters as the cause of her unhappiness! It is you who murdered my father, and drowned in tears and blood the hopes of a wife and mother! I am a Borgia! The thought will drive me mad! Hear me! I have a mother's wrongs to avenge, and on you, my aunt! Your life has been blackened by so many crimes, it must be hateful to you! I will rid you of its heavy burden! I, Lucretia Borgia, am to slay you; therefore commend your soul to God, for your fate is sealed!

LUCRETIA.

Gennaro, Gennaro! you are as yet innocent of crime! Oh, have mercy! Your hands are yet free from innocent blood, your heart yet unclogged by crime; oh, keep it so! I entreat you, commit not this murder!

GENNARO.

Murder! crime! My head wanders, my sight darkens! Is it with the thought of crime? No, no; am I not a Borgia? My heritage is murder! shall I disgrace my name by mercy to another? No!

LUCRETIA.

I will call for help.

GENNARO.

Do so! No one will answer! You yourself forbade it; and if they did, ere they could reach you it would be too late.

LUCRETIA.

Gennaro, would you assassinate a woman, — a helpless woman, — and you a soldier? You have a soul too noble for so vile a deed! You call me vile, criminal, wicked; if I am, cut me not off thus; or, if I must die, it cannot, must not be by your hand!

GENNARO.

I will not, dare not hear more. Are you not my aunt? Lucretia Borgia, where, where is my mother?

LUCRETIA.

Oh, my heart! I cannot tell him all. Spare my life! I will submit to any infliction! Shall I hie to a cloister? Say you so, I'll do it. Yes, to obey you, I'll look for the last time on the bright world; for you my head shall be shorn, my bed ashes, my raiment sackcloth, while my bare feet shall tread the flinty floor of my cell, and my hours shall be passed in prayers for forgiveness of Heaven for past sins, and for blessings upon you. Gennaro, hear me. [*He seems faint.*] Ah, you turn pale! Why have we wasted the precious moments? Quick! drink that antidote! It is not yet too late; save your own life — spare mine! Do not, I beg, implore you, perpetuate crime to your name, and by such a deed as will forever blast your peace while living and your memory when dead! Speak! let me hear your voice! and do not, do not kill an unhappy woman, who kneels and supplicates for mercy!

GENNARO (*moved and softened*).

Madame!   [*Drops knife.*

LUCRETIA.

Ah, you relent! your eyes fill with tears, your hand trembles in mine; you will not, cannot slay me!

MAFFIO (*within*, C.).

Gennaro!

GENNARO (*starting*).

Ah! what voice is that? Who is it calls me?

MAFFIO.

It is I — Maffio — your brother! I die, Gennaro! Avenge me!

GENNARO.

Avenge thee, my brother? I will, I will! Lucretia Borgia, you've heard your doom! A voice cries from the grave, "Revenge!" Hark! You must die! [*Raises knife.*

LUCRETIA (*struggling*).

Mercy! One word more!

GENNARO.

No ! it is too late !

LUCRETIA.

Oh, spare me ! spare me !

GENNARO.

No !

LUCRETIA.

In the name of Heaven !

GENNARO.

Fate decrees it !   Die !   [*Stabs her.*

LUCRETIA.

Gennaro, you have killed me !   I AM YOUR MOTHER !

GENNARO (*with a scream of despair*).

O God ! my mother !   [*He falls dead before her.*

LUCRETIA.

Gennaro ! dear Gennaro !   My son, I do forgive thee !
It may not be too late yet ! the phial !   [*Crawls to his
body.   She takes the phial, puts it to his lips, then exclaims.*]   Dead !   [*Kisses him.   Monks within chant,*
"*De profundis," etc.*]   Gennaro !   [*Dies.*]

THE END.